The man blinked in surprise.

"Don't know where you got that," he said, referring to her sword. "Nice one. I think I'll keep it when I'm done with you." He handled his machete with practiced grace.

It looked as if he had some skill and wasn't just a hired thug. He became the aggressor and lunged. Another fencing move, a fast strike that she deflected with her sword. From the blow she could tell he was strong, stronger than her, but not quite as agile. He stepped back and gave her an evil grin.

"This is fun," he said. "You're feisty."

Fun? A part of her was pleased to have a challenge, but mostly she was disappointed. She'd hoped to clock him into unconsciousness like she had the first attacker she'd come across. The noise was likely to draw more men and set the odds in their favor...not hers.

Titles in this series:

ROGUE ANGEL

Alex Archer

RIVER OF NIGHTMARES

A GOLD EAGLE BOOK FROM

WORLDWIDE®

TORONTO • NEW YORK • LONDON
AMSTERDAM • PARIS • SYDNEY • HAMBURG
STOCKHOLM • ATHENS • TOKYO • MILAN
MADRID • WARSAW • BUDAPEST • AUCKLAND

Recycling programs
for this product may
not exist in your area.

First edition March 2014

ISBN-13: 978-0-373-62167-5

RIVER OF NIGHTMARES

Special thanks and acknowledgment to
Jean Rabe for her contribution to this work.

The
LEGEND

...THE ENGLISH COMMANDER TOOK
JOAN'S SWORD AND RAISED IT HIGH.

The broadsword, plain and unadorned,
gleamed in the firelight. He put the tip against
the ground and his foot at the center of the blade.
The broadsword shattered, fragments falling
into the mud. The crowd surged forward,
peasant and soldier, and snatched the shards
from the trampled mud. The commander tossed
the hilt deep into the crowd.
Smoke almost obscured Joan, but she continued
praying till the end, until finally the flames climbed
her body and she sagged against the restraints.

Joan of Arc died that fateful day in France,
but her legend and sword are reborn....

1

The beast followed the river, staying well back from its edge. Mysterious and hiding all manner of scaly creatures within, the river was the center of her world. Her life—all life—was tied to it, and she knew that to venture too far from it, too deep under the layers of leaves where the shadows forever ruled, was to risk captivity and death. The shadows were the domain of men.

The river was a place of great light this morning. The sun streamed down and made the surface shimmer and brought out all the amazing colors that rose above and beyond the thick forest. So very wide at this point, she could not see to the other side of the river. Birds skimmed low over the swirling current; she liked to watch the ones with wings the shade of wet moss. Some had yellow patches on their crests, as if the sun had sketched on them. The birds called to her sometimes, as they were doing now, the ones wearing pieces of sunlight mimicking her own shrill voice.

The beast thirsted, but waited until she reached a spot where a stream fed into the great river to drink her fill. She trusted this thin water, as she could see to its bottom and could stand in it without worry. It flowed around her massive three-toed feet and made her happy. On a bright day like this, the beast could admire her reflection in the stream. She resembled both monkey and sloth, front legs longer, back sloping, and all of her covered with thick, matted fur, the skin beneath tough like an alligator's. Her snout was long and beautiful and filled with tiny sharp teeth that could easily puncture flesh. But the beast ate fruit and leaves only. She was taller than a man when standing on her hind legs, a pose used to frighten those who ventured to the bank to fish. Sometimes she would rip apart a tree to add to her ferocious image, exude a ghastly stench, and cause the fishermen to run away in panic. The beast preferred to be alone.

At times, though, she would tolerate the friendly dawn-colored fish that could at night become men— or rather something *like* men. They would sit on the bank and sing, and she relished the melody. And sometimes she would get quite close to a river creature that looked like a child but was not. It had backward feet, and the beast had watched this creature lead hunters to their doom.

The beast had not seen the backward one in some time, and wondered if perhaps the creature was dead. She had, however, in these recent days, seen more and more men come to the river to fish and hunt. They had tried to catch her. Others of her kind had been caught in the past. The foul men had tugged her sisters through the forest. She'd followed them once. The men kept her kind in little villages and had forever stolen their freedom, making them carry things upon their broad backs.

She worried that someday enough men would find her and that they would not fear her stench and shriek, and would tug her to one of their villages deep under the layers of leaves where the shadows always ruled. She brushed the troubling thoughts away and continued to follow the river, listening to the music of the birds and admiring the bright colors the great forest gave her this fine morning.

2

Roux felt old today.

He was a tall fellow of moderate affluence, white hair draped past his shoulders, neatly trimmed beard edging just below his Adam's apple, gray suit well-tailored and light blue shirt nicely pressed. A retired farmer perhaps, likely in his late sixties or early seventies, who'd come to visit the big city. His skin had that look, like a worn piece of leather weathered by the sun and the wind, his fingers calloused. He was, in truth, more than five centuries old, and his vocation had been swords rather than plow shears. As he stared at the rising spires of Cathédrale Notre-Dame de Rouen, he swore he could feel every one of those years pressing down on his shoulders.

There were three spires: Tour Saint-Roman; Tour de Buerre—or the Butter Tower, so named because the wealthy paid for it in exchange for being allowed to eat butter during Lent; and Tour Lanterne—this the most recent, having been finished in 1876 and containing a carillon of fifty-six bells. Roux had watched the workers that year put the finishing touches on the seven-hundred-and-forty-ton work of art.

One entrance illustrated the martyrdom of St. John the Baptist. The main door depicted Jesus' family tree. The other entrance was dedicated to St. Stephen, considered the first martyr.

No tribute to St. Joan here, and she had been—in Roux's estimation—the most noble and sacrificing of all of Christendom's martyrs. But she would not have approved of the ostentatious pomp this cathedral offered. Joan had been a rather humble soul. Like the years, she weighed heavy on him this day—May 9.

The wind gusted and he wished he'd worn a proper coat. The temperature was in the low fifties, quite cooler than usual for this month. A quartet of young American women brushed past him, chattering and pointing, one of them taking pictures, one of them oohing and ahhing at the massive cathedral. Tourists. There were plenty of them in such a picturesque setting as Rouen.

"City of a Hundred Spires" the city was nicknamed and for good reason. The Gothic architecture was an added bonus.

Roux had walked these streets when the city was greater. It had been second only to Paris until the 18th century. It was a place of wealth and power then because of its impressive wool industry. Later, the Normans named it their capital. William the Conquerer had called it home. Roux had, too, for a brief time.

Roux had been back numerous times since then, the last in the late 1980s when a storm toppled one of the cathedral's pinnacles. The choir stalls and vault were damaged, too. He thought the cathedral's interior, with its vibrant stained glass, was even more impressive than the outside, and that was where he'd intended to pray this morning.

He changed his mind.

Instead, he took slow, measured steps around the side of the Cathédrale. At the back of it, he faced the Palais de l'Archevêché—the Archbishop's Palace, Joan had been tried at the palace in 1431, and "rehabilitated" posthumously there twenty five years later.

She had been captured, accused of heresy, but Roux knew it was all politics—condemning her was merely an attempt to undermine her king. The trial began in January and took a winding course before the unfortunate, but never-in-doubt end. May 9 stuck in Roux's mind because he'd been in the Castle of Rouen trying to visit her that day, but had been denied. He'd a plan to break her out. That day she'd been threatened with torture lest she decry the "voices" and yield to the city's clergy. Roux had made it as far as the prison tower and was close enough to hear her screams.

Je refuse! Je désavouerai tout ce que vous me ferez dire!" I refuse! I will retract anything you make me say!

So strong of mind and body, Joan was. There were many words of hers that he would never forget.

Sometimes he came to Rouen in May to pay his respects to Joan, though sometimes he purposely stayed away because the memories were too thick here. One of Joan's knights, Roux had failed her. Unable to save her, he witnessed her horrific burning. He'd shared a special connection with the Maid of Orléans.

And now he had a different connection—with Annja Creed, the woman who'd inexplicably inherited Joan's sword. Today he was here for Annja, not Joan. He'd thought—sensed—that Annja was here. And he'd sensed serious trouble brewing.

But something was wrong with his thinking. She was nowhere in Rouen, or in France for that matter, and the special connection they shared—and that somehow usually let him know where she was—at this moment, had become a frayed thread that stretched...to where?

Roux's dreams the past several days had been troubling. Annja's and Joan's faces had been merging, one woman interposed over the next, and Annja's form becoming more indistinct with each passing night. Merely dreams? Or some sort of omen?

He wasn't responsible for Annja; he had his own life filled with the simple pleasures of young women and fast cars, and only occasional complexities. But he was tied to Annja...somehow, and maybe his future was linked to hers. Roux enjoyed his immortality, but once in a while genuine worry crossed his thoughts. After Joan's death, her sword had shattered and seemed lost to the ages before it mysteriously reformed and landed in the grip of Annja Creed. If Annja died, would Roux age like a normal man? He wasn't obliged to look out for her, but perhaps she was responsible for his continued existence.

Where was she?

He walked the streets, alternately musing about Joan and Annja, eventually arriving at Vieux-Marché, where Joan had been tied to a pillar and burned to death. He sat on a bench and tipped his face up to the sun, reached in his pocket and pulled out a phone. Roux didn't call Annja often; he didn't want her to think he was checking on her or meddling. Today, it was to ease his soul.

The dreams, and this city, and the fragmented, troublesome memories....

No answer in her apartment or on her cell phone. He used the number for her satellite phone, his concern building with each ring.

Finally.

"Hello? Roux?"

"Annja, where are you?"

There was a pause, and in the background he heard men talking, something about a boat. A bell rang—a clunky sound, not musical like a church bell. Horns honked, taxis maybe. Laughter, music.

"In Belém."

He had difficulty hearing her for the ruckus.

"Did you say Bethlehem?"

"No." She spoke louder to compensate for all the background noise. "Though yes, I suppose. Belém. The city's name literally means Bethlehem. What's this about, Roux?"

He paused. "I am in Rouen, and I was thinking of you."

"Listen, we landed about a half hour ago, and we're waiting for a van. I'm in the country for three weeks," she said. "So when you're thinking about me, think about little biting insects. I've been told to expect a lot of them. We're filming a series for—"

"—*Chasing History's Monsters.*" Roux thought it an

alternately interesting and silly television program. He watched it avidly, though he did not admit that to Annja.

"I'm pretty busy here, Roux. We have to get to our boat."

"This boat—"

"*O Seguro.* It's Portuguese, means the dependable boat. And my crew is depending on me to keep us on schedule. So do you need something? Is anything wrong or— Ned, don't leave your bag just sitting there. Ned! Sorry, Roux. Didn't mean to shout in your ear."

"Nothing's wrong. I was just thinking of you, that's all. Be well, Annja." He ended the call.

She sounded well. Her voice was strong.

But the connection he felt, the thread that somehow let him know where she was…he still couldn't feel it.

Roux shivered, and not from the brisk wind. There were four places open for lunch in his line of sight. He selected *la Couronne,* built in 1345 and functioning ever since that date as a restaurant; it was perhaps France's oldest. Being one of the first patrons of the day, he was able to sit on the main floor near the window, where he could at the same time admire the view and the room's old wood paneling and array of photographs displaying its famous guest.

He made pleasant small talk with the waitress, saying he'd just arrived in Rouen this morning and hadn't bothered with breakfast. Hungry, Roux ordered a salad, the Dover sole, Calvados soufflé for dessert, and a glass of Bordeaux, only a small part of him registering how delicious it all was.

He used his phone to look up "Belém," discovering

that it was a large port city in Brazil with a five-hour time difference. It had been just shy of 8:00 a.m. there when he'd reached Annja.

He ordered a strong cup of coffee, paid the waitress, and asked if she could recommend a good travel agency, as he'd prefer to deal with a person rather than making reservations with his phone. She gave him an address, 12 Rue De La Champmesle, a woman in the hotel there handled bookings.

"I make my vacations with her. She finds the best prices. But why do you want to leave our beautiful city so soon? You said you just got here." The waitress tsk-tsked. "We have so much to see."

"I've seen everything," Roux returned. More times than he cared to count. "And I need to be leaving as soon as possible." For Brazil.

3

"Ned!" Annja hollered at the stills photographer who'd set his bags down and drifted away, snapping pictures of an artful mosaic pattern embedded in a bush-lined sidewalk. She and the rest of the *Chasing History's Monsters* crew stood outside the Val de Cans–Júlio Cezar Ribeiro International Airport, a paved lot stretching in front of them, the city beyond it and the river to the north. They were waiting for a van to whisk them to the docks. The area was crowded this morning, and she'd only moments ago watched airport security hustle away a young man who'd tried to steal a traveler's briefcase. "Ned, you better—"

Too late, in a heartbeat her photographer's leather satchel was scooped up. The thief swung it over her shoulder and dashed across the pavement, dodging cars as she went.

"What?" Ned Lundock turned toward Annja. "What's so— Hey! That's my stuff. Stop!"

Annja hadn't waited for Ned. She'd shoved her own duffel into the arms of one of her crew and took off after the thief. The sounds inside the terminal had been wonderful, the speakers playing a track of rain gently drumming—it was the rainy season after all. But outside it was standard big-city cacophony, mixed with the rumble of an approaching storm. Behind her she heard Ned call for security, heard a shrill whistle. Car horns blared all around, and she narrowly avoided becoming the hood ornament on a limo. Music spilled out taxi windows, and there was the slap-slap-slap of feet pounding in her wake, maybe Ned, maybe security. She wasn't going to lose time to look over her shoulder, and she wasn't about to lose sight of the satchel; she knew he had camera equipment in there that might be needed for their filming.

"Ladrão!" Annja knew only a smattering of Portuguese, which had similarities to Spanish, "thief" or "scoundrel" being on her list…at least she hoped she was hollering "Thief!" She spotted people milling on the pavement ahead. *"Ladrão! Impedi-la!"* But they didn't try to stop the young thief. They just stood and watched as both the girl and Annja raced by.

"Detener al ladrón!" A taxi driver standing outside his car tried to help get the attention of the police—Annja spotted a police car he waved to on the far side of the lot.

"Policía!" someone shouted in Spanish, and then in Portuguese.

She even heard English in the mix, all calling for the police…and all the people in front of the girl jumping out of the way rather than lending a hand to try to stop her. A siren piped in, similar to police cars in the States, but higher pitched. Thunder came louder.

The thief—Annja only got a look at her backside—was probably in her early teens, slight, wearing a T-shirt, jeans and scuffed tennis shoes. The girl was nimble as a monkey, and fast. Annja was in top physical shape, but she wasn't catching up, just keeping pace. The girl had the satchel over one shoulder, and in the other hand she held a large leather clutch purse...probably also stolen. Clearing the pavement and the sidewalk beyond, the girl darted through traffic and headed into the city. Her legs pumped out a rapid rhythm that Annja matched.

Annja heard a siren crescendo, a police car approaching. The footsteps on the pavement behind her slowed, and then stopped. Whoever had been joining her in the chase gave up. Annja wasn't about to give up.

The thief looked over her shoulder and Annja caught a glimpse of her face. A kid, probably twelve or thirteen, dark brown hair with glittery pink highlights, freckles splayed across her cheeks. The girl grinned widely and raised a hand, throwing Annja a foul gesture before going faster still.

That only spurred Annja to dig down and lengthen her stride. She had a soft spot for kids, growing up in an orphanage in New Orleans. Annja'd had young friends who occasionally resorted to shoplifting to get special treats or to get a little money so they could buy something. But the thief's grin and the rude gesture wiped out Annja's sympathy for her. The thief had braces, and that wasn't cheap—someone had invested money in the girl.

The buildings that stretched ahead and above were

a mix of modern skyscrapers and decades-old colonial charmers, many of them painted tropical shades of peach and pink, flowers hanging from porches and lining the street. All of it was a blur of colors and angles.

The sidewalk they dashed down was crowded, businesspeople heading to work, shops and restaurants opening. The thief exercised no care, rudely shoving folks, pulling some down in Annja's path to slow her.

Finally someone tried to lend a hand. A businessman at the next corner dropped his briefcase and made a grab for the girl, but she swung a leg out and kicked his feet out from under him. Annja shouted "thanks" as she leaped over him and gained a little ground on the girl who had just gone down an alley that was too narrow for the police car to follow. Annja heard the squad pass her and skid to a stop. Annja slipped through the gap between the buildings, continuing the mad dash after the thief.

A policeman who'd gotten out shouted something about leaving this to the police. But Annja wasn't sure they could catch the thief. The girl barreled through a side door of the nearest building, and disappeared from sight.

Annja almost lost her balance, her foot catching on something and costing her a few seconds. She followed through the same doorway the girl had entered.

She paused for only a heartbeat while taking everything in. It was a long, busy kitchen, cooks preparing breakfasts, waitresses carrying trays, collecting dishes. The scents were amazing. There was a trail of debris to show the girl's passage, plates and broken mugs on the floor down one aisle, cartons of eggs spoiled. One of the cooks, a blond-haired man with green eyes, pointed toward a door.

"Get her!" he said in perfect English. "Get the little monster!"

Rather than risk adding to the damage in the kitchen, Annja instead darted back out into the alley and raced to the end of the building, seeing the girl…who was now speeding down another alley that was at a ninety-degree angle to the first. The girl kicked up dirt and gravel and cackled in laughter.

"This isn't a game!" Annja hollered, continuing to give chase. Two sets of feet coming behind her, the police, she confirmed with a quick glance. Both of the officers were a tad on the pudgy side and she doubted they could keep up.

Annja felt a welcome burn spread up from feet and fill her chest. An adrenaline junkie, she loved running… but for pleasure, to work out, to participate in marathons. Not to chase a kid through an unknown area of a foreign city that she hadn't been to in more than a few years.

The girl rocketed out of sight again, turning onto a busy street. Annja kept going, and caught a glimpse of her quarry. Annja could more easily *hear* where the girl was going—cars honking, people shouting in a variety of languages for her to "watch where you're going!" Annja had to wait for cars to pass, and then sped out during a gap in traffic and hurtled the curb. She smiled at the applause of a group of people who'd just gotten off a bus.

"Catch the thief!" a woman hollered.

"I intend to catch her!" Annja ground out between clenched teeth.

A park came into view, and Annja saw the girl sprinting across it, knocking a man with a cane to the ground. The girl had dropped the clutch purse somewhere and was swinging her free arm, feet chewing up clumps of grass. The park was a mistake for the thief; it let Annja lengthen her stride and close some of the distance. Annja jumped over a hedge and angled toward a fountain. Thunder boomed, and fingers of lightning shot through a darkening sky, matching Annja's mood.

Annja was angry; not only had the girl stolen from her crew and sent their trip off schedule, but she had no regard for the people she was knocking over. Still, a part of Annja was enjoying this. A chase always had an element of excitement. The thief looked over her shoulder again, this time a snarl on her face. She made another rude gesture at Annja and cut in a different direction, head down.

A police whistle shrieked, and Annja saw that one of the officers was still in the chase, but he was about a hundred yards behind her. She changed directions to follow the girl, who'd just charged across one more street and into the Ver-o-Peso Market. Annja realized from a previous trip that more than a thousand stalls made up the market, traders hawking their wares regardless of the weather. If Annja didn't catch up now, she'd lose the girl in the jumble of stalls and tents and shoppers.

Fortunately, this early in the day, many of the vendors were still setting up, and the piles of boxes and carts that spread across the aisles made it impossible for the girl to race down any one path with a great amount of speed. The thief tried to push a cart out of the way, but an angry vendor confronted her. The girl pushed him down, but that had cost her precious seconds. Annja was on the thief, sending her flying into a table with jewelry and bright colorful scarves. Vendors cursed and threw up their hands, shoppers gathered to see what the ruckus was. The police whistle cut through all the voices.

Annja tugged the girl to her feet.

The thief struggled, and for a brief instant Annja got a glimpse of her sword in a deep, dark corner of her mind, as if it wanted to be called. But the thief was little more than a child, a nasty tempered one, but a child. And there was a growing crowd to consider.

The girl spoke so quickly Annja couldn't make it out. Portuguese, something about being a poor, poor girl who had to steal to live, followed by a string of expletives that would make a sailor blush. The tennis shoes were high-end Nikes, and her belt buckle sterling silver and turquoise, the chain around her neck gold. She probably wasn't poor—the braces had little gems set in them like a rapper might have—she probably just stole for the rush…because she could get away with it.

Annja passed the girl to the policeman who arrived. He was walking, face red, huffing. He handcuffed the girl, nodded to Annja, then bent and put his hands on his knees to catch his breath. In that instant the girl tried to make a dash for it, but a shopper blocked her way, grabbed her by the shoulders and spun her around back to the officer.

"I believe this belongs to you," the shopper said. An American tourist, he had a Southern accent. Annja judged by the clothes and chatter of the crowd that had gathered that there were quite a few Americans in the market today.

"Obrigado," the officer replied. "Thank you."

Annja picked up Ned's camera satchel and hoped nothing was broken inside.

"Queixa?" the officer asked. He switched to English. "Will you press charges, miss?" At the edge of the market a police car pulled up, and the cop's partner got out. Rain started to fall, gently, sounding like the track that had played inside the airport.

"Sim," Annja said. "Yes, I most certainly will press charges."

The officer smiled and the crowd cheered.

Annja pulled out her phone and called her crew to tell them she'd recovered Ned's bag. "The van's there? Good. Have breakfast without me and then get everything loaded on the boat. I'll catch up as soon as I can." Paperwork always took a while.

4

Arthur Dillon was the shopper who'd briefly held the thief. He watched the officer prod the girl toward the police car, the woman who caught her followed them.

"Blimey! A bit of excitement today." Dillon's British companion drew his trench coat tight and adjusted his hat. "And with a celebrity no less. The lovely lass who caught that thief, I see her on the telly every now and then. Do you follow it?"

Dillon consulted a list he held close in an effort to keep it out of the drizzle. "No, I don't watch TV much."

"She's Annja Creed, a famous archaeologist. Chases mummies and the like. Did a special on vampiric goat suckers or somesuch in Mexico. I caught it the other day. I'll never go to Mexico because of that."

"Chupacabra."

"Eh?"

"The vampiric goat suckers, they're called chupacabra."

"Ah, you have watched her! Television doesn't do her justice."

"Never saw her before." Dillon shook his head. "I

read a lot. Chupacabra are mythical monsters in Mexico, southwest United States." He stopped at a vendor selling all kinds of beans and put in an order.

"Wonder what brings her to Brazil? What monsters might abound in this city, don't you wonder? I should've got closer, Artie. Asked you to take a picture of me and Annja Creed."

Dillon scowled. "I don't have time for such folly, and you don't need any notoriety. I have a helicopter at the airport that I have to be on in two hours." At the next vendor he bought a gallon jar of jaca pulp, dried chuchu, and a couple of bags of oranges.

"And so you need your shopping to be all done with, I know. But did you have to drag me out here in the rain? I could have stayed in my nice, warm flat."

"It's the rainy season. You said you had something to tell me. I swear you won't melt." Dillon checked off the items he'd already arranged for and scanned the market for the rest. He spotted a tea and coffee vendor he favored and headed that way, trying to shut out the sounds of the sellers and buyers, the traffic shushing by, and the Brit's constant, annoying chatter. The Brit made a chuffing sound.

Dillon could have placed his orders through a broker in the city, but he needed a brush with civilization every once in a while; the green of the rainforest became overpowering sometimes. He needed reliable Wi-Fi so he could see his emails and catch up on reading the Atlanta Journal-Constitution. He required an occasional stint in a four-star hotel, a long soak in a hot tub, and female companionship that asked no questions and was willing to experiment if the money was right. Above all of that, he'd needed to meet with his British partner, who hadn't the mettle for venturing into the wild and was crucial to their endeavor.

"So, a rather short stay, then?" The Brit picked up a warty-skinned piece of fruit, made a distasteful face, and replaced it. "Back to the…uh, salt mine, as the American expression goes?"

"Salt." Dillon laughed. "Yes, so we have just enough time for coffee and our conversation." He placed one more order, directing all of it to be taken to the airport; then he picked up his cup of coffee and had a sip.

The Brit made a show of drinking from his cup, coughing after having a long swig of the strong brew. "Artie, everything we talked about yesterday morning, it's handled."

"Already?" Dillon rubbed at a spot on the back of his hand. "I didn't think you'd get it locked down for a few days—at the earliest." He edged away from the growing crowds. "I'm impressed, outdone yourself."

"I was lucky, is all. Right people in the right places at the right time."

"And—"

"The shipment we sent a few weeks back netted a tidy sum, all tucked away in the accounts, and got us more lookers for future deals. The next batches, we'd do better with at auction, I think."

"Will that be difficult to arrange?"

The Brit looked offended. "I've set that up. And we've a bidder already on the big one, more than one, I think, especially if we start it low…say at two? If we play it right we should get twice that. How fast can we supply the smaller batches? I think I should cut some."

Dillon held the hot liquid in his mouth, savoring the rich flavor before finally swallowing. "Tell them three weeks. That gives us a good margin. I have the other customers to handle in the meantime."

"Ah, yes, those fellows in Atlanta and Dallas."

Dillon gave his partner a foxlike grin. "They are footing most of the bill for all of this."

"And reaping only a smidgen of the reward." The Brit raised his cup in a toast. "Thank God for nasty, incurable diseases, what?"

5

It was almost noon when Annja reached the docks—dealing with a few of the police department's *Chasing History's Monsters* fans meant she'd stuck around much longer than she expected. It had rained while she was at headquarters, but the sun was out now and sent the temperature up into the high seventies. A haze hung low over the ground, and the riverbank smelled of earth and damp wood. All the sounds of the city were behind her, substituted for fishermen returning from an early morning catch and sightseers of all nationalities…Canadian, Israeli, American, German and French. The cloying odor of city traffic was replaced by the not-as-heavy scent of diesel fuel.

The boat wasn't what she'd anticipated. She gaped at it, a mix of emotions dancing through her head—surprise, pleasure and overriding that a thick layer of ire.

Ned practically flew toward her, snatched his satchel and set her off balance. He caught her and tried to hug her. "Thank you. Thank you. Thank you, dear Annja.

My lenses, all my memory cards, spare camera, water-proof camera. I—"

"—will never again set my bag down unattended in a big airport," Annja finished, putting him at arm's length. "Because I will not retrieve it for you a second time. You'll have to look through it to make sure nothing's damaged."

His dark blue eyes sparkled. "No, I certainly won't leave it unattended again. Seriously, thank you."

She wanted to be mad at him, but his boyish grin sunk that notion. Ned Lundock peppered her with questions—how did she get the satchel back, did police arrest the thief, where had she been for the past several hours. Ned was new to her crew. He'd been picked up to shoot stills for the website. A photojournalist for a wire service, he'd spent three years in Afghanistan and Iraq embedded with the troops, and had come back to the States a month ago when *Chasing History's Monsters* made him a lucrative enough offer to lure him away from hard news. The desert had bronzed his skin and lightened his hair; it was such a pale shade of blond that at a distance it looked white. On the flight here, he'd said his time with the soldiers had also bulked him up because every day had been a workout to stay in step. The muscles in his arms strained the seams of his khaki shirt.

"This isn't the right boat," she said.

"No, it's a better one!" This came from Wallace Carper, lead cameraman. Wallace was sixty-two, twice Ned's age. His gray hair was short, and he was bald on top, as if he had purposely adopted a tonsure; the hairless spot gleamed in the sun. He clunked across the plank to the shore and waved an arm to happily indicate their substitute ride. "Thank the heavens for sick Baptist ministers!"

She raised an eyebrow.

"The so-called dependable boat that we'd booked…it had some serious engine problems, so Doug approved spending a little more and getting this. Not much choice, Miss Creed, almost everything else is for tourists or is already rented. We lucked out with this baby. A group of Baptist ministers from Georgia had her booked for a two-week retreat, but flu swept through them and they canceled this very morning. Lucky, eh?"

"I suppose," Annja started. "We could use this for a while and—"

"Already paid for two weeks. Doug wired the money. We're getting a refund for the other one."

"The *O Segura*. Not so dependable after all. This one isn't as sleek as the one we'd planned on, Wall." Annja's voice was flat.

"Look, it was this or wait around a few days until something else opened up or the *O Segura* got repaired. Or I suppose go to another city on the coast and find something. But I'm liking this boat. I'm liking it a lot."

The boat's name was in faded red paint: *Orellana's Prize*. Annja had studied up on the Amazon before suggesting this series. She knew Francisco de Orellana was a Spanish soldier who'd been the first European to explore the river. Orellana had helped Pizarro conquer Peru and served as a governor for a time. After his sojourn down the river he finally returned to Spain, where his tales of gems, spices and native women resembling the Greek mythological Amazons contributed to the naming of the river. Eventually he came back here, but his ship capsized at the mouth and he drowned. Annja shuddered, a boat named after a drowned man…who would do that? And paint the name in the color of blood.

"C'mon, Miss Creed, I'll give you the tour. I already put your duffel in your cabin. Gave you the nicest room." Wallace led the way.

Cabin? Annja had expected to be roughing it. The boat they'd originally chartered had a common room for sleeping that doubled as the dining room. She'd selected the *O Segura* after contacting a charter company she'd found on the internet and followed up on with a few phone calls. This series was wholly Annja's idea, and she'd thought that particular boat would come over great on film, make it look like taping these segments was dangerous, that taking an antique-looking tug into the tributaries was a big risk. More drama. This boat was probably three times the size of that tug, practically luxurious.

"According to the captain, *Orellana's Prize* is one of the oldest still navigating the Amazon. Maybe *the* oldest. Built in France in 1876."

Annja felt a tingle on the back of her neck. Roux had called her from France this morning, said he was thinking of her. Odd connection, this boat to France.

"She was originally a Peruvian naval ship, was in the campaign to expel the invasion of Ecuador back in 1902, or maybe it was 1903. I should've written all of this down, might be a good tidbit for the website promo.

Maybe we'll do a clip just on the boat, for the 'extras' on the DVD."

That had been part of Annja's proposal, too. Release the segments as a DVD around the holidays, include bonus features on their boat, the river itself and any other tidbits that struck their fancy.

"We'll double-check it all, the dates and history, with the captain when we start filming. He's quite the character. I want to do a little piece on him. Anyway, apparently in the early 1900s, this boat was used for exploration of some tributaries—maybe the same ones we're going down. She was fully restored four or five years ago." He stroked his chin. "We're sailing on a piece of Amazon River history, Miss Creed. Maybe it was a good thing our other charter didn't work out, eh?"

"Steam powered?" Annja noted that keeping with the boat's apparent history, the original brass ornamentation here and there was reasonably polished. But the paint was weathered and faded all around, the tropical climate taking its toll despite the restoration.

"Captain said they switched that out a couple of years back. Has a diesel engine and two generators."

They circled the deck; Annja put it at a little more than ninety feet long and sixteen or seventeen feet wide. It had two upper levels, giving it the look of a Mississippi riverboat, and the roof served as a viewing area, complete with safety rail and padded benches.

"We each have our own cabin," Wallace said, beaming. Annja remembered him grumbling about the shared sleeping quarters in the dining room of their original charter. "Air conditioned, private bathrooms with showers. And there's a big dining room, and off of it a library."

"A library?" Annja did the math. The boat had at least six private cabins for guests, because counting herself, there was six in the film crew. Wallace; Ned; a second videographer—Marsha Carr; logistics—Ken McCullough; and sound—Amanda Hill.

"Six cabins," she said.

"Yeah, six exactly. Worked out perfect. The captain, well, I'll intro—"

They were outside Annja's cabin. "I suppose there's a laundry, too."

"A small one. Well, one of those stacking washer-dryers. It's next to the dining room. I doubt your 'dependable' boat had a laundry."

"I'd never inquired." Annja was adept at doing her laundry in a bathroom sink, or at the edge of a river.

"Well, um—" Wallace seemed as if he wanted to say something else, but stopped and screwed his face into an expression that looked comical.

"I'm going to change." And take a shower, Annja thought. The race through the downtown to retrieve Ned's satchel had made her sweaty; she didn't like the smell of herself. "How about we meet in the dining room in about an hour? Can you arrange for something? There's grub on board, right?"

"Actually, there's a cook. A late lunch and go over our schedule? Sure." Wallace nodded. "I'll tell the captain we're good to go. We can shove off? Ask the cook to fix us something."

"Fine." Annja closed the door, stripped and discovered the shower didn't have a lot of water pressure, but the heat felt good running over her back. She'd managed to squeeze a half-dozen changes of "camera suitable" clothes, hiking boots, tennis shoes, a rain poncho, insect repellent and an overlarge sleep shirt in her duffel—along with her laptop and a spare battery. She'd been warned regarding the "dependable boat" that internet reception would be spotty at best, but she suspected that *Orellana's Prize* had some sort of Wi-Fi. She sat the laptop on the nightstand and hung up the clothes, figuring the dampness from the river would take any wrinkles out of them. She hadn't counted on the luxury of a closet. She selected a pair of jeans and a long-sleeve shirt and decided a washer-dryer on board was probably a good thing so she wouldn't be washing things out by hand. A little luxury would be helpful after all.

Her satellite phone rang; she figured Doug wanted to make sure they were underway.

"Roux?" Two calls in one day. "What's going on?"

There was a pause on the other end.

"Roux—"

"I was thinking of you."

"Yeah, that's what you said when you called this morning."

"And everything is still fine?"

"Sure." Annja talked while she dressed, shifting the phone from one hand to the other as she wriggled into the jeans. "Other than this boat being a little too lavish, and me being too accepting. My jog through the downtown resulted in my getting a private bath with a shower and a closet. I wasn't here to pick a different boat."

"A *different* boat?"

"Never mind. You don't know what I'm talking about. What's this about, Roux? What's going on?"

"Probably nothing."

"Probably?" She stopped dead. "Still in Rouen?"

"Still France," he said.

"That's where this boat was made."

"Pardon?"

"The boat I'm on, named for a drowned man, *Orellana's Prize*. Made in France about a hundred and forty years ago. It even has a washer and dryer."

Annja paused, waiting for him to continue talking. The back of her neck tingled, something was amiss. She slipped on the shirt and buttoned the sleeves at her wrists. "Are we done with this conver—"

"I'm at Charles de Gaulle Airport, Annja. There wasn't a direct flight from Rouen."

"Direct flight?"

"To Belém."

"Roux, what is going on?"

"Probably nothing, Annja, like I said. Probably nothing. I'm probably being a silly old man."

"You've got the old man part down."

"Watch yourself, all right?"

"Always."

"This boat that you're—"

"*Orellana's Prize*. It's not waiting for you, Roux. I felt it leave the dock. Your flying to Belém is a waste of your time and money. You're probably not going to be able to catch up with us…let alone find us. The Amazon is a big, big river."

"It wasn't cheap, the flight. Fifteen hundred Euros for an open return ticket, and that was for a seat in coach."

Annja's brows knitted together. Roux had a bad feeling about something if he was willing to sit in coach for an international flight. And giving her that tidbit about the cost was his way of telling her to worry.

"I'm fine, Roux. The boat's fine. Whatever your intuition is telling you it's off the mark. But, yeah, I'll watch myself." She ended the call and sat on the bed, head in her hands. "I don't need this." She didn't need Roux following her down the Amazon River. She closed her eyes and searched for the sword, finding it in the *otherwhere*. She wasn't going to need her sword on this trip, she thought. Or was she? Something had spooked Roux. "Are you being a silly old man?"

She tried to push thoughts of Roux out of her mind, but they hovered there, like the sword. Sometimes the old man just showed up, unannounced, conveniently helping her with one problem or another, somehow knowing she was in danger. But Roux had oddly announced himself in advance this time and warned her to take care, and so something was bothering him more than a little bit.

And that bothered her.

Annja left the phone next to the laptop and headed to the dining room. She didn't want to deal with another Roux call for a while. She hoped lunch was something significant. Her stomach was rumbling like crazy.

6

When Annja met the captain, the nagging displeasure over this "luxury cruise" vanished. Wall had mentioned doing a little feature on the captain for the DVD extras…absolutely. She was instantly mesmerized by Captain Belmiro Almeirão and not only wanted him in Wall's sidebar, but in some segments for the actual series. His charisma was palpable. He had a presence.

She figured Almeirão was in his mid-to late-forties, with skin that looked like tree bark. He had a short, coarse beard the color of wet shale that was bisected here and there by heavy scars where no hair grew, hinting that he'd either gone through hell or had lived through an incredible adventure. It was as if he'd grown the beard to cover up the disfigurement of his face, but instead it only added to the ugliness. His nose was wide and crooked, obviously broken at some time, his head shaved, and a thick, ropy scar wrapped down the side of his neck like a cord. He was missing the thumb and index finger on his left hand, the scarred, knobby remains looking like a surgeon had done a poor job patching the injury.

Almeirão smiled, but it was a polite one, an expression that didn't reach his coal-black eyes, which looked to be thoroughly studying Annja. He shook her hand, the grip strong and dry, the fingers and even the palm heavily calloused. Then he took his spot at the head of the dining table, not saying a word but commanding all eyes on him.

Vatapa, a shrimp dish with peanut sauce, and moqueca de peixi, a coconut fish stew, was on the menu. Annja watched Wallace pick at the unfamiliar food; she'd been on enough projects with him to know he was hesitant to try anything that bordered on exotic and that he'd probably packed several boxes of granola bars. His favorite meal was a hamburger with a side of macaroni and cheese. While she'd always had a healthy appetite, her metabolism had shot up since inheriting Joan of Arc's sword. Annja dove in, found everything incredibly delicious, and asked for seconds of both.

In between bites, she took in the casual conversations of her crew. Marsha Carr, the second videographer, was talking about her rescue cats she'd had to put in a boarding facility because of this trip. Marsha had recently celebrated her twenty-first birthday. She'd dropped out of film school after her second year, and worked freelance for one of the NYC news stations a few months. Her footage of a warehouse fire caught Doug's attention because of her sharp camera work and obvious willingness to wade into a dangerous situation. She wasn't quite five feet, kept her red hair trimmed short like the cap of an acorn, and never wore a trace of makeup. Annja had liked her immediately and asked for her on this shoot. While Wallace was top-notch, he was sixty-two and stubborn, and Marsha would no doubt be willing to climb a few trees or go where the older film man would balk.

Amanda Hill, the sound technician, hadn't been Annja's choice. She came across as a debutante, fitting because her father was an investment banker on Wall Street. Although she wasn't the most cordial soul, Amanda was the best "sound man" Doug had. Annja knew sound was more important to this series than video, at least in terms of quality. Viewers of documentaries and programs like *Chasing History's Monsters* were more apt to accept spotty camera work as long as they could hear what was going on.

Lastly was Ken McCullough, in charge of logistics and settings. Annja had worked with him twice before and found him competent. He was in his mid-thirties and had jumped from job to job, although always TV related. He loved it and it showed. Ken sat to the left of Captain Almeirão and was futilely trying to engage him in conversation.

However, when the chatter drifted toward their planned series, which would focus on the various historical monsters rumored to live along the river, Almeirão finally spoke.

"In my earlier years I spotted creatures that defied explanation, certainly the things you are looking for. Big. Dangerous maybe, I'd never gotten close enough to test their proclivity. But lately it is all monkeys, parrots, alligators and snakes. A lot of snakes. But those beasts from my childhood, I believe, are still in the forest, hiding. And the Amazon people who are mostly hidden see them from time to time. I hear their stories." His voice was craggy and seemed forced, reminding Annja of longtime smokers she'd known; but he didn't have a trace of smoke on him. The scar on his throat— perhaps some injury had affected his speech. Amanda might have to finesse the sound to make him clearly understood when they got him in front of the camera. She'd wished Marsha or Wall had brought cameras to lunch and could have recorded him.

Annja and Wallace stuck around after the others left.

"Captain, Wallace said he's given you our planned schedule and—"

"Belém to Macapá to Manaus to Iquitos." He waved his fingers, reminding her of thick flying beetles. "I know where you want to go and what you want to do. We can do all that. I've taken charters to those places. But these films for your television series, they will be better if we go elsewhere… Talk to the Amazon people who have seen your hidden beasts."

The skin on the back of Annja's neck started tingling again. Still, she was intrigued.

"Oh, I dunno," Wallace said. "We've pretty well got this arranged and—"

"Where would you take us?" Annja leaned over the table and watched Almeirão's finger trace a thread-fine tributary on the map that disappeared into a dense patch of green.

"We are still in the rainy season and so the river and its veins are swollen. My *Orellana?* She drafts shallow and can navigate here and here and here. At least for three more weeks." He pointed to places that looked like solid forest, no trace of the blue river lines. "There are tribes living here, little places that have no names. These are the forest people that time has changed only a little." The captain stood, and Annja noticed his right shoulder was lower than the left, the length of his legs uneven. Maybe later she would press him about the injuries that shaped him.

He continued. "Because the river and all of its parts are so deep and wide right now, I can take you. We will go where the water is cut by low slivers of land like stretching fingers. Where the sun sets early because the forest is so high and dense, where zebu-cattle stand like ghosts at the water's edge, white against green, against black when night comes to swallow them. Where the channel gets ever narrower and narrower." He put the thumb and index finger of his right hand together, as if he was squeezing something. "Places where the river's tributaries are only a memory during dryer months."

"Yes," Annja said, caught up in his magnetism and the notion of going seriously off the beaten track. "Take us. I'll inform my crew our destinations are changing."

"You do not understand." The captain shook his head. "The destination is the river, and so the destination does not change. It is the stopping points that will be different. It is the people that you will meet who will be different." He said something in Portuguese that she couldn't understand, and then he turned and left the dining room.

Wallace folded the map. "I don't know about this, Miss Creed. There aren't any place names on these maps, not along the route he suggests. Nameless villages? Nameless tributaries? Doesn't even look like the river goes where he's pointing. Maybe we should call Doug, check with him."

"No. That won't be necessary, Wall. And it's really not Doug's call. This is all on me. Besides, I'm sure he'd agree."

"But what if this is a bad idea, going where the captain says?"

Annja countered. "What if it isn't?"

7

The first village was nothing more than a collection of huts made from woven reeds and wooden poles. Half of the small buildings were at the very edge of the river, with people standing in the doorways, water above their knees. There was a larger building farther back, but Annja couldn't make out the details. The lowest canopy was so dense that the shadows were thick and effectively cloaking the structure.

It had taken them nineteen hours to reach this stop on the unnamed tributary that Captain Almeirão steered them down. Annja had spent quite a few of those hours with the captain, Wallace discreetly recording parts, and Amanda flawlessly finessing the voices to make them as smooth as possible. Annja learned that the captain's various injuries and resulting disfigurements hadn't come from any one episode…an alligator a dozen years ago, anacondas more than once, an arapaima—a monstrous carnivorous catfish responsible for one of his legs being shorter than the other. The captain had a prosthetic foot. Yet he had no fear of the river, only respect, if not outright love.

"It was at this very village a year ago," he said, "and a big, big paco came to take a taste." He laughed and slapped his hands together. "Thought they ate only nuts and seeds. This one, he made a mistake and should have stuck with nuts and seeds. I fed him to the people here."

"And these people are—" Annja prompted.

"These people are Kayabi," Almeirão replied.

Annja looked for Wallace, who had moved behind the captain, so he could film the village as the captain saw it, as if viewers were looking through his eyes.

"This village, it has no name, most of the people in it have no names. I stop here once, twice during the rainy season to trade between charters." He shouldered a large duffel and whistled as the *Orellana*'s anchor caught.

Annja did a quick head count: sixty villagers that she could see. The Kayabi, many of whom had waded into the water to greet the boat, had deep brown skin, their clothes were scant, loincloths on some of the men and women, but most were naked, and save for the smallest children, they were all tattooed.

Annja heard the constant hiss-click of Ned's digital camera. Wallace was getting pan shots. The river lapped against the boat, and an odd howl cut above everything. She spotted the source: a monkey, about four feet tall, hanging on a branch that dangled low over the water. He had a humanlike face and a big saggy chin that served as a resonating chamber. A howler monkey, its throaty hoots could reverberate for miles. He swung to a higher branch over a group of Kayabi that had perched on the shore, and then he urinated on them and howled again. The howl was answered a moment later from across the river.

"Miss Creed, I take back what I said, about it being a mistake our taking this route." Wallace continued, "This place is quite promising, good to photograph. Beautiful people, adorable children. And they all look so friendly." He turned to the captain. "Do any of these people speak English? Portuguese?" He'd switched off the sound when he asked the questions, but put it back on and aimed the camera again at Captain Almeirão.

The captain gave a throaty laugh. "Just as this country has the greatest diversity in plants and animals, it has the greatest number of distinct tongues in the world."

"So that would be a no on the English or Portuguese. How do you communicate?" Wallace had flicked the sound off and then on again.

"Some Kayabi tribes indeed understand some English, what with all the tourists who come to buy their beads and crafts. But not this group of Kayabi," Almeirão said. "I told you, these are hidden people. No one else comes here, no need to learn any other language." He waved at the gathering and a few of the children excitedly waved back.

"You're from one of these villages?" Wallace was recording the children on the bank.

"The Apiaká. But that was a long time ago. I understand, but do not like the primitive life."

"I thought the Apiaká and Kayabi didn't get along," Annja said.

The captain's smile reached his eyes this time. "So,

miss, you study a place before you visit? Admirable. And not what I expected. Television is so baseless sometimes."

Wallace sniggered.

"We try to make our programs entertaining and educational," Annja pointed out, though sometimes the education part was a stretch.

"I see. Well, the two tribes used to be enemies, but that is all done with now. And when you find the Kayabi it is usually farther west. But these people here, they came east to hunt and they stayed, established gardens and found the area suited them. I know enough of their words, I'll translate for you as best as I can."

"You speak English so well," Wallace cut in. "Where did you—"

"I have a teaching degree in economics from the University of Campinas in Brazil. I studied English there. Portuguese, my father taught me. But I discovered I liked this boat and the river more than a crowded classroom."

"Wow," Wallace said.

"Where's the raft to go to shore?" Ned asked.

"My charters usually go to villages that have docks. Someday maybe I will buy a raft to keep my feet dry when I go to villages with no names and no docks." Almeirão grasped the railing and eased himself over the side, the water up to his waist, the pack held above his head. "But now, we will not have dry feet. Watch your step," he advised. "Alligators and piranha in here, the latter will give you a… No, never mind, but step on an alligator and you will know it. Get blood in the water and everything changes." He looked over his shoulder. "I'd say only half of you should come. These Kayabi are mostly friendly, but let's not press them right away."

"Can we bring cameras?" Ned climbed over the rail, pausing for a nod from Almeirão, then following him to the shore.

Annja went next and motioned to Wallace to follow. The older cameraman squeezed himself beneath the rail, holding on to it with one hand, and his camera and bag with the other.

"Fine with me, everyone. I'll stay here." Amanda turned her face up to the sun. "You don't really need me anyway. I'll clean up the sound when you get back." Ken stood at her shoulder.

Marsha rocked back and forth on the balls of her feet, clearly anxious. She had a camera in one hand and gave Annja a less than pleased look.

"Later," Annja told her. "Get some color shots from the boat for now."

Almeirão slogged ashore and greeted the kids and adults alike. Then everyone was talking, and in a language Annja couldn't fathom. It sounded beautiful and harsh at the same time, filled with lots of hard consonants and clipped words. It was punctuated with hand gestures and head bobbing. She could pick up Almeirão's craggy voice in the mix.

Wallace and Ned moved into the throng, with Wallace keeping a visual bead on the captain. The villagers closest to Annja politely fingered her clothes and sniffed at her. She looked toward the boat, seeing Marsha and Amanda leaning against the rail. Ken was at the bow, talking to Almeirão's first mate. Some of the children had waded into the water and were tracing the letters painted on the side of the boat, one was reaching up to grab the railing. The insects were thick along the shore, seeming to prefer the newcomers over the villagers. Probably something in the Kayabi diet or something they put on their skin kept the pests away. Annja weathered the bites, finding the insect repellent she'd liberally sprayed on wholly ineffectual.

Annja slowly moved through the village. A thin girl, maybe eight or nine, grabbed onto her hand and guided her. Away from the river, and behind the largest hut, which Annja took to be a communal building, was a vegetable field that spread out like the spokes of a wheel between rows of trees. Tapir hides were being tanned and stretched on a frame to the north, a cloud of insects over the apparatus. Closer, she saw a thick green-black snake cut through the ferns. She hadn't seen its head, but watching its body and mentally counting, she knew it was at least twelve feet long. Unconsciously, she took a few steps back and scanned the area around her.

She guessed an hour or more had passed when Almeirão came over to her. His canvas pack was smaller now, his trading with the Kayabi done, and whatever he'd gotten in return took up far less space than what he'd bartered away.

"Ask your questions," Almeirão said. He gestured to an older man who followed close behind. This Kayabi appeared to be the most tattooed of anyone, and he looked to be about forty—though appearance was a deceptive thing with people in remote locations; he might well have been ten or more years on either side of that mark. "This is Jywa, the chief, one of the few here with a name, though the name seems to apply to all those in his family. I explained that you are looking for monsters."

Jywa grinned, and pointed at himself. The tattoos on his legs and chest were black and looked more like runes. A boxy tattoo outlined his mouth—similar to designs many of the other adults had, and there was a stippling over his eyebrows and across his forehead.

Annja launched into a brief introduction she'd planned. Almeirão translated for the chieftain's benefit. She was nudged from behind, some of the villagers crowding in. "We search along the Amazon River for beasts cloaked in mystery and legend," Annja explained. "Among them a magical child with backward feet and the mapinguari—"

"Guari," Jywa pronounced, the word sounding harder coming from him. He bobbed his head. "Guari."

"You've seen one of them?" She didn't disguise the excitement in her voice. Almeirão translated haltingly.

"Apparently he has seen one," the captain said.

More vigorous head bobbing. The adult villagers around them nodded, too, and began chattering. Annja knew Amanda would have her work cut out for her filtering the voices to a manageable level so she and the chieftain could be clearly heard. Annja's heart raced. She'd read several reports of some of the Amazon's so-called mythical beasts actually being spotted—it lent a little more credence to the notion that at least some of the creatures might exist.

"Where did you—"

Almeirão talked, and Jywa pointed away from the river and spoke rapidly.

"One roamed beyond the gardens, past the growing grounds," Almeirão translated. "One mapinguari. Never two such beasts together. Only one. A singular creature. They spot it by accident, have never found it while actually looking. Saw it last year. Not at all this year. He thinks their mighty spearmen frightened it away."

The chieftain continued to talk, and Almeirão's brow furrowed. Annja could tell he was trying to find English words to give her.

"Jywa says your beast has long claws and the skin of a…" He paused and listened to Jywa again. "Skin like a caiman, a second mouth on its belly. One eye." He waited again while the chieftain went on. "An ape or a giant sloth, it is neither of those beasts and yet it is both of those beasts, but much larger. It stands taller than a Kayabi when it rears on its back feet, and it is covered in thick matted fur." Almeirão lowered his voice. "He describes something I saw when I was a child, but that was a far distance from here. Your beast, though, is real."

Wallace edged closer, the camera trained on Annja now.

Annja said, "The mapinguari is believed to be traced back to prehistoric times, yet scattered reports of it surface today. People have claimed to see the beast in the remotest locations along the Amazon, that they can rip trees in two, ferocious and dangerous."

Almeirão was quietly translating this for the villagers; Jywa nodded the entire time.

"Some accounts—"

The chieftain interrupted, his voice rising in excitement. With his hands he made slashing gestures.

"Jywa says the guari is louder than a howler monkey, that it stinks worse than a basket of long-dead fish, and that spears bounce off its hide. It travels near the river, but will not venture in. And it stays away from people, like it is afraid of them, and also afraid of the river."

Annja segued into something else she'd prepared. "We have to look to 1937 to find an incident where a mapinguari encroached on civilization. In central Brazil there were reports that one of the beasts went on a rampage, slaughtering more than a hundred cows in villages, with farmers providing a fearsome description of the creature. In all the research, we found no evidence of it attacking humans. It is our endeavor, at *Chasing History's Monsters,* to find and record images of this beast and any other rare species in the region."

Wallace clicked off the camera. Ned continued to take stills, and Annja hoped he had more than a few memory cards with him.

"What do the tattoos mean?" Ned caught the captain's attention. He pulled back his own shirtsleeve displaying his tattoo, a snake that coiled around his arm and was chewing on its tail. "Got that in Kabul." He held the camera with his other hand and pulled up that sleeve. It showed a skull with a dagger thrust through the eyes. "This one on vacation in Saigon."

"I do not think you want to know what those mean," Almeirão said.

Now Annja was curious. "Fish?"

Almeirão let out a breath and nodded. "Sure, sure, some of the designs are fish. Some represent animals and forest spirits."

"What about the dotted boxes around their mouths? Not all of them have that. You don't have that, have any that I can see." Ned took more pictures.

"Men can have that tattoo after they earn the right to eat human flesh. The Kayabi, like the Apiaká, used to practice ritualistic cannibalism." Almeirão frowned. "And the next time I tell you that you don't want to know something—"

"We'll not press," Ned concluded. "Some of those box tattoos look like they were inked recently, Annja. Look at the redness."

"Come! They have invited you to the midday meal," Almeirão said. "These people do not have a lot. It would be rude to—"

"Of course we will join them," Annja said.

"Depending on what's on the menu," Ned quipped, as he traced a boxy outline around his mouth.

8

"My cook is providing a treat to the village," the captain said. "But, Annja, you cannot eat until after the men have had their fill. It is the Kayabi way. Men first, women get the leftovers."

The midday meal was served in the large hut, and Marsha had replaced Wallace, who said he wanted to go through his recordings and do a little editing. In truth, Annja suspected he didn't want to eat whatever the Kayabi were serving. A man so finicky should not be so quick to accept assignments to exotic places, she thought.

Annja inwardly seethed at the blatant gender discrimination the tribe practiced, but she held her tongue and sat outside the doorway next to Marsha, both of them watching what transpired inside. Just once she'd like to feature a tribe where the women made the rules and men had to eat the leftovers.

Almeirão's contribution included a platter of pancakes. "This is cupacu, a local dish made from tree pulp," he explained for Annja's benefit. Marsha filmed the men eating. "Cupacu is one of my cook's specialties. The pulp, it can also be made into juices, jellies, and I have had cupacu liquor." A pause. "Too much of the liquor a few too many times." He also provided a few bowls of freshwater crab, which was served in the shell with the claws attached. Annja's mouth watered, but she stayed silent.

The Kayabi offered up a sort of mash, that Almeirão called "manicoba." He looked to Annja. "It takes a long while to prepare. Manioc leaves are ground, cooked, served with manioc flour and sweet pepper. You ladies will undoubtedly get to try some of this, but my crab and cupacu…it seems these men will not leave any of that."

"So unfair," Marsha whispered.

"They can't understand you," Annja said. "You don't have to talk so low."

"I'm not saying this is unfair to us, sitting outside like stray cats waiting for scraps. It doesn't matter to us. We're here for a visit, tonight or tomorrow we leave, and this—" she pointed at the men still eating "—this will be only a bad memory. I'm talking about how unfair it is to the women in this place. How can they live like this?"

"I've seen worse," Annja said. "Besides, we're not here to start a revolution, just observe."

"And ask about monsters." Marsha let out a hissing breath that fluttered her bangs. "Doesn't mean I'm not bothered."

"It's good that you're bothered."

"So many people are naïve. They don't realize that

oppression still exists. Is our program going to show any of that? Even a hint?"

"We will." Annja rose. The men had finished eating and motioned the women and children inside to dine on what was left.

Almeirão pulled Annja aside. "Jywa and some of the other men, they say there is a village around the turn in this tributary. It takes them a day to reach it in canoes. They say there are two white people like you there, that it is a dreaming village. Sometimes Jywa dreams there when he has something to barter. He says maybe if you dream you will find your monsters. Dreams lead to things."

"Dream?" Annja sat and reached for a leaf she smeared with the manicoba. She put the leaf in her mouth and used her teeth to scrape the mash off, like she would if she were eating an artichoke appetizer at a fine restaurant. It looked like plain oatmeal but was surprisingly tasty. "What sort of dream? Hallucinations?"

Almeirão shuddered. "We can stop there, at the dreaming village. I have been there before. You can dream with them if you like. I have dreamed once, but never again. The dreams along this river, with these hidden people and the old, old ways…dreams here can be nightmares."

Marsha looked at Annja. "We're going, aren't we?"

"Absolutely."

9

It was early evening when Roux's plane arrived. He found the sound of the rain the airport featured throughout the terminal disturbing. He located a money exchanger and switched his Euros to colorful Brazilian reals, stopped at one of the shops, and bought a sturdy canvas carryall. Then he took a shuttle to the Hilton in the heart of the city, knowing he likely wouldn't be able to charter a boat until the morning, and so he'd get that proverbial good night's rest. There was a shop off the lobby, and in it he picked up toiletries, two pairs of over-priced jeans, three shirts and underwear, suspecting that the dress clothes he'd carried in his bag to Rouen and subsequently brought here would not be appropriate for a river excursion.

Checking into his room, and musing that this trip was an expensive venture to quell his worries—Annja always managed to take care of herself, didn't she?—he called her satellite phone.

It rang and rang, no pickup, no voice mail. Same problem he'd had when he'd tried from the airport. But if she was busy she wouldn't answer, maybe didn't even

have it on her. People walked through the hall outside
his door—he guessed they were young judging by the
sound of their voices; the burst of laughter had a youth-
ful energy. The elevator chimed; he'd wished he would
have asked for a room at the end of the hall where it
would be quieter. He needed that good night's sleep. Too
much turbulence to rest on the plane. Leaning against
the window, he looked down on the street and faintly
heard the hum of traffic, a sound that was the same all
over the world. A siren, too. There were always sirens,
save in the remotest of places. He remembered back to a
time when there were no sirens and no cars, only horses.

I'm so old, he thought.

He waited a half hour and called again.

Finally Annja picked up, but she didn't speak at first.

"Annja—" Roux started. "I am in Belém now,
and—" He heard birds squawking. No doubt there were
an abundance of parrots along the river. A throaty howl
cut above the noise. He had no clue what it was, an animal maybe. It was odd. "Annja," he persisted. "Where
are you? Is there a village you can name? I'm going
to—"

His throat tightened when he heard a gasp. Someone
started talking rapidly, but in a language he couldn't
understand. There were other voices, too, muffled, the
howl again, a cry—either of surprise or pain. He tried
to pick out Annja's voice, his sense of worry growing.

"Annja—"

Words were rapidly spoken in an unfamiliar language and then the line went dead.

Roux called repeatedly, but Annja would not pick up.

This wasn't the first time he'd had trouble contacting her, and in the end there had always been an easy rationale…poor reception, she was in the midst of something important and would get back to him later.

But this didn't have an "easy rationale" feel.

He called again. Nothing.

Roux stuffed his phone in his pocket, packed everything into the carryall, checked out, and left the hotel to head to the docks. He'd camp there overnight if he had to just to find a boat to rent and a captain.

Annja could well take care of herself, right?

Joan of Arc had been able to take care of herself, too.

In the back of his mind he saw Joan's face, Annja's wavering next to it before he blinked the image away.

Roux had failed Joan. He wouldn't fail Annja.

Still, he had no idea where she was. So when he managed to charter that boat…where would he ask the captain to take him?

The howl he heard over the phone ran over and over through his mind.

10

The captain was right about night coming early to this part of the Amazon, the trees so high that they cut the light when the sun started to set. Annja stood on the observation deck with Ned. He took pictures of the boat lights reflecting on the black water. Something large splashed at the edge of their vision.

"My satellite phone is missing," she said.

"Along with four pairs of my socks and all my Juicy Fruit." Ned laughed. "Did you tell the captain?"

"He said Kayabi kids probably slipped on board while we were in the village. I saw one climbing on the boat. He said that every time he stops there, he's always missing little things…though nothing that really matters to him, usually food. He said he makes sure to put anything valuable under his bed and in drawers, says he doesn't think they look there."

Ned lowered his camera. "My mistake for leaving my duffel open. At least they left me two pair—the cheap white ones. And good thing I had my camera bag with me."

"I wouldn't have retrieved it for you a second time."

Ned brushed at the insects hovering around his face. She saw that insect bites were plentiful along his neck. "Captain Almeirão could have warned us, though, about the Kayabi taking things. Marsha had placed a little picture of one of her cats on her nightstand. She's furious it's gone. Gave me an earful about it. Just a silly cat picture, but she's steaming."

As if in response to that comment a cat snarled, the sound carrying across the dark water. A jaguar or leopard must be hunting along the shore, Annja thought. A second snarl was followed by the flutter of wings, birds shooting up, briefly caught in the light of the boat, and then disappearing in the darkness. Something else splashed, the ripples caught in the shimmering light.

"I was expecting a call from Doug on that phone, and if by chance he gets a Kayabi to push the button and answer it, he'll not understand the language."

"Wallace has a sat phone, doesn't he?"

"Yeah. Doug will phone Wall when he can't reach me." She scowled. "They're expensive, sat phones, and that one was mine, not the station's. And then there's the hassle of trying to keep the same number."

"Cost more than socks and chewing gum, that's for certain." Ned snapped a few more pictures of the reflected light, and then took a few of Annja. "Marsha asked the captain to go back to the Kayabi village. She really wanted that photo. But Almeirão told her to be sure to stash her stuff away when we stop at the next village…and to picture the cat in her head. She told me she was only picturing wringing the neck of whoever swiped the photograph, in her head."

Annja studied the shore, but could see nothing beyond bands of gray and black, the rainforest hiding its mysteries. "I was just hoping one of the team had borrowed my phone, to call home or something."

"Did you poke around the boat, make sure it's not here? That somebody in the captain's crew doesn't have sticky fingers?"

"Yeah. I looked," Annja said. "And I'm very good at looking."

"And you're very good looking, too."

Annja's eyes were instantly daggers. Despite the limited light, her expression of ire was clear.

"Sorry. Sorry. Once upon a time, a woman would take that clever comment as a compliment. Now I'm sexist, eh? No harm in a little flirting." He paused. "Or are lady archaeologists only interested in men that have been dead a few thousand years?"

Annja didn't reply. Ned was good looking, but he seemed too superficial, and she wasn't going to entertain any notion of romance on this trip. She pushed away from the rail and left for her room, took a quick shower, and crawled into bed. Thunder boomed and within moments rain was pelting down.

Sleep didn't come easy. Her mind was filled with the image of a fence that had swords for railings. The fence circled a village where a woman burned in agony at a stake. The people gathered were tattooed and mostly naked, some of them wore the faces of the Kayabi she'd seen earlier today. One held a satellite phone, another wore a pair of argyle socks. She heard the fire crackle, the throaty howl of a monkey, and then the ship's horn sounded, waking her.

A heartbeat later there was pounding on her door.

"Annja, we're here." It was Marsha's voice. "I'm going ashore with you, since Wallace isn't feeling so good. Annja—"

"Give me a few minutes."

"Damn a few. Your breakfast is getting cold, and I'm ready to go."

11

"These are Dslala, and many of them do not bother with clothes," Almeirão said. "This group is completely isolated except in the rainy season, when boatmen stop here to trade when this tributary is swollen. The boatmen call these people Cacateiros, 'clubbers' in Portuguese. But they hunt with blowguns and spears, and they are not Cacateiros, they are the Dslala."

"No tats," Ned observed.

Marsha was filming the captain and Ned, and then turned her camera toward the shore, where a group of women stretched a piece of colorful cloth and folded it.

"No," Almeirão said. "Not many tribes tattoo themselves anymore."

Ned whispered, "Hopefully because they don't eat—"

"Let's get to work, shall we?" Annja was the first one over the rail. "Then I'm going to schedule some dreaming time."

ANNJA STRIPPED OUT of her clothes and climbed into a large earthenware tub, pulling her legs in close. The water was warm, and slightly oily, and it smelled of something she couldn't identify…similar to rosemary, but sharper and settling strongly on her tongue. She'd interviewed several villagers—getting her work for the show out of the way. Happily she'd found a tribesman surprisingly and reasonably fluent in English and who translated for his tribe, regaling everyone with tales of the mythical Amazon beasts. He said there were two Americans living with them, but they were away at the moment, "pestering a businessman harvesting plants."

The highlight of the filming had been the reveal of a big piece of fabric that Dslala artisans had stained some years ago with an image of a mapinguari; the chieftain traded it to Annja's crew in exchange for a pearl necklace Amanda offered.

The tapestry tucked safely on the boat, Annja had slipped away to soak in this tub and "dream." She was at the far end of the village, where the rainforest encroached. Snakes draped from the lowest tree branches. Higher up toward the sky, monkeys cavorted and parrots watched her curiously. She found it all idyllic.

"All of you," D'jok said. He was the English-speaking Dslala she'd found. "All of you in the huito bath, Annja Creed."

Annja took a breath and dipped under the water.

When she came up for air D'jok placed a blindfold over her eyes, and directed her to step out. She patted herself dry with a coarse cloth he'd provided, and he guided her to a second tub.

"Into this, will you please, Annja Creed?" D'jok set

Annja's hands against the rim and she climbed in. It felt as if she was wallowing in warm oatmeal.

"What is this?" Annja liked the feel of it, relaxing, as if it were drawing out all her concerns.

"Clay," he said. "White clay from under the earth. Foreign dreamers only can come to this village in the rainy times when the river will let them pass and the chieftain decides to…hmm, I need the word…tolerate. When the chieftain decides to tolerate the strangers."

Annja had surrendered her watch in trade for this experience. The chieftain found the watch curious and was quick to put it on his own wrist. "What does the clay do?"

"What you need it to," he answered. "All of you, Annja Creed."

She held her breath and went under, finding that the clay pulled at her, trying to keep her in its embrace. She stayed that way for as long as possible, then when her lungs screamed for air she climbed out and scraped as much of the clay off as she could. It was a difficult proposition since she couldn't see.

"Sit here, Annja Creed."

"Should I keep the blindfold on?"

"Until I remove it, Annja Creed. The blindfold is so you listen to the forest. Open eyes keep you from paying close attention. Annja Creed does not listen so well with open eyes."

D'jok said something in the Dslala tongue and Annja heard shuffling footsteps, a grunting, and then she was doused with water that smelled like gardenias. The process was repeated.

"To remove the rest of the clay," D'jok explained. "To wash away the bad that was pulled from your skin."

He tugged Annja to her feet and another pair of hands wrapped a coarse cloth around her. D'jok led her across ground dotted with rocks and twigs that dug into her soles. She clamped her teeth together to keep from crying out. How many thousands of dollars did people pay for this type of experience in a spa? Then she felt the cool smoothness of ground cover between her toes.

One part of this ritual was proving true: the sounds and scents of the rainforest did seem more intense with the blindfold on. She still heard the monkeys and parrots, but she also heard the breeze playing across her skin and picked up a hint of rain in the air, like another of the frequent storms was on its way. Softer, as if from a great distance, was the snarl of the cat. Closer came high-pitched laughter and splashing…probably children playing along the bank. Some type of fish was cooking, the odor stirring her stomach. She'd been so busy with the filming and interviews that she'd skipped lunch.

"Inside, Annja Creed."

Annja remembered seeing a hut surrounded by trees beyond the village, no other huts near it. This was probably that hut. D'jok had told Marsha and Ned not to take pictures of it, as the shaman who lived inside would be so angry he would cast a bad spell on them.

"Home of Ch'det," D'jok said.

She bumped her head on the top of the doorframe and ducked, shuffling forward until D'jok pressed on her shoulders and she sat. He pulled her blindfold off.

Annja felt instantly dizzy. It was dark inside. The hut

had no windows, but there was a small hole in the roof, through which a stream of smoke spiraled up, looking like a thin, writhing serpent. Leaves burned slowly on a wooden plate that sat between her and an old man. Actually, he seemed ancient.

"Ch'det," D'jok said as an introduction. "Our most wise man." He said something else in the Dslala tongue, then he pointed at her. "Annja Creed of America."

Ch'det's voice sounded like the river gently lapping at its banks. She could make out none of the words, but appreciated the resonance.

"Annja Creed, I told Ch'det you bathed in huito and are ready for ayahuasca. In your words ayahuasca means 'vine of the soul.' Some of the boatmen who dream here, they call it 'dead man's root.' But I do not like the sense of that, though dead men you may see."

The shaman picked up a long pipe and inhaled, the glow at the end a pale orange and whatever was in the bowl adding an acrid touch to the air. He rested the pipe on his feet, reached behind him—Annja realized he wore no clothes—and brought forth a bowl with liquid in it.

"Prepared only for you, Annja Creed," D'jok said. "It will make you ill, but that is necessary for healing and dreaming. You will need all of it."

Ill? Annja accepted the bowl. She was usually more curious than cautious. The shaman gestured for her to drink it, and then spoke at length.

"Ch'det says if the spirits allow, you will meet ghosts, see your death, and become aware."

And if the spirits don't allow? Annja wondered as she downed the vile-tasting mixture.

"If the spirits do not allow, you may see your death anyway, Annja Creed. No matter the journey you take, you will first feel like you are dying. Only close to death can you truly love life and be open to all possibilities. Being so close to death makes us more alive."

Annja had been close to death many times. She managed to choke down the last of the liquid.

"Death and life," he said. "They are not so far apart. The thickness of a flower petal. That is the space between the two."

In the space of a heartbeat, Annja felt death rushing at her.

12

She'd never tasted anything so utterly awful. The liquid had gone down her throat, but was starting to crawl its way back up again. Gagging and fighting for air, she was suffocating on the ghastly concoction.

That she'd traded her classic waterproof watch for this ceremony…was madness. Thankfully, she'd told Marsha not to record any of this, to let her have a little privacy.

Let her die alone.

Annja leaned forward, saw that a large empty bowl had been placed in front of her, and retched. When she thought she'd given up everything in her stomach, she retched again.

And again.

The world spun and she felt sucked down with it.

She fell on her side and convulsed, her legs and arms gyrating despite her best efforts to control them, her face involuntarily rubbing against the dirt floor. Her tongue felt swollen and she tried to talk but only an unintelligible moan escaped with a line of drool. She tasted blood and more of the vile mixture she'd been all too willing to swallow.

Suddenly her chest felt as if it were on fire, and her head pounded. The thunderous rhythm of her heartbeat slammed against her eardrums.

What had she done to herself? She gulped in air and retched once more. Roux's words teased her ears. "Be well, Annja. Watch yourself, all right?"

She wasn't well, and she hadn't watched herself.

Waves of fire and ice chased each other from her toes to the ends of her fingers, and then a cloud of black appeared and engulfed her.

As the imaginary wind screamed like a chorus of howler monkeys, she thought she heard the shaman cackle before oblivion claimed her.

SHE AWOKE ALONE.

The shaman and D'jok were gone, and whatever leaves had been burning on the plate were out. All traces of her vomit had been cleaned up, and she was dressed in her jeans and a long sleeve shirt that felt good against her skin.

Her stomach was empty, and the headache was gone. She listened, hearing the chattering of parrots and the shush of the trees rubbing against each other in a strong breeze, the bones clacking on strings in the doorway. No human voices.

Annja tentatively got to her feet, fighting the momentary dizziness, and shifting her weight back and forth to make sure she was okay. In the light that slipped in through the curtain she caught the details of the hut.

She'd been so focused on the shaman before that she'd not noticed his surroundings. The place was perhaps ten feet square, spacious for a home belonging to only one man. There was a sleeping pallet at the back, shelves to the right holding an odd collection of things—dried plants, earthenware bowls, monkey and parrot skulls... things one might find in a medieval alchemist's lab. But there were modern pieces, too, probably from the boatmen who traded with the tribe or who'd "paid" for a dream...and who actually got a dream, unlike Annja who'd only gotten a terribly upset stomach. There was a large aluminum cheese grater, a set of drinking glasses, a commemorative crystal paperweight with an image of the American flag in it, and on the top shelf a plaster bust of Julius Caesar—what dreams had been bought with those things?

Taming her curiosity, she didn't touch anything. Annja stepped outside. It was morning, and she'd undergone the ordeal in the middle of the afternoon, so she'd been unconscious for well more than a few hours. She felt rested...felt better, actually, than she had in a long while. Maybe surrendering her watch hadn't been too high a price.

She felt *good*.

Someone had put shoes on her—her favorite tennis shoes. Twigs crunched under her feet as she retraced her steps from the shaman's hut back to the earthenware tubs—empty now, though it looked like rainwater had gathered in the bottom of each. Then she went to the village proper, which was also oddly empty. A glance at the river...*Orellana's Prize* was gone. Maybe it had just floated downriver, her camera crew looking for more footage.

Was this part of the ritual? Leaving her alone in some nameless village somewhere on an Amazon tributary after she'd drank the worst cocktail ever and got nothing from a supposedly mystical experience?

Nothing except an exceptionally good night's sleep.

Padding to the shore, she saw a turtle bob its head up. The details she picked out on the creature were amazing, all the little ridges around its eyes and the variation of color, as if every shade of green that existed in the world had been dabbled on the head of the creature.

Annja listened for her heartbeat, but all she heard was the lapping of the river against the bank. She held her breath. What was the tiniest and most meaningful measure of time? A heartbeat? An inhaled breath? Was she suspended in that infinitesimal space between increments of time?

She took in the scent of the river and the damp earth, the flowers that hung on the vines draped from trees—more fragrant in this instant than the most expensive perfume. She exhaled, but the odors of the rainforest remained a part of her. Annja picked up a shiny rock with her left hand, the sword forming in her right. The ground damp, the rock wet, all evidence it had rained. But this was the rainy season…of course, it had rained.

She squeezed the rock against her palm and felt it warming, a piece of the world she'd claimed just for herself.

Was this a dream?

No. This had to be real.

If she was dead or dreaming she wouldn't feel the rock, would she? Wouldn't feel anything or smell anything. The sun would not be kissing her forehead.

"Watch yourself, all right?" Roux's voice.

She spun, eyes searching the foliage and hut entrances. The old man had called her—called her before her phone had been stolen—said he was coming to Brazil. Had he somehow found his way here? Caught up?

"Watch yourself. Watch yourself. Watch yourself."

Roux stepped out of the closest hut, squinting in the bright sunlight, reaching into a pocket and pulling out a pair of sunglasses. He looked to study the glasses a moment before putting them on and coming toward her.

Roux could not have gotten here so quickly. Annja released the sword and it fell. She stared at it, seeing her eyes reflected in the blade. The sword should have vanished. She'd mentally dismissed it. The blade should have been whisked away to the otherwhere.

"I *am* dreaming," she said.

"Which is preferable to being dead," Roux returned. "If you were dead, that would mean I'm dead, too. And last I checked I still had a pulse. I had a devil of a time finding you, Annja."

She carefully studied him. There was something different about him. It took her a minute…he was younger, just a little, fewer lines on his face. Maybe it was because he was relaxed, the setting easing him. His shoulders did not look so square and stiff. "How did you get here, old man? More to the point, how did you find me?"

"How did *I* find you? Annja, you brought me here."

"Not possible." Annja sucked in a breath; Roux smelled faintly of some musky cologne.

"This is your dream, you brought me here. And where is here, Annja?" His bright eyes held an eagerness she'd never noticed in him before. She waited and watched as his hair darkened. Black now with gray highlights. The years were melting off him. He was getting younger by the minute.

"Madness." Annja dropped her gaze from Roux and looked to her sword. This time instead of her reflection in the blade, she saw the eyes of a stranger. She fell to her knees and checked it closer. The reflection disappeared entirely, replaced by wavering shades of green. "What did I do to myself? What the heck did I drink?"

Roux stepped out of his shoes, and the shoes disappeared. Barefoot, the pads on his feet thick like a Dslala's. He extended a hand. "I brought some people with me. I want you to meet them." The calluses she'd remembered on his fingers felt fresher, coarser.

"People?"

"Venez avec moi, Annja," Roux said.

She picked up her sword and let him lead her. She could hear everything, the fabric of his pants brushing, the leaves rustling in the trees around the village, the water flowing behind her now. A glance back and she saw the turtle had come up again. The chatter of the monkeys and the parrots came so loud now it was hurtful to listen to. And when she thought about it, the odors of the village were overpowering, too. There was her sweat, the river, the rich fragrance of the loam, the scent of flowers, and the tantalizing aroma of fish cooking. The scent of Roux's cologne was heavier as well.

He led her behind a hut where two incongruous stone benches were separated by a bowl-shaped depression filled with dark water. The benches had not been in the village when she'd toured it with Marsha and Ned. But they were familiar. It took her a moment to place them...exact replicas of the garden benches outside the Hôtel de Sully in Paris. Annja took a whiff of the liquid in the small pool—huito, the stuff that filled the first tub she'd immersed herself in.

She sat. "I don't see anyone else, Roux. Who did you bring along to my dream in this nameless village?"

He sat next to her and pointed at the opposite bench. A heartbeat ago it had been empty.

"Cette épée, ma chère amie, a déjà tué par ma main," the newcomer said. *This sword, my friend, once slew men by my hand.*

Who are you? Annja thought.

"Charlemagne." He patted a sword that appeared in his lap. "Joyeuse." He was dressed out of date and rather plainly. He wore a gray linen shirt and matching breeches. Over the top he wore a dark tunic trimmed with a pale silk fringe, everything looking expertly hand-stitched. He was in his sixties or seventies, tall, and with a thick neck and a nose that belonged on a bigger man's face. His hair was snow white, and there was an abundance of it. The curls stirred in the wind. He had on a heavy fragrance that warred with Roux's and disturbed her nostrils, and under that was the scent of dried blood. *"Joyeuse, très chère amie."*

Charlemagne was long, long dead. Annja remembered D'jok saying that she might be talking to ghosts. Why would her mind conjure up this man? He looked solid, though, and he cast a shadow. Her mind had fabricated a very real image.

"Et vous êtes?"

Annja was fluent in French. "I am Annja Creed," she said in answer to the question.

"Vous possédez une épée de Jeanne d'Arc." His eyebrows rose.

"I don't know why I have Joan of Arc's sword," Annja said. *And I don't know why you know it's Joan of Arc's sword. And I don't know why I'm dream-talking to King Charlemagne.*

"Cette épée...c'était le mien."

It was Annja's turn to raise her eyebrows.

"Jamais mon préféré. C'était Joyeuse."

He'd just told her that Joan of Arc's sword could have belonged to him. But Joyeuse, the blade in his lap, had been his favorite and he carried it until his death. He was not sorry that he'd never wielded Joan's sword in combat.

"I don't understand," Annja said. "You could have had this sword? This one?"

"I'd even like to think it was once mine. But I don't believe it was ever truly meant to be my sword—though it was offered to me and I held it in my hands. A good balance, that sword." Charlemagne spoke English now, a language he couldn't possibly have known during his lifetime. But since this was her dream, she supposed she could make the characters speak whatever language she wanted. "God-touched, that sword is young woman. In my heart I knew it was meant to be Joan's all along. You know, it once belonged to my grandfather—Charles Martel, and so I could have inherited it. I don't know who had it before him. Maybe God. Maybe an angel. I held it when my hands were young and the blade felt too heavy for them to carry it. Too heavy and yet not heavy enough. My grandfather...he asked if I could change the world with the sword. I was too young to consider such a proposition, and so I handed it back. A boy does not fill his head with notions of saving France or changing the world. A young boy is interested in far more simple things."

"The story is true then," Annja said. Or true as far as her vision was letting her believe. "Of it being Charles Martel's, then Joan's."

"Briefly mine between."

"Briefly."

"My grandfather was a righteous man. He took that sword and put it in a place where someone willing to change the world would find it." Charlemagne stood and stretched, rotated his head as if working a kink out of his neck. "Joyeuse better suited me in any event. It helped me save enough, eh? Change enough things, don't you think? Joyeuse and me are in the history books."

He extended a hand and she hesitantly took it, keeping hold of her sword with the other.

"Let us walk, would you mind?" His eyes twinkled. "Indulge an old man and a king, eh? I've not been out for a walk in a long, long time, and I've not seen such a beautiful forest. Perhaps we will find a deer. I love to hunt deer. Perhaps if we see one you will summon up a bow so that I can shoot the deer. Roast venison. Ah, my favorite. My doctors…they told me to avoid roast meat. But boiled venison is not near so tasty. Had I listened to them, I might have lived longer. Though I might not have enjoyed it quite so much, young woman. Besides, I think I lived just long enough."

The blood Annja had smelled on him, it could have been from an animal. Deer perhaps? It had a bit of a gamey odor.

"While we walk, I think I will regale you with a tale of one of my many great battles. Perhaps you would like to hear about that final push I devised to conquer Saxonia and to convert the barbarians to Christianity. That…that is a very good story. And you, Annja Creed, you must have equally good tales since you have the sword that was once, very briefly, mine."

The rainforest closed around them as they stepped past the final group of huts. An eerie silence took over.

"Vous possédez une épée de Jeanne d'Arc?" Charlemagne asked, slipping into French again.

"I don't know why I have Joan of Arc's sword," Annja replied. *And I don't know why I'm dream-talking to King Charlemagne.*

When he appeared to tire of the walk, they returned to the benches. Roux was waiting. Charlemagne bowed and kissed her hand.

"Il a été très agréable, Annja Creed. Traiter l'épée bien. Jusqu'à ce que nous nous reverrons…"

"Yes, until we meet again."

Then he was gone. She closed her eyes and listened, hearing Roux pacing nearby. Annja wondered what he would look like when she opened her eyes again. Different? A little, she confirmed. He had yet darker hair and even fewer lines on his face, more years disappeared. On the bench across from her was a slip of a girl. She hadn't heard the child approach, though she could now smell her—flowers and youth.

At first Annja thought it was the thief she'd chased outside the airport. She was the same size and had the same smile. But there were no braces, and the clothes were plain, like an extra at a Renaissance Faire might wear.

Roux bowed deeply to the child and then faced Annja. *"Annja Creed, rencontrer mon cher, cher ami de Jeanne d'Arc."*

Annja shivered. Joan of Arc? Annja often thought of Joan, but never had thought of her this young. The girl was probably twelve or thirteen. At first she seemed plain, unremarkable. But the longer Annja stared, the more beautiful she realized the child was. Her eyes were clear and wide, face unblemished. The girl looked perfect and innocent, yet her mien was determined and her lips set firm.

Annja had no words for her imagined encounter with Christendom's youngest martyr.

"My sword," Joan said. Her voice was small, musical, but it could be heard easily through all the other sounds of this spot. "Only a moment ago, and yet so very long ago that was my sword you have in your lap. When I walked the earth at Chinon I sought a blade.

It was in the Church of Saint Catherine of Fierbois. It was behind the altar with other weapons, all covered with rust. I knew the sword was there, the voices...*my* voices...told me it was there. Five crosses on it, and not deep beneath the ground. The prelates cleaned it for me, said the rust fell away like dust. And I was given two sheaths for it, one made of red velvet and the other of a golden cloth. Lovely, but not appropriate, thoughtful though. I thanked them for the gifts. But I had another made of strong leather, more practical. I told the inquisitors about it, the sword, and they asked where I had gotten the blade. They asked so many unnecessary questions. I told them the truth about the sword. But not *all* of the truth, for they were not of a mind to understand."

Annja found her voice. "Understand? Understand what?"

"That I loved that sword like a mother would love a child. I loved Saint Catherine, and it was found in her church. They would not have understood that God delivered the blade to me when I was ready for it. And they would not have understood its purpose."

By having Charlemagne's grandfather bury it inside a church? Was that how it was delivered?

"And now you have the blade, since you were ready for it."

"I can't save the world," Annja said. "And I can't change the world with this sword." Charlemagne said his grandfather asked if he could change the world with it. In her way, Joan had effected changes that stretched from her birth to her death…and that had ramifications for centuries beyond.

"You have saved many lives, dear Annja," Joan said. "And saving even one person means that in their eyes, the world is forever changed." She raised her chin. "And that, I believe, is the sword's purpose."

Are you real? Is any part of this real? Annja rubbed at her temples.

Joan had aged in the moment Annja had looked away. She was still young, in her teens, but there were scars on her arms and she looked weary. Her clothes—pants and a discolored tunic, what a farmer might wear—were soiled. Annja had seen enough blood to know that the garments had been spattered with it, and the attempts to wash it out were not wholly successful. Yet, she didn't smell blood on the girl, only the soft scent of sweet flowers. French flowers—fleur-di-lis.

Joan looked at Roux, and in that instant Annja saw his face soften and eyes become watery. His hands relaxed, and he mouthed something. Annja did not try to make it out, although this was her dream. Roux had been Joan's knight. Annja looked down at the tips of her feet. Insects scurried along the ground in all directions, intensely colorful beetles. A butterfly lit on the ground, large and amazingly beautiful. Annja swore she could hear the gentle beat of its wings. Her gaze followed it as it rose and landed on the bench opposite her.

Joan of Arc was gone…Roux was at Annja's side, looking older now, the decades rushing back upon his frame. She stood and took his offered arm. There were lines at the edges of his eyes, and they deepened as he escorted her through the village and to the earthenware tubs and then beyond them to the shaman's hut. His hair was long and gray by the time he pulled the curtain back and gestured for her to go inside.

"Until we meet again," he said.

Annja went inside and woke up to screaming.

13

A dream! Joan of Arc, Charlemagne, Roux...all of it really had been a twisted and yet magically wonderful dream. Soul-satisfying.

Annja picked herself up from the hut floor. An oil lamp burned, revealing the hut's interior—simple furnishings, animal skulls and primitive knickknacks. She was wearing the coarse piece of cloth, wrapped around her like it was a bath towel. Annja was alone in the shaman's hut.

A look outside told her it was night. So she'd slept a few hours. That would explain why she felt so rested. And it probably also meant she'd slept so much that she'd have a hard time drifting off later tonight.

She stretched and looked to her pile of clothes, reached for them and stopped when a scream interrupted the chorus of insect sounds.

She thought she'd dreamt the scream.

But there it was again, and what she'd heard hadn't been part of her dream. Wearing only the coarse cloth, Annja dashed outside. Immediately she felt the sword hovering anxiously. She summoned it, finding the feel of the pommel in her hand reassuring.

The foliage was so thick here that it was nearly impossible to make out the trunks of the closest trees. Her eyes adjusted to the darkness, and in the distance she saw the glow of a torch or a cook fire from the village. She hurriedly stumbled toward that, free hand out to her side to guide her and fingers brushing tree trunks, vines, a snake; feeling first the cool dampness of ground cover beneath her feet, then the biting rocks and broken pieces of wood. Her foot caught on a raised tree root and she went flying, the unseen ground rushing up to meet her. As she slammed into the earth, the air whooshed from her lungs and she instantly got back up and kept going, the sword still held tight in her hand.

Another scream, long and painful.

To her right, half the village was shrouded, but to her left the huts in the water and at the river's edge were clearly visible. An incredible number of stars in the sky above the Amazon River glimmered like shiny silver sequins against a stretch of black velvet; they let Annja take in the grisly details. She raced forward.

The captain had warned them about alligators, and there was a large one on the shore, a villager firmly in its mouth. The unfortunate man screamed once more as Annja closed the distance. There were other villagers nearby, throwing rocks. Four men with spears jabbed at it, but it refused to release the man. It had already killed three men, bitten them in half, their blood and organs spilled on the bank and gleaming in the starlight. If she'd had anything left in her stomach....

Annja rushed past the spearmen and brought the blade down on the beast's neck. It was a caiman, not an alligator, and twice the length of any caiman she'd seen, probably two dozen feet long and maybe two thousand pounds. It was squatter in appearance than an alligator, resembling a black armored tank on stumpy legs.

And it was fast.

Her sword bounced off its hide and she swung it again. She hated the notion of killing such a creature, but there was no choice. Its eyes were black marbles the size of billiard balls, unreadable but locked onto hers.

"Run!" She recognized D'jok's voice.

"The captain!" That was Marsha, somewhere behind her. Annja kept her focus on the huge caiman.

"Annja, Marsha, the captain's dead!" hollered Ned, who was on the deck of *Orellana's Prize,* anchored a few yards out from the bank. A camera to his face, he was undoubtedly taking pictures, recording the grisly tableau for posterity. The channel certainly wouldn't use the images.

The caiman spat out the dead villager and came toward Annja now, head swaying as it trundled, maw opening and fat tongue covered in blood.

Midway between the bank and the boat Annja saw a body—or rather part of a body—floating face-down in the river...what was left of Captain Almeirão. While she'd been dreaming with Joan and Charlemagne, and talking about swords...enjoying her mystical experience, people had been dying. Her "me time" had proven fatal to others.

"You have saved many lives, Annja." She recalled the

line from her dream, yet she hadn't saved any of the caiman's victims. Because she'd selfishly indulged herself.

She stepped in and redoubled her attack on the beast, darting one way and then the next, nearly slipping in the blood and feeling a stone hit her back that had been meant for the caiman. A few more stones pelted it, and the spearmen jumped in, but could not effectively pierce the thing's thick hide. One lucky tribesman managed to lodge a spear into the caiman's side, but it seemed to serve only as a minor irritant.

The spearmen skittered back and she continued to swing.

The creature could have filled the starring role in one of those cheesy SyFy movies, but this wasn't animatronics; it was angry flesh and flashing teeth, she could smell it, a fetid odor that reminded her of death and rotting. A wave of the smell surged up from its belly and she gagged.

The spearmen yelled and jabbed, retreated and yelled again.

The caiman raised its head and opened its cavernous mouth wide, its teeth sparkling in the starlight.

"Annja! What are you doing?" Marsha's voice called to her and she heard footsteps behind her. "It'll kill you. Run! Get out of there!"

"Marsha, stay back! I'm okay."

"Don't get so close!" Marsha swept to Annja's side, but stayed well away from the caiman. She had her video camera pressed to her face—more footage that even Doug would veto. "Keep away from it!"

Annja's throat constricted when the beast turned, its eyes on Marsha now.

"Oh, no," Marsha muttered. "Annja! Help me!"

Like lightning, the caiman shot toward a weaponless target, snout and tail brushing aside the spearmen who'd darted in again, sending one of them into the river. Annja leaped, barely registering a snapping-chittering sound that came from the water—piranha feasting. She pointed the sword down and wrapped both hands around the pommel, drove the blade as hard as she could as she fell onto the caiman's back. The rough ridges of its carapace dug into her like a hundred little knives, and she clamped her teeth tight to keep from screaming. She pushed with all the strength she could summon, the tip of the blade digging even deeper into the caiman's neck, then sinking in farther—through it and into the damp ground beneath.

Annja managed to drive the blade in all the way up to its hilt, pinning the caiman like an insect collector might pin an elephant beetle. The beast thrashed and threw Annja off, its tail striking her in the face. Annja felt dazed, and its tail lashed her again. She felt herself drifting, but Marsha slipped past its snapping jaws and pulled her away.

"Stay awake, Annja. Stay awake!"

Annja fought to stay conscious and focused so the sword would remain in this world. If she lost consciousness, the sword would vanish, the caiman would be free, and who knew how many more people it would kill.

The snapping-chittering from the water grew louder

and a glance showed the surface choppy from the feeding frenzy.

"Those are piranha, aren't they?" Marsha pulled Annja back even farther, falling once, but getting back up and pulling again. "Piranha, and they're eating the captain."

Something was eating the captain and any other villagers that had been tossed in the water. Annja protectively pushed Marsha behind her; the dizziness had passed. Starlight reflected off the blood pouring from the wound on the caiman's neck. It continued to thrash and the sword wiggled like it was working itself free.

"Black!" Marsha shouted. She'd picked up her camera again. "It would have to be black, wouldn't it? Black monster. Black river. Damn night. It'll take some finessing to get it to show up on screen. But it'll be awesome footage to go with our series."

Annja's empty stomach roiled. The loss of life, and Marsha was thinking about *Chasing History's Monsters*. No wonder Doug hired her…they were very much alike. But even Doug would refuse to show all this death.

The entire village had turned out by now. Men and women continued to throw spears that bounced off the caiman's hide and pelt it with rocks. Annja picked up a dropped spear and hollered for everyone to stay back.

The scent of the creature and its blood, coupled with the blood of its victims, filled her senses and made her lightheaded. She shifted her weight from foot to foot and edged closer, mindful of its tail and snapping jaws and ignoring the nervous talk of the villagers. The caiman remained pinned at the neck, but Annja could tell it wouldn't for much longer. And she concentrated to keep the sword in this world and not let it vanish to its resting place.

"Okay, I'm ready," Marsha called. "I've got new batteries in and everything."

"Oh, come on," Annja said, annoyed. "Put the camera down." Time to end this, she decided. She sprinted forward, avoiding its buffeting tail, and landed on its back. She crouched to keep her balance. The thing gyrated, trying to throw her off.

How to kill it quickly? The caiman's hide was impossibly tough. It had taken all her strength to jab the sword through its neck, and this spear was a poor weapon. The sword then; it was her only recourse. She'd try using it again, aiming for the spine this time. Sever the spine and kill it.

Now! She dropped the spear and with both hands grabbed the pommel of her sword, gritted her teeth, and yanked with all the strength she could put into it. At first the sword defied her efforts. But she tried again and was finally rewarded.

The blade came up, but the act set her off balance and she slipped from its back.

"Annja!" Marsha screamed. "Annja!"

The beast was on her, whirling one way and slapping her with its tail, then bending the other direction so its jaws could reach her, its teeth scraped her leg as she scrambled out of the way. She raised the sword again as it shot forward and it didn't miss this time. Its teeth clamped onto her leg. The pain was excruciating, white-hot daggers sinking in and burning like acid. She screamed, sweeping the sword down across its snout, trying to make it release her. The blade bit in, but not far enough to cause serious harm. She swung again, but the blade bounced off.

The beast dragged her through the blood of its previous victims, then into the water. The caiman's jaws were locked so tight that she couldn't free herself. She felt her heart pounding, as if it were bursting from her chest.

"Annja!" Marsha splashed into the water, spearmen at her side, some of them hurling spears and almost hitting her. Marsha retreated and kept filming.

A part of Annja prayed the caiman would actually bite her leg off so she could crawl away, but that didn't happen. It tugged her out farther, where the water was turbulent from the feasting piranha. She swung once more, feeling the blade sink into its flesh.

She jerked the sword free and Annja had just enough time to grab a breath before the caiman took her under, beneath the feeding frenzy. It dragged her across the rocky bottom, objects she couldn't see scraping her arms and face and adding to her agony.

She could no longer effectively swing the sword, the water a barrier that slowed the blade's course. Annja shifted her hold on the weapon, at the same time kicking at the caiman with her free leg—another exercise in futility. Using the blade like a spear, she jabbed at it again and again. But she couldn't see and didn't know if she was hurting it. Everything was black. She was effectively blind.

Be well, Roux had told her, take care of yourself.

He'd been worried about her for a reason, though unknown at the time. Fate or whatever was telling him that Annja would die on this trip, that the sword would be lost until it landed in the grip of yet another warrior. How many centuries would pass in the meantime?

Annja was losing.

She didn't fear death…or rather she hadn't until this point. Fear coursed through her now—as firmly rooted as the pain radiating from her leg. But there was no direction to the fear, her sense of terror chaotic and unfocused and all-consuming. How much longer would she suffer? When would the real blackness come? And was there something on the other side?

The river was at the same time turbulent and caressing, and the caiman's stumpy legs churned the water into a roar. What would it feel like, she wondered, when she came to the boundary of death, would oblivion be fragile or hard as stone?

Annja didn't want to find out—not here anyway, not now. Not in the Amazon and not to a hungry caiman that had already slaughtered too many people.

She couldn't quit just yet.

Her lungs screamed for air as she jabbed the sword where she figured the beast's jaws must be. She'd cut off her own leg in the process if she had to. One leg in exchange for her life? A fair price.

Eyes wide open, the world was utterly black. What was it D'jok had told her about sight blocking her other senses? She listened, and thought she heard the caiman moan in pain.

She couldn't tell how far down below the surface

it had pulled her, but she felt the pressure of the river against her ears.

Her senses still achingly acute from the dreaming experience, she felt things brush her skin...plants, fish with tiny scales. Each touch was distinct and lingering. She felt the warmth of the blood that continued to pour from the wound on her leg. The captain's words came to mind about the dangers of getting blood in the water and how it changes everything.

Well, there was plenty of blood in the water now.

Slicing her leg in the process, she managed to work the blade between the caiman's jaws, and she heard it scream, an unnerving spine-jarring sound. She'd seriously hurt it this time. She jammed the blade in farther, pulled it back, then once more and—

Freedom! The beast had released her!

There was more blood—its blood mingling with hers, mingling with the river. She could smell it, feel it, the blood warmer than the water. And there was more movement, too, more fish with tiny scales brushing up against her, the caiman gyrating nearby. All these things she pictured as...

The piranha! There are piranha down here! Not content with the bodies on the surface.

"Watch your step," the captain had advised.

Everything changes.

Everything had changed.

Death is close to life.

The sword floated away, her grip weakening. Her fingers fluttered, not finding the pommel, even when she concentrated and called for it. Instead, she found a swarm of biting fish. She kicked and tried to surface, but her injured leg wouldn't work, and instead she felt herself sinking. She thrashed more violently, battering the piranhas. The bites became fewer.

She sank deeper still and the biting stopped altogether. Likely the piranha were feasting on the caiman.

Lightheaded, deprived of oxygen, and her lungs on fire, Annja fought to stay alive. But the weight of the river pressed down on her.

Again she called for her sword, but couldn't even sense its presence. Was she at the boundary of death? Was she about to discover whether the border of oblivion was fragile or hard as stone?

Would Joan of Arc be waiting to greet her?

Charlemagne?

"Be well, Annja." Roux's voice a memory that flickered.

Holding the last trace of air inside, she gripped a rocky ledge and frantically pulled herself up.

She crawled toward what she guessed was a cave. Please let there be air to quench the fire in my chest, she thought.

Joan had died in fire.

There was light ahead and she was getting closer to it; in desperation, she went faster. Caves like this could hold pockets of air, and that's what she prayed for, air… and then a way out.

Yes!

Her head cleared the surface and she gulped in stale air that to her oxygen-starved lungs tasted so very sweet. Minutes…she'd been without air for minutes, had nearly drowned. Her head ached so much, and when she closed her eyes Annja saw white pinpoints. She took a breath and held it, then took in more, releasing it and then repeating the process.

Finally sated, Annja paused, listening. The water sloshed around her, against the walls of the cavern. She clawed the ledge and the wall to get herself upright. Leaning on an outcropping, she waited until the shakiness passed. When she called for the sword again, this time it came, forming in her hand, comfortable, an old friend returned. Her muscles bunched to keep a hold of it, and at last she let the tip down. She'd spent so much energy that the blade felt heavy and unwieldy.

Keeping her free hand against the wall, she edged toward the light to take stock of herself. The leg where the caiman had bit her looked horrible, the flesh in tatters. She could see the white of bone; it was only her iron will that let her walk on it. No wonder she felt so faint; she'd lost a lot of blood and would need an emergency room. If she didn't possess such an amazing ability to heal, she would have died at the bottom of the river and be digesting in the bellies of the Amazon's beasts.

Best-case scenario, she'd make it back to the *Orellana* and could use Wallace's satellite phone to arrange for a helicopter to take her to a hospital. Worst case, she'd never make it out of this cave. She tore a strip off the cloth that had miraculously remained tied around her and used it to staunch some of the bleeding. The piranha bites were minor compared to the damage the caiman had done. She used another strip to make a bandage and cover the worst of the wound so she wouldn't have to look at it.

Now to see about getting out of here. She padded forward and took in the details of an enormous cave. There was some sort of phosphorescent lichen high on the walls that kept the darkness at bay.

There was something else, too. Paintings! Primitive, but discernible, remarkably preserved, the colors—red, black, green and violet, all reasonably bright. They depicted amazing creatures. And there was more than just the paintings. There were bones!

The pain in her leg became inconsequential at the discovery of large skeletons that could well be the remains of mapinguaries and other animals she had no names for. The skulls were unlike anything she was familiar with.

"Incredible. This is wonderful."

She'd need to get her crew down here to film this, and then she'd contact some archaeologist friends, and they could work the site together, expand the show's series on the Amazon River. Ned could take stills of everything. It should be easy to get the necessary permits. Her mind spun.

There was so much to do! But first she'd have to get out of here. Get out of here and get mended. She stumbled, her leg throbbing to the syncopated beat the pounding in her head provided.

"So tired," she muttered. The fight with the caiman had robbed her strength, the loss of blood compounding it. She tried to ward off the fatigue.

"Death is close to life," D'jok had told her.

How close to either was she? Could she heal from this devastating wound? Not on her own. Whatever enhanced constitution the sword provided her, surely wasn't going to be enough.

"Marsha, Wallace." No doubt they thought she was dead. Would they have the captainless boat turned around? Would she be stranded in a nameless village… provided she could get out of this cave?

Annja desperately needed to escape, let her crew know she was all right, and tell them about this unprecedented discovery. It would be the high point of their series, a ratings bonanza that would make Doug swoon.

Mourn for the captain and the villagers lost to the caiman, she would do that, too.

"There's got to be a way. There—" High overhead she saw a gash in the rocks. She could swear light was filtering down. Her heart raced with hope. The wall was climbable, not easily, but Annja had free climbed scarier walls than this.

Her body had other ideas, however. A few more steps and she collapsed on a stretch of cool sand that fit her as well as an expensive mattress. She struggled to stay awake only for a moment. Then her exhaustion won out and she slept.

And woke…inside the shaman's hut.

14

Annja's vision adjusted to the dim light, and she noted the details were the same as the first time she'd woken up, or rather thought she'd woken up—right down to the drinking glasses.

No trace of D'jok or the shaman, or the wound from the caiman. Her clothes were neatly folded next to her. She dressed and tied her tennis shoes, seeing that her skin looked black as ink.

Yet one more dream.

Where would this one take her?

Annja pushed back the curtain and stepped outside. It was twilight. Cook fires burned in the village. Soft sounds of birds and other animals could be heard. She tentatively walked down the path, listening for any screams.

"Annja! Dear God!" Marsha had been talking to D'jok, who was eating something charred on a stick—snake from the looks of it. Marsha reached into a sling bag, pulled out her video camera and aimed it right at Annja. "Wow. Oh, just wow. You're blue."

Annja crossed her arms and let a hissing breath escape, looked down, and saw that her hands were not black, like she'd thought inside the hut, but a shade of midnight blue. "Let's see how this dream plays out."

D'jok smiled warmly. "The huito," he said. "It can turn the skin blue."

Marsha giggled. "It'll wash off, won't it? D'jok, tell Annja that it'll wash off."

"Of course it will wash off. Two, three weeks, longer if you do not bathe each day. The blue takes you out of your world, Annja Creed. The color, the blindfold, the dreaming. It makes you aware. Was it a good dream?"

"I'm still dreaming," Annja said flatly. "Actually, I'm having a nightmare, and I'm just waiting to see what happens next."

"Oh, my lord!" Ned spotted her and started snapping pictures. "What happened to you?"

D'jok gave her a serious look. "The dream? It is over, Annja Creed. I promise. If you were not happy with the experience and wish to dream again—"

Annja's stomach growled. She was famished. "No. I am not happy with the experience." If this *was* real, if she *was* blue, filming the rest of this *Chasing History's Monsters* special wasn't going to happen. She couldn't go on film looking like this, despite Marsha continuing to record her. Doug would probably be furious. *Please let this be a dream.*

It took several more minutes of D'jok's convincing before Annja finally believed this was reality. The sounds of the village and the rainforest were not as intense as when she was dreaming, and the feel of her clothes against her skin, the air that played across her face was not so extreme, her senses back to normal. She couldn't hear her heart. Emotions flitted behind her eyes—anger at herself, amusement, frustration. She shoved them down.

She'd surrendered an expensive watch to have dreams...the one was a pure nightmare, and to be turned a shade of navy.

"Can I get something to eat?"

"Yes. Yes. Of course, Annja Creed," D'jok said. "The Americans...the ones living with us...they came back while you were dreaming. They are anxious to meet you, Annja Creed."

Annja was not anxious to meet anyone. In fact, she considered returning to her cabin, but her stomach won out.

Captain Almeirão was near a fire pit, and he laughed when he saw her.

Ned took more pictures.

D'jok whistled and got the attention of two raggedy-looking Americans who'd been hunkered over the cook fire. The pair jumped up.

"You've been dreaming!" the young woman said, as she raced to Annja and thrust out her hand. "Wonderful! Did you see any dead people or—"

Annja endured the small talk, but avoided discussing anything from her visions. Her stomach continued to grumble, and it took three helpings of charred snake to quiet it.

Becca Mooney—"Moons," and her companion Edgar dominated the dinner conversation. They looked similar—thin, sunburned, hair scruffy and hanging to their shoulders, both dressed in jeans and long-sleeve T-shirts. Edgar had a short, uneven beard, his hair was mud-brown. Moons had unnaturally black hair that was brown at the roots, like she usually dyed it for a Goth look, but hadn't in a while.

"There's a pharma camp about a half day's walk from here," Moons said between bites. "We came back from it an hour ago. We can take you there in the morning and you can get pictures for your television show. You can prove to the world how corporate greed is destroying the Amazon basin."

"They're certainly up to no good, the pharma, harvesting what should belong to this tribe. I don't think they have the right permits," Edgar said. "Baladi and F'yd—"

"—our people," D'jok cut in.

"—haven't come back yet," Edgar continued. "They went with us and they should be back by now. Said they were going to look around a little more. But they should be here. It's getting dark."

"Soon, I hope," D'jok said. Annja thought he looked a little worried.

"We'd still be there with them," Moons added. "But the big guy kicked us out. Again. There's something they don't want us to see. I know it. He ran us off, didn't notice Baladi and F'yd. Just us. Said he was gonna kick our sorry—"

"Because you couldn't be quiet," Edgar said. "He saw us 'cause you couldn't shut up."

Annja tried to focus on the other sounds, the Dslala conversations that she couldn't understand, the clicking of Ned's camera, the monkeys. The snake had been tasty, spiced with sweet pepper.

Marsha nudged Annja. "We could go with them, right? To this camp? Let me get some spare batteries and—"

"Doesn't have anything to do with mapinguaries," Annja said. "But we might find something for a sidebar." She reached for a gourd D'jok passed her, sniffed, and then drank. It was some sort of fermented berry juice.

D'jok wagged his finger. "Not now, lady. This forest, with the night here now, you must stay. Leopards, jaguar. In the dark you would get lost. In the dark you might get eaten. Caiman in the dark, too."

Annja shivered at the mention.

Edgar nodded. "Yeah, we can't go back at night. It's hard to see your hand in front of your face out there after dark, and the insects. You think they're bad during the day? Out there, away from the fire at night, you might as well donate half your blood to the Red Cross. Have to go early in the morning. Maybe F'yd and Baladi are hunkered down somewhere, waiting for morning and feeding the insects."

Annja took a fourth helping of snake. "All right, we can stay here another day. See if I can get some of this blue to fade, and the pharma camp might be worth a spot on the show."

"Wonder if there's enough makeup to—"

A glare from Annja cut Marsha off.

Two or three weeks? Had D'jok really said she'd be blue for two or three weeks?

She closed her eyes and listened to a nearby howler monkey. Why, oh, why, couldn't this be a dream?

15

Baladi and F'yd were still absent in the morning.

"The big guy did something to them," Moons insisted. "Killed 'em, I bet."

"We don't know that," Edgar countered. "But maybe we can poke around when we get to the pharma camp and—"

"How about you two just concentrate on your piece with Annja." Ken went to work on checking the equipment. He looked at Annja. "We good?"

"We're good."

Ken leaned into Annja. "I looked through our supplies, nothing there to help you…all that blue. But maybe Wall, when he's feeling better, maybe he can recolor whatever gets shot today. Some advanced photoshopping and you might be your peachy self."

"You're gonna use what we say, right?" Moons turned to Edgar. "I look okay?"

Nice, he mouthed.

"You're gonna get our message out there, right? That the pharma is up to no good? The world needs to know what goes on in places like this. I know it's not just them, there are other companies, loggers. But they're here and we're here, and…we have to do something." Annja admired that Moons spoke passionately. "Maybe the big guy killed F'yd and—"

"Let's go." Annja set her hands on her waist. She'd like to investigate the missing tribesmen, but the Dslala could do a far better job searching for their own in a rainforest they were familiar with. "I make no promises on what we'll use."

"Not her style to make promises," Marsha cut in. "Be happy we're doing this. Be happy Annja dyed herself blue or we'd be onto the next village chasing monsters."

Annja shook her finger at the camerawoman. "Edgar, Becca—"

"Moons."

"Moons. We'll follow you into the rainforest as you point out some of these valuable plants. I'll try to sell my producer on the notion of a companion segment about the rainforest being endangered, a webisode if nothing else. The station's website gets thousands of hits because of our interactive content. Listen, you can't come across as starry-eyed tree-huggers or militant eco-rights activists. You won't be taken seriously, and Doug won't use the content. Let the situation speak for itself, and I'll have an easier time getting it on the air." Annja really did want to convince Doug to use a piece like this, as she sympathized with the threats to the rainforest. Moons and Edgar's concern was infectious.

Moons bobbed her head. "Okay. Okay. I get it. And it's not like the world doesn't know this place is in deep trouble. I mean, there are magazine articles, blog postings. documentaries. But more exposure will help, and you have so many fans all over the world, Annja. People who don't watch the other stuff…well, they watch you. And maybe those are the people who will end up helping us make a difference."

Edgar added, "You're friggin' famous with your Chasing Monsters of History."

"*Chasing History's Monsters,*" Marsha corrected.

"Yeah. So this would help," Moons said.

"Big-time," Edgar said. His grin was lopsided and endearing.

Annja swirled her index finger in the air and Marsha started recording the pair as they walked.

"We're ruining this amazing, beautiful country," Moons said matter-of-factly. Annja thought she had a good, strong voice. Amanda wouldn't have to finesse the recording much. "Before outsiders came here, like Orellana that your boat is named for, there were probably five million indigenous people. Five million. Conquest, disease, most of the tribes were wiped out. Statisticians are guessing about five hundred tribes remain. Five hundred thousand indigenous people are all that's left. Sounds like a lot, huh? Not when there were five million."

The forest provided its own music, though Annja suspected Amanda would lay a soft, new age track behind it, something with drums to simulate the cadence of walking. There were parrots squawking, people talking, water lapping at the river's edge. It was wonderful, but something felt…unsettling. Annja had the sensation they were being watched. Maybe a big cat, curious.

Maybe something else. She'd learned not to dismiss such trepidation.

"Speaking of millions," Edgar chimed in as he followed a path toward Annja. "There's more than two million square miles of Amazon rainforest, the diversity of plants and animals incredible. No richer ecosystem on the planet, and we're destroying it. Me and Moons are doing what we can to help. We'll leave when we catch a ride on the last boat that passes by when the tributary dries up. Hopefully by then we will have gained a better understanding and can pass that along to others."

Annja stayed behind Marsha and her camera, but knew the mic would pick her up. "On *Chasing History's Monsters'* trip to the Amazon, we encountered Becca Mooney and Edgar Schwartz, recent college graduates who have been living with some of the indigenous people to learn more about the problems facing the rainforest. Becca, what drew your interest here?"

"Actually, it started as a vacation last summer. We did the tourist bit first, starting in Belém with a cruise, did some birding."

"Fantastic birding, actually," Edgar said.

"Visited native villages and watched some of their ceremonies. But that was all part of a tour package we'd found advertised in the college newspaper, one of those go here-to-here-to-here things that fit with our student budget. Caught a game, too." She pointed to the logo on her gray T-shirt. It was a green and black soccer ball and the shape of Brazil across the center of it. Edgar's T-shirt featured a harpy eagle, a rare Brazilian bird of prey.

"At one of the stops we heard about the deforestation, the exploitation," Edgar said. "We were biology majors, so it hit home for us."

"Hit hard. We came back in December, right after we graduated. Yeah, took four and a half years for Edgar, six and a half for me, not the so-called standard four-year degree for either of us. But Edgar…his story is he didn't take enough hours during a spring semester. My story? I worked full-time all the way through, and when you do that you can't take enough hours in *any* semester 'cause there aren't enough hours in the day."

Edgar draped his arm around Moons's shoulder. "Our visas are good for another seven months, so we might go elsewhere along the river until our money runs out. But after that, it'll be off to Virginia where we'll knock on the Nature Conservancy's door and try to get full-time jobs. With luck, the Conservancy hires us and sends us back here, but—"

"We'll go pretty much anywhere in the world if it means making a difference," Moons finished. "We have to do something to help the balance."

Martha shifted the camera. "Balance?"

"Yeah, balance. Man and nature, there's a delicate balance between the two, and in a lot of places it's out of whack," Edgar explained.

Annja continued to listen as the two talked and walked and periodically turned around to face the camera and point at various plants. She swatted away swarms of gnats and was mentally editing the piece, deciding which parts to cut because the pair went on a little *too* passionately here and there. She was distracted though because she still had the sensation of being shadowed. Maybe someone from the Dslala village was following out of curiosity…but she doubted that would raise the hairs on the back of her neck. Her companions, however, were at total ease.

"There's an operation nearby we're having fits with." Moons frowned as she shifted directly to the pharma camp. "It's a pharmaceutical company, even the head honcho is here." She paused. "Can you cut that sentence out? Let me try again." She straightened her shirt and looked all serious. "Dillon Pharma is about a half-day's walk from the Dslala village. They're stripping some of the most valuable plants in the area, the ones the Dslala harvest rely on. Edgar and me have been chased out of their camp several times. All we want is to see their permits…and they've refused. If we can prove they're not here legally, we can catch a boat to the city and alert the authorities. Instead of us running, it'll be Dillon's researchers who will be the ones chased out."

Marsha clicked off the camera and cradled it in front of her. "Let's get closer to this camp, so I can get footage of damaged trees, something to illustrate your point."

The moss covered ground had give, like one of those old-time dance floors with spring. But unlike those flat dance floors, this ground had slopes, cliffs and hills and was interrupted by a waterfall that Annja spotted through a rare gap in the trees. Receiving nine or more feet of water a year, the ground was always moist, and the going was slow because the tree roots spread across the ground rather than growing deep into it. Walking was a bit of a chore, but Annja relished the exercise.

Her younger camerawoman, however, was obviously starting to tire.

Two hours later, Edgar announced they were close.

Marsha, huffing and rubbing the fronts of her legs, asked to stop for a moment. "When we get back to New York, I'm gonna start hitting the gym." She pulled up the video camera and squared her shoulders. "All right, guys, point out some of the plants Dillon Pharma is interested in."

"Dillon Pharmaceuticals Ltd., actually," Moons corrected.

"Like this?" Edgar pointed to a thick vine that had wrapped itself around a tree trunk. There were other vines on a nearby tree, but what was left of them were all high up and dying, the lower portions obviously removed.

"Barbasco," Moons said. "You can see where these vines have been harvested. Here and here and here. All harvested by Dillon because the Dslala don't take all the vines on any one tree. They know how to conserve. But Dillon doesn't care. To them it's all about the green—and I mean money, not plants."

Annja touched one of the vines; the blue skin of her hand was pretty next to the green foliage. She grimaced and pulled her hand back when she saw that Marsha was recording her. The vine had felt smooth and tough, like the stem of a big sunflower. "What do the Dslala use this for?"

Edgar took a turn. "To help them get by in the dry season. 'Cause, yeah, there is a dry season despite all the rain now. It's basically when the river's down and fishing is tougher. They pound the roots until it turns into this sap that looks like milk. They dump it in a stream and wait. The sap is a toxin that messes with fish respiration, stunning them."

"They float to the surface, and the natives scoop them up." Moons pantomimed the action. "I suppose used in a certain way the toxin might have some medicinal value. Or maybe some sort of sleep remedy."

"And this tree is the annato."

"Achiote," Moons corrected.

"Fine, achiote." Edgar made a face.

Annja spun away, certain she'd seen someone or something mirroring their path. But the shape melded into the green, frustrating her.

"Look there," Edgar said. "That fruit, spiny and not very tasty. I know, I've tried it. I've tried to eat just about everything here. It's the seeds Dillon wants out of that fruit. They're used as food color and in cosmetics all around the world, and now they're researching medical applications. Some of the natives use it as face paint, sometimes they streak their hair red with it. Moons used it once, but it didn't show up much since her hair is so black."

The pair continued to talk, Marsha kept recording, and Annja drifted back. She'd heard something, a branch snapping. Leaves rustled, but not from any breeze. The plant growth was so tight here the wind couldn't reach down. The air was still. She stared toward the source of the sounds, seeing a darker patch of green…maybe a man…maybe one of the tribesmen who'd gone in search of F'yd and Baladi…maybe something else. Maybe more than one man or creature was dogging them.

Edgar fingered a low-hanging leaf. "Basically, what everybody should know, is that rainforests cover a little more than ten percent of Earth's land area. More than half of the world's species of everything—plants, animals, insects—live in rainforests, but things are going extinct because of interference from us. We're killing species, and in the end it'll kill us."

Marsha began to speak, but what sounded like two gunshots rang out.

Annja and Marsha pressed themselves against a tree trunk. Annja reflexively opened her hand, waiting a beat before calling the sword, but in the same instant it started to form, she banished it, hearing Moons giggle.

"Nobody's shooting at us," Edgar said.

"Possumwood tree." Moons gestured east and up.

The tree was massive, and Annja couldn't see the top of it.

"That one's probably a hundred feet tall." Edgar started looking on the ground.

Another sharp bang sounded!

Marsha recorded Edgar as he prodded something with his foot. There were three more bangs in rapid succession, silence, then the howl of a monkey and the squawk of a big blue macaw that landed on a low branch and regarded them curiously.

Annja glanced at the canopy, and then back to where she'd earlier heard a branch snap. She still had the definite feeling she was being watched.

"Here. Over here." Edgar picked up something that

resembled a gourd, about the size of a big apple. It was cracked open and stuffed with seeds. "When these pop—and they do when they're ripe—it sounds like a gun going off."

As if the tree wanted to illustrate the point, Annja heard another succession of bangs. Again she thought she saw something moving—someone maybe—from the corner of her eye. Two shapes this time.

"The tree can shoot these things a few hundred feet," Moons said. "Besides the pods, Dillon's interested in the tree's sap." She rested her hand against the trunk, smiling sadly for Marsha and her camera. "The Dslala dip their darts in it and use it as a mild poison when they're hunting. But Dillon's looking at it as medicine. They're tapping the trees around here." She indicated a few places on the trunk and pulled her finger away, liquid glistening on it. "Tapped today, I'd say. And the one over there is dying, looks like it's been tapped dry. See?"

It reminded Annja of tapping trees in the northern United States for the production of maple syrup, but the operation she'd seen there was easier on the trees. The hairs on the back of her neck stood up.

"Speak of the devil," Moons said.

There was another possumwood just beyond Moons, and a man in dark green coveralls stepped from behind it, perhaps the source of the eyes Annja had felt on her. But she'd thought there might be two people.

"Hey! You're not welcome here! We told you to stay out." The man was tall and skinny, the coveralls hanging on him in folds. He wore a hard hat with a big brim that shadowed his heavily bearded face. Annja couldn't see his eyes. But she saw his hands, gloved in black leather, each holding a Taurus pistol. "We warned you kids. Yesterday, in fact. And we're tired of warning you. We're done warning you." He waved one of the guns for emphasis. "Maybe I should just shoot you, leave your carcasses for the leopards and monkeys. The blue one ought to be tasty to a big cat, you think?"

Annja knew a lot about guns, having had more pointed at her in the past several years than she cared to remember. These were Brazilian made, double-action, with magazines that when full carried a dozen shots.

Her palm itched, waiting for the sword to form against it. She almost called it. One man with two guns, Annja could take him if he turned the guns on them. She judged the distance between her and him, how many steps, the angle to strike. She'd do it…if she had to.

"Look, Hammond," Edgar started. So he knew the man by name. "Don't you know who we've brought with us? A celebrity. Annja Creed. Ever hear of her? You're going to wish you'd never heard of her after she—"

"Shut up," Hammond said. "Just shut up."

"Hammond, we want to talk to Mr. Dillon," Moons said. "We just—"

"I said, shut it!"

Annja could tell that Hammond didn't know quite what to do. She heard a faint click from over her shoulder followed by a bang that didn't come from a possomwood tree.

Annja whirled to see a second man; he had only

one Taurus pistol, and he'd shot in the air to get their attention.

"That's the big guy we told you about," Moons said. "Don't know what his name is."

"All right, let's go talk to Mr. Dillon," the "big guy" said. He was dressed similarly to Hammond, but this one filled out the coveralls better; his shoulders were so broad they strained the seams. Clean shaven and without a hard hat, Annja took in the sharp planes of a face that wore a cruel expression. He looked more like a hired thug than a botanist interested in plants.

Marsha had the camera up; she was recording all of it. "This is some awesome footage, Annja," she said.

16

An eggshell-white tent the size of a double-car garage took up a good bit of a large clearing, a generator sat next to it, alongside a mound of crates wrapped in a heavy net with a hook on top, likely brought in recently by a helicopter. There were also two tents a little less than half the size of the big one and four pup tents sat behind them.

The trees that had been cut down to create the clearing had been turned into logs. They ringed three sides of the camp, forming a four-foot-high wall that was bolstered by mud that had been pressed up on both sides. Barbed wire was strung to complete the enclosure. Annja thought it looked more like a military camp than anything, drab and forlorn, stern men walking around with guns. A thin cloud of insects hovered over everything. Past the enclosure was a stretch of ground that had been cleared and burned, ugly amid all the green of the forest that rose around it, large enough to accommodate a helicopter.

No heavy equipment, but Annja saw chainsaws on a crude table, along with machetes and overlarge pli-

ers. There was a sheet of plastic covering objects on the
other half of the table—who knew what was under it.
Another table was empty, benches on either side. And
near that was a muddy horseshoe pit with a post that
canted at a forty-five-degree angle.

"Move," Hammond said. "You got enough pictures.
Too many pictures." He prodded Marsha with his pistol; she was still recording images. He took her video
camera and dumped it onto the empty table. "Right up
to the wire, then inside. All o' you."

"Sorry, Annja," Edgar whispered. "Didn't mean to
get you caught up in this. Well, not quite like this anyway. But see what we're saying? These guys are up to
no good. They got guns. If all you're after is plants,
why do you need—"

"Shut up, punk," Hammond directed to Edgar. "Just
shut up, unless you want me to shut it for you." He
opened the gate and nudged them inside.

Annja saw that the barbed wire was rusty and blood
and feathers hung on it near the gate, suggesting that a
low-flying parrot had met its demise.

There were four men in the clearing, all in coveralls, all with hard hats, and all watching Annja and her
crew. She heard them talk in soft voices, about "the
kids," and the "blue lady."

"Boss!" Hammond shouted. "Trespassers! Them
damn kids came back. Told you they would."

"We weren't trespassing!" Moons said. "We're not
kids. We were minding our business, and we—"

Annja recognized the sound of another couple of possumwood pods bursting. One of the men in the clear-

ing jumped and reached in his pocket. Maybe he was armed, too. Maybe they all were.

"Boss!" Hammond shouted again. "Trespassers!"

A middle-aged man in khaki trousers and a sweat-stained muscle shirt emerged from the largest tent. He had thinning red hair and a pencil mustache, dirt smudged on his high forehead. He brushed his hands on his pants and regarded the entourage for a moment before approaching. He looked vaguely familiar, like she'd seen him in passing somewhere. He stank of sweat and insect repellent.

"That's Dillon," Edgar whispered.

"Keep your hands up," Hammond cautioned. "Higher. Followed them all the way from the village. They're like boomerangs. Throw 'em out and they keep coming back."

So Hammond had been the shape Annja had noticed on their way here, watching the Dslala village and dogging them, responsible for the hair rising on the back of her neck. He'd been relatively stealthy. Why hadn't he pulled out the guns earlier and told them to turn around? Had he wanted them here so his boss could take action?

"I told you to ignore them, Ham," Dillon said. "You shouldn't have been messing around the Dslala village. You should be here working. I wondered where you were."

"Hard to ignore the kids. Tired of 'em." Hammond shrugged. "Joe and me…we were watching for them, in case they were up to no good. This time they had company. Company with a camera. That's the 'no good' they've got going, taking pictures of our trees. Get a load of the blue one. I think we—"

A howl burst through the clearing, and Annja saw a pair of monkeys cavorting on a wide branch. From somewhere a good distance away, another answered.

The possumwood went off again.

Dillon crossed his arms. He wasn't muscular, but he appeared reasonably fit. "The blue one has been dreaming with the Dslala, Hammond, something that might do you a world of good. In a place where mysticism is as thick as mosquitoes, I would recommend you avail yourself of some of their thinking."

"Mr. Dillon, I—"

"Since you seem so interested in the village, Ham, you ought to trade them something for a dream."

"No thanks," Hammond said. "About these dumb kids—"

"We weren't trespassing," Moons repeated. "And your goon had no business following us."

Hammond growled.

"Honest," Edgar said. "We weren't even all that close—"

"Annja Creed, right?" Dillon swept his arm toward the table. "The television archaeologist? Chupacabras and all that."

Annja noticed that the four men who'd been milling in the clearing went to work; one picked up a chainsaw, another a machete, the other two carried folded burlap sacks. She watched them leave and head west, and then she quickly lost sight of them.

"Ham, don't you and Joe have something better to

do? Like collect the root samples we're scheduled to ship? I'll talk to our guests." He indicated the table with the camera. "Join me, Ms. Creed?"

From the moment they'd been escorted into the camp, Annja sensed Moons and Edgar's tension. Moons had her hands clenched, knuckles white. Edgar had rabbit eyes, not locking onto any one thing for more than a second, nervously trying to watch everything.

"Annja Creed. Please, join me." Dillon thrust out a hand, but Annja didn't take it. He gave her a hurt look, but she didn't find it genuine.

"You have me at a disadvantage," Annja said. "You know who I am. I don't know you."

"Arthur Dillon, and this is my outreach base for Dillon Pharmaceuticals. We're a research company with offices in Atlanta and Dallas. Small, but we're cutting-edge." Judging by his accent he was from the south. "We focus on finding cures, not just treatments."

Annja stepped ahead of him to the table, getting a good look at the remaining chainsaw and machetes on the other table. Marsha followed, sitting next to her. Dillon took the opposite bench, and Moons and Edgar stood behind Annja. Hammond and the big guy kept a respectable distance.

"We're gonna stick around just a bit, Mr. Dillon," Hammond said. "In case you need help with them."

"Fine."

Annja saw movement in the large tent, shadows darkening the tarp. At least two more people were in there. After a moment, one of them poked his head out, saw Dillon seated at the table, and then retreated inside.

There was more movement toward the north, beyond the log barricade. Maybe a large monkey? Again she had the unnerving sense of someone watching her.

"We weren't trespassing," Moons insisited. Annja picked up the brittle tone in her voice. "We actually weren't all that close to your camp—"

"—when your goons pulled guns on us," Edgar finished. "They brought us in here. So we were herded, not trespassing. Not this time."

Dillon kept his eyes on Annja. "I apologize for Hammond and Joseph. They are my security, and—like me—they've grown very weary of your young companions."

Annja studied him. His careworn face was tanned, the lines around his eyes and mouth marking him as on the far side of middle age. It was an old tan, one he'd probably brought with him from the States, no hint of sunburn. His hands had a delicate appearance, but the nails were chipped with dirt beneath them—a boss who worked at the side of his employees. She was certain she'd seen him somewhere before.

"Listen here, Dillon—" Moons's voice rose.

"No, ma'am," Dillon said. "No, I will not listen." Definitely from Georgia, Annja decided; his voice had that gentle lilt. "*You* will listen. Hammond overstepped his bounds, and I apologize for that, but you've pushed him. You break into my camp and destroy my equipment. You cost me time and money."

Annja glanced over her shoulder to see Edgar reddening.

"The damage the two of you have done has been

significant. Not that the lab equipment by itself is all that costly, but getting replacements brought in by helicopter is, and you have added weeks to my work by your shenanigans. You have destroyed plants we've processed, burned my men's sleeping tents. And yet you say I'm the one who is the menace. I've been civil to you. I've not contacted the authorities. But if I catch you one more time—"

"Authorities?" Moons stepped to the side of the table and put her hands flat against the wood. "I'd love for you to contact the authorities. I'd really, *really* love for you to contact the authorities. 'Cause I bet they'll haul you right out of here."

Dillon let out a breath and steepled his fingers under his chin. "So we do this dance again, for Annja Creed's benefit. I'm here legally. And I'll continue to stay here legally. I have all the permits and—"

"You've not shown them to us," Edgar said.

"And why should I? Same dance. Same music. I don't answer to you. I answer to the people of Brazil. You're American teenagers, ill-mannered thieving college students—"

"We're not teenagers," Moons offered. "And we're not students. Not anymore."

"Meddlers, then," Dillon said. "Vandals. How about we agree on those terms? Far more appropriate. Meddlers, vandals, thieves. I'm hurting nothing and no one. And believe me I know just how very precious this rainforest is. And now you've got a television archaeologist roped into your sabotage schemes. You'll paint me as some villain on your show when all I'm trying to do is help the world. You have Annja Creed out here to—"

"—not do anything about your biology research operation." Annja gripped the edge of the table. "Mr. Dillon, I'm here filming a series on beasts of the Amazon. I stopped in the Dslala village—"

"—where she dreamed and turned blue," Moons supplied. "I'm dreaming that we're gonna take you down with television exposure courtesy of her. I'm dreaming of your sorry self being—"

Annja's eyes were ice when she glanced at Moons. "Can you stay out of the conversation a minute?"

"Yeah, give it a rest, you two. You're only feeding the fire," Marsha put in. "Give the adults…or rather the people who are willing to act like adults…a chance to talk." She nodded toward Hammond. "I'd like my camera back."

Moments later, Annja and Marsha were shown into the largest tent, Hammond keeping an eye on Moons and Edgar outside.

"Film anything you like," Dillon offered. "Hmm. You don't use film anymore. So what's the word?"

"Film works fine," Marsha said. "I get the drift." She panned the interior, which was crowded with tables, equipment and a pair of refrigerators. "So if you're all scientist-types here, why do you need guns?"

"Leopards. Jaguars. Caiman the size of a VW Beetle," Dillon answered. "And as a precaution against any guerillas, and I don't mean the animal kind."

"Guerillas in this part of the country?" Annja asked. "I thought that was settled." In the close air inside the

tent, Dillon's sweaty odor was stronger. Annja backed
up a few steps. She noticed cases of batteries stacked
on the opposite side of the tent. The printing on each
side showed there were 336 D batteries per box, and
there looked to be twenty boxes—though how many
were full was a mystery. She did the mental calculation:
roughly five thousand batteries. Boxes under the center table were marked double-A batteries, again, cases
of them. Dillon had a generator; what did he need *all*
these batteries for? The quantity was obscene and more
than a little suspicious.

"Guerillas are still around. Though we haven't seen
any here specifically, but I've heard rumors. And I'd
rather keep me and my employees safe. Seems those
kids are the worst threat."

"They have a cause is all," Marsha said. "All fired
up and righteous." Annja detected the sympathy in her
tone. "They want to protect the rainforest."

"I say again, I well understand how valuable this
rainforest is," Dillon said. "Ladies, my brother died of
bone cancer in his senior year in high school. His pain…
the drugs didn't work in the end. My grandfather died
of Alzheimer's. I promised my grandmother I'd find a
cure for the disease. I fully intend to keep that promise.
Lymphoma later took her, and that one is on my hit list,
too. My son…my *infant* son…died of neuroblastoma.
Apparently cancer runs in my family."

"I'm sorry to hear—" Marsha started.

"Not just in my family. Hammond's father, he died of
non-Hodgkin's. It's in a lot of families." Dillon waved
her pity away and spoke louder and with passion. "I

know the secret is in plants. The secret is here in this rainforest. All the medical miracles are right here. It's just a matter of finding them. I've had a bout with melanoma. So it has personally touched me, too. The cure for cancer is here. Alzheimer's. The cure for a lot of things. I'm counting on finding the cures to so very many of the world's most wretched ills right here along this big river. But those two kids out there, they have blinders on. They see trees, and they don't see the people that can be helped by those trees. I'm taking only pieces of this forest. Only little pieces."

Dillon demonstrated that the plants were vacuum sealed, some dried, some refrigerated, some frozen. Some had been liquefied, roots pulped. Cartons were marked for laboratories in Atlanta and Dallas. He showed them how they processed roots, and Marsha recorded everything.

"I send a shipment out once every seven to ten days," he said. "Even the CDC's got a stake. And despite what those kids would have you believe, I am careful with my harvesting. My men range pretty far, not taking all the samples from any one spot. What the kids should be going after are the industries cutting down the trees for lumber and oil. They clear the land for cattle and to grow commercial soybeans. The real value of the trees is keeping them alive. Many of the trees here are hundreds possibly thousands of years old."

"So the kids," Marsha prompted. "Why do they think you're up to no good?"

Dillon looked exasperated. "I don't know. Maybe they think I'm the enemy because I've cut down *some* trees—I had to for this camp. I have a smaller camp about thirty miles due west, and no trees cut there. I cull plants and roots in the hope that scientists will discover cures, new life-saving drugs. Does that make me a villain? Or a hero? A sedge root we discovered early on can treat headaches, muscle cramps, dysentery and fever. This place is the world's pharmacy…if we use it right."

Marsha turned off the camera and reached in her pocket for more batteries. "Some great quotes here, thanks."

"Please, film as much about this camp and our activities as you'd like. And tell your eco-minded young friends that next time they cross my path I *will* contact the authorities. And I will press charges." He tapped a satellite phone holstered at his waist. "Maybe I should've reported them, got them out of my hair the first time I caught them destroying my equipment. Maybe I still will report them."

"What *actual* damage have they done?" This from Annja. "You mentioned equipment."

"What damage haven't they done? They've busted microscopes, liquefiers, ruined one of my freezer units—and thereby destroyed all the prepared samples inside, set fire to sleeping tents—clothes and personal belongings in the process, destroyed roots we'd processed—why do that if they're so eco-minded? They tossed one of my chainsaws in the river…and how is *that* helping the environment?" He squeezed down an aisle to the lone desk, rifled through a tub drawer, and came out with a folder. The pages inside were in plastic sheet protectors. He spread them out on the only empty space. "My permits. Take a look."

Annja did just that, skimming quickly, noting the permitted locations, length of stay, fees, signatures. It all looked legitimate. "Why didn't you just show this to them?"

"Because it wouldn't have made a difference," Dillon said. "They would've come up with some other thing to go on about."

"I suspect you're right." When Annja was finished looking through the papers, she handed them back.

"Tell your young friends to leave me alone, Ms. Creed, or—quite seriously, I won't leave them alone. I'll get them tossed out of Brazil."

They returned to the table outside, and he offered to brew tea. They'd been inside about a half hour, and in that time the sky had darkened and the scent of rain hung in the air.

"We need to get back," Annja said. "Apparently it's not wise to be in the forest after dark, and we've got a few hours' hike."

"I understand. And it looks like it'll go dark very soon. A storm's coming." Dillon looked at his watch. "Will you be in the area much longer? You could film my men taking samples. You could go with them tomorrow if you'd like."

Marsha shrugged and pointed at Annja. "She's in charge."

"I think we have enough footage from your camp," Annja said. "Like I said, really we're here for a series on river monsters." Edgar muttered something under his breath. "But we'll be sticking around a few more days at least. The Dslala have tales of some of the creatures we're highlighting in this segment. They've been quite cordial."

"But two of them are missing," Moons said. "The two Dslala who came with us yesterday. You did something to them."

Dillon closed his eyes and sighed.

"Time to go," Annja said. "Mr. Dillon, thank you for your hospitality."

When they could no longer see the camp, Annja whirled on Moons and Edgar and put her hand in front of Marsha's camera, not wanting the confrontation recorded. "Vandalism? Really? Destruction of his property? Fires?"

Edgar shrugged. "We were sending a message. He shouldn't be here."

"You're the ones who shouldn't be here," Annja returned. "A chainsaw in the river. Really? Whose good idea was that? How good for the river's ecology is a chainsaw?"

Moons looked deflated. "Well, maybe that we shouldn't have done."

"You think?" Annja slowly simmered. Thunder rumbled, complementing her mood, and the large drops of rain started to fall.

Annja and Marsha fell in step behind Moons and Edgar, letting a few yards separate them. Annja heard something moving through the foliage to their right, probably Hammond making sure they really were going back to the Dslala village. The hairs stood up on the back of her neck.

She should have paid more attention the moment they left the pharma camp. But she was distracted, wondering about the two men in the tent she hadn't gotten a good look at. There'd been two shadows, two men moving around in there when she'd first arrived. But those two men weren't inside the big tent when she and Marsha got the tour. They'd obviously slipped out the back before Dillon escorted Marsha and her inside. Why had they left? Had they taken something out that Dillon didn't want her to see?

"So Dillon wasn't such a villain," Marsha said. She stopped and got some footage of a pair of scarlet macaws flying below the lowest canopy; despite the failing light their brilliant plumage stood out starkly against all the green. "He's all fired up about finding cures for Alzheimer's and cancer, keeping a promise to his grandma. Nice to run into someone so driven. Kind of inspiring, huh?"

Annja didn't doubt Dillon was sincere in his desire to discover some medical miracle, but there was more to the man.

Marsha put her camera away. "So maybe the sidebar should be about him, do you think?"

"Actually, Moons and Edgar are right," Annja said, keeping her voice low. "Dillon is very definitely up to something." She felt it in her gut. And nothing was going to prevent her from going back on her own and finding out what.

17

"They could ruin everything," Dillon said.

"So you want me to kill them? Those kids?" Hammond stood just outside the main tent, looking in at Dillon, the rain pinging off his hard hat. "Joe and me can take care of it tonight, like we did with them two nosey—"

"They'd be missed."

"But never found, Mr. Dillon. Caiman and piranha eat the evidence around here. Could drop them in the hole, too. They'd die down there."

Dillon managed to keep the smirk off his face. Hammond had that part right; it was effortless to dispose of bodies in the Amazon. Not even a finger bone would be found. "The authorities aren't going to spend even a handful of seconds looking for missing tribesmen from nameless villages, but U.S. citizens? That's bad for tourism. They might send some people out to poke around, parents raise a fuss in the media, and we need to stay under everyone's radar."

"Then what do you want us to do? Scare 'em? Run 'em out of the forest like we should've done a while back? They can't keep coming back here, especially if they have a television reporter along. Make 'em hightail it to—"

"The kids aren't the problem, Ham." He heard the soft rumble of thunder; he liked the sound. Soon the rain would play against his tent. "The kids are insignificant. A burr is all."

"A burr? A pain in the ass is what they are."

Dillon chuckled. "They're a nuisance, I'll grant you that…but Annja Creed and her photographer?" Something worried Dillon about that pair. He didn't understand it, and couldn't explain it, but her presence did not sit well, and he was always one to play to his instincts. He didn't like the way she walked through his tent, looking so close into the corners, skimming his documents while her eyes kept drifting. She was observant, maybe too observant.

"They could be trouble. They're television people." He really didn't want any attention, despite his invitation to them to "film anything you want." He hadn't meant one word of that, and he didn't like her comment that they'd be in the area another few days. He wanted them long gone—now. He considered waiting it out.

His British partner would have been pleased to have seen Miss Creed, though; he'd been all happily enthused at seeing the TV archaeologist in the Belém marketplace a few days ago. Had wanted his picture taken with her. What odd circumstances had brought her to his camp in the middle of nowhere? It was a fateful encounter that made his teeth ache.

"You're resourceful, Ham. They had to come in by boat, right. And the boat has to be at the village."

"So I should do something to the boat. I could sink it."

"Heavens, no. I want them to be able to take that boat out of here…and the sooner they take it, the better. Like I said, an American goes missing, people will come looking. We just need them gone. Safe and gone."

"I got you." Hammond pulled his lips into a thin line. "I'll make it so they need to leave soon, then. Like at first light. I've a few ideas."

"As I said, you're resourceful." Dillon held the tent flap open. "You'll need the night goggles and a transmitter. I'll want to watch if you don't mind."

"Nah, I don't mind. Be glad to have you along for the show. I'll need a few other things, too."

"The lab is at your disposal." Dillon suspected Hammond was looking forward to the night's activities.

IT WAS ALMOST like going himself. Dillon was dry and ensconced in the lab tent, fingers wrapped around a large mug of Darjeeling, eyes fixed on his laptop screen. The rain was white noise, a constant tat-tat-tat-tat against the canvas that he found soothing.

Hammond's goggles had a viewer fitted onto the bridge, and so Dillon watched as his loyal and capable assistant started down the narrow path that Annja and her videographer had taken—a path created by Moons and Edgar's numerous forays from the village to this camp. Then Hammond left the path and cut at a right angle, forging into the thick vegetation. Dillon

shuddered; as much as he loved what the rainforest provided, he disliked trudging through it. He was pleased
Hammond never minded such excursions.

Hammond was ex-special forces, a key hire. Back
from Afghanistan, living with a brother in Atlanta,
looking for work, Dillon snapped him up for security
a year and a half ago. Hammond was used to travel,
liked violence, and was unswervingly loyal, never ques-
tioning orders; Dillon paid him very well.

Dillon sipped the tea and split the screen, the left side
showing Hammond's slow and steady progress through
the rainforest, everything looking eerily green-black
with the night vision goggles, the sounds haunting—the
rain in stereo from the mic in the goggles and drumming on the tent, frogs chirping like birds, big cats, who
knew what else moving through the vegetation. Good
that Hammond wasn't afraid of anything. Dillon turned
down the volume and concentrated on the right side of
the screen, information and images of Annja Creed and
Chasing History's Monsters.

Chestnut hair, green eyes, lived somewhere in Brook-
lyn, and the sole reason *Chasing History's Monsters* was
successful and beamed into television sets around the
world. She was radiant in a series of promotional stills
he flicked through. Most of the pictures showed her in
a khaki shirt with numerous pockets and often with a
tan broad-brimmed hat, he mused. In one she was accepting some sort of television award and was radiant
in a long blue gown, close to the color she'd turned herself with the Dslala dreaming ceremony, trimmed with
sequins and with spaghetti straps. He considered her

gorgeous. He stared at that picture a moment more, and then moved to the next result.

Chasing History's Monsters episodes were available online for watching. He noted one on chupacabras, another on Mayan relics found in a Wisconsin lake. Interesting and perhaps would provide some future amusement. He bookmarked that site and kept looking. A link to a map showed all the places where the series had been filmed. She got around. And it appeared that trouble followed her. He checked newspaper archives that matched the times of her visits to various locals, his scowl deepening as he skimmed the articles. It was indeed fortunate he sent Hammond out tonight; he didn't need Annja Creed snooping around his base camp. It wasn't like he could move this operation, and he wasn't ready to abandon it just yet. There was too much money to be made.

He clicked open a link that traced to a Belém travel writer's blog. It was dated a few years ago, and it took some work to find a cached file, as the original page no longer existed. Apparently Annja had been hired to find a lost city named Promise in Brazil, where legend said there was a key to eternal youth. No mention if she found it, but links off that post suggested she was a part-time treasure hunter.

Dillon definitely needed her out of Brazil. He didn't want her uncovering his treasure.

He dropped the split screen and focused on Hammond. It was close to midnight when the man reached the boat. The rain had intensified, and was now pelting the river, loud enough to drown out the sound of the frogs that had been singing a loud chorus. Dillon was impressed with the size of the boat; he'd expected a tug, something along the lines of the *African Queen,* not something that looked like a Mississippi riverboat, sans the paddlewheel. There were lights on the bow and stern, a light glowing from a window on the second tier, but otherwise the boat was dark. He made out part of a word on its hull, but then Hammond was moving.

Annja Creed might be prone to venture to dangerous places, but it seemed she liked to travel in style and comfort.

Hammond slogged out into the river, and Dillon sucked in a breath when he saw a caiman surface and come close. Hammond stretched out a gloved hand and pushed it away, and the caiman got the message and floated out of sight.

He suspected Hammond's heartbeat had remained steady. The man truly was afraid of nothing.

Dillon guessed the water was about up to Hammond's waist. He circled the boat, until he was on the side that faced away from the village and pulled himself up. The railing groaned softly and the wood deck creaked under the man's weight.

"Be quiet," Dillon urged. "So very quiet." He could talk to Hammond if he wanted; there was an earpiece attached to the goggles, but Dillon hadn't turned his mic on. He didn't want to be a distraction. He finished the Darjeeling, yawned, and discarded the notion of a fourth cup of tea; it might keep him up, and Dillon wanted to get to bed soon. He had a big day planned and wanted to be well-rested for it.

He could only see Hammond's arms from the elbows down, and his hands. It was like one of those popular video games, where you looked out through the eyes of whatever character you'd picked to run through an electronic gauntlet. Hammond was an exceptional "character."

The rain sounded angry striking the boat. Dillon followed Hammond's progress, into a dining room that had books and maps spread out on a table. There was a camera bag on a chair. Hammond's night vision goggles distorted things, but it looked like the bag that Annja Creed had rescued from the thief in the Belém marketplace. Hammond picked up two of the maps, along with some other papers—Dillon could not read what was on them—folded them, stuffed them in the camera bag, and carried it outside. He eased it over the side by the strap and let it sink in the river. Then he returned to the dining room, went through it and into the kitchen, and methodically dosed sauces, soups, a breakfast casserole and bottles of juice with some extracts from the lab. It was similar to ipecac syrup, but to the tenth power. It would make whoever ingested it violently ill. The effect could linger for days and would no doubt force the boat to turn back toward Belém with its state-of-the-art hospital facilities.

Hammond continued moving through the boat. He crept into a lower cabin, where someone slept soundly, snoring—the videographer who'd been at the camp with Annja Creed. Dillon watched Hammond pan around the room, seeing a suitcase and opening it, and then looking through a few drawers...probably looking for the camera bag she was carrying when she and Annja Creed had come to the camp. That would be a nice touch, Dillon thought, getting rid of all their footage.

Apparently Hammond gave up the search, pulled back the mosquito netting, and uncapped another vial. He dosed a cloth with the contents, and pressed it to the woman's face. Her eyes flew open, but his free hand clamped over them. She struggled for a second, and then lay still. Hammond held the empty vial up in front of the goggles for Dillon's benefit.

Indeed, Dillon had hired well. The dose would put the woman into a comalike state for a least several days, especially given her small size. Give her a fever that ought to prove worrisome to the others, the dose a derivative of the poison the Dslala used to fish in the dry season. Hammond saw a T-shirt draped on a chair by the bed, took it and wiped the floor where he'd walked and left wet boot prints. He retraced his path, diligently wiping the floor, down the stairs, and back into the kitchen and dining room, then out onto deck, covering his tracks again before he went over the side, the rail creaking ominously from his weight.

Dillon had been worried that Hammond might take matters a little too far, as the man had a churlish streak. He shouldn't have doubted his man; Hammond would be due for a sizeable bonus when this was all done.

The comalike state of the photographer should be enough by itself to turn the boat around and send everyone into a tizzy thinking it might be contagious. The other passengers getting ill after eating some of the drug-laced food would be icing on that very sweet cake.

Nothing would be detected, as the drugs would be too far through the victims' systems by the time any tests could be run. Everyone should eventually recover—so no lasting harm done; and this tributary would start to dry up and prevent a return trip. Dillon would be finished with his work before the next rainy season.

No fingers would point in his direction. Illness was not uncommon among foreigners in the Amazon basin: malaria, yellow fever, typhoid, hepatitis, influenza and more. Something could sweep through a group without raising eyebrows. Dillon couldn't keep the Cheshire cat grin off his face.

No more Annja Creed and the potential for media coverage and undue scrutiny.

Hammond settled himself on the shore west of the Dslala village, back against a peppertree, and eyes trained on the boat. Dillon knew his man would keep the post until morning, when, if everything went well, the big boat would turn around.

Dillon clicked on his mic. "Good job, Ham. Exceptional work, actually."

"Couldn't find the woman's camera," he whispered.

"Doesn't matter," Dillon replied. "The woman won't be able to use it."

"Good night, boss."

Time for bed. Dillon turned off his computer, stretched, and stepped out into the deluge. He stripped, letting the rain pummel him and wash away the sweat and malodorous insect repellent. When he was satisfied that he was clean enough, he retreated to his sleeping tent and toweled himself dry. He expected that his dreams would be pleasant ones.

18

"Dengue fever maybe," Captain Almeirão said. "There was an outbreak on the river ten years ago, a first mate I had back then caught it. And years before that there were outbreaks. Scattered cases since, but not among the boatmen that I have heard. This? It looks like Dengue. But I am no doctor." He stood in the doorway to Marsha's cabin, shaking his head. "There's no vaccination for it, Dengue. She couldn't have prevented it with shots. Dengue is very bad."

Ned was behind him, looking around his shoulder. "How'd she catch it?"

Almeirão shrugged. "Insects. Usually always insects. So many insects along the river, and they spread many, many things."

Annja peered through the mosquito netting. Marsha was completely still, except that her chest rose and fell regularly, but shallowly. Her skin gleamed with a thin sheen of sweat. Her eyes were moving behind the closed lids, but that was the only hint of activity. Marsha had been so eager to go with Annja yesterday, traipsing through the rainforest to the pharma camp, insects and standing water everywhere. Maybe if she'd stayed in the village she'd be all right, Annja thought. But she had been gung-ho.

"We were going to get shots of the Dslala village waking up this morning." Ned backed up. Annja couldn't see his face. "It was her idea—Marsha's. We were going to meet in the dining room about four, grab something to eat and wade over before the rest of you got up. Get some shots of Annja coming ashore with the captain. But I couldn't find my camera bag. Came here thinking maybe I left it in her room last night. She'd stuffed hers under the bed, said she didn't want any kids to sneak on board and take it." He paused. "I hope no kid stole mine. I really don't remember leaving my bag here. Just my shirt."

Annja raised an eyebrow at that.

"This was how I found her." He stepped closer and pointed to the bed. "I couldn't wake her up, so I went and got you. Is she going to be all right?" Ned paused and looked to the captain. "Is she contagious? Last night, we…uh—"

"No," Annja said. "Dengue is not contagious. If that's what it is."

"She was fine when I left her last night. Honest." Ned ground the ball of his foot against the deck and cursed. "I left a little after midnight. We'd been up… talking and stuff."

"Dengue is treatable." Annja sat on the edge of the bed. "Like I said, if that's what it is. But Marsha should be in a hospital, and somebody should call her folks and her boyfriend. She lives with a guy in Greenwich.

Can we arrange for a helicopter? I can use Wallace's sat phone to call for one."

"I have such a phone as well, but they won't come this far out. The risk of being here. We must get closer to the city." Almeirão shook his head. "I'll turn the boat around and we'll go back to Belém at full speed. That is the best course and—"

"Wallace is sicker than a dog." Amanda showed up talking louder than anyone. "He's puking. His cabin reeks. And I'm not doing so good myself. Hey, what happened to Marsha?"

"Turn it around now," Annja said. She touched Marsha's arm through the mosquito netting, then she reached under the bed and retrieved her camera bag. "When Marsha eventually comes to, tell her I've borrowed this." To the captain she said, "Just give me five minutes to grab my duffel and Wallace's sat phone. I'm staying with the Dslala."

"Say what?" Amanda exclaimed. "Are you nuts? You're friggin' nuts, Annja! We all need to get back to what passes for civilization."

Almeirão left, his uneven footsteps fading.

Annja squeezed by Ned and went face-to-face with Amanda. "No, I'm not nuts. This series has to be salvaged. If I can get a little more footage, enough to give us at least one good episode, it'll justify us all coming here. I can't do anything for Marsha by going with her. But I can do her justice by adding enough material so what she's already shot isn't tossed."

"In short," Amanda growled, "you're making sure

Doug gets something for the money he's tossed at this. The almighty dollar trumps compassion for your crew."

"Wow, that's cold," Ned said.

Annja walked past both of them.

"Hey! How will you get back?" Amanda followed on Annja's heels. "Are we just supposed to all fly back to New York without you? Or—" She turned, grabbed the rail and leaned over the side, retching into the river. "Breakfast isn't agreeing with me. Why did I ever get up so early?"

Annja stopped and over her shoulder gave Amanda a sympathetic look. "Get yourselves checked out in Belém. The station's insurance will cover it. Then you can fly home to New York." Annja dashed up the stairs and into her cabin, haphazardly throwing things in her duffel and grabbing her laptop. Next stop was Wallace's room.

The senior cameraman was on his side in bed, hands pressed against his stomach. His cabin smelled of vomit; he'd puked into the trash can. He watched Annja as she set her laptop on his nightstand and made a show of grabbing his satellite phone. "Hate to take this," she said. "But Captain Almeirão has one, and he's going to call a hospital in Belém. Marsha's in bad shape, and you and Amanda need to get checked out. Use his sat phone if you have to. Make sure Ken and Ned get checked out, too, before going home. You're in charge, Wall. And please take care of my laptop. It's not going to be any use to me where I'm going."

He opened his mouth to say something, but she was in the doorway, waving. "I'm going to stay behind a little while. I'll find a way back." Resourceful, determined, she'd find a route to Belém; she'd either catch another boat going by while the tributary was still swollen, or hitch a ride on one of the helicopters that apparently visited the pharma camp. She wanted to return to the camp anyway…something wasn't right there. Arthur Dillon was up to something and the notion was making her hands itch. Annja was always one to follow her instincts. More than wanting some additional footage for *Chasing History's Monsters,* Annja wanted to chase down whatever Dillon was into.

Once her curiosity was sated, she'd leave. She sprinted back down the stairs and practically flew to the port side of the *Orellana.* The ship's engine had caught, and the boat had swung around.

"What about taking your own advice and getting yourself checked out?" Ned grabbed her arm at the railing. "What if you're sick, too?"

"I'm not." Annja had a remarkable healing rate, which was somehow connected to her having Joan of Arc's sword. It was as if the sword wouldn't let her be sick—or at least not sick for long. "I'm just blue, and apparently the only cure for that is time and a lot of showers. Or maybe wading through the river."

"I could go with you," Ned volunteered. "I haven't found my camera yet, but I can use Marsha's." He pointed to the camera bag on Annja's shoulder.

The boat started moving.

She almost said "yes," as it would be nice to have the company. But she shook her head and was quick over the side, holding the duffel and camera bag out of the water, and sloshing to the bank. Her stomach growled with each step. She'd been heading into the dining room for an early breakfast when Ned had hollered about Marsha, and so she'd skipped eating. Annja really was hungry, but how could she possibly think about food at a time like this anyway? Marsha and Wallace sick, Amanda from the sounds of it. Maybe some parasites in something the cook prepared. Maybe insects. Most certainly bad luck. It was a good thing she hadn't eaten.

"Be well," Roux had told her.

So far she was feeling fine.

19

D'jok invited her to stay in his family's hut. She accepted, pleased it was one farther back and not in the river so her stuff would remain relatively dry. And the experience would finally be the roughing it that she'd expected when she'd booked the original boat.

"Doug—" Annja managed to reach him on the satellite phone. She'd woken him and he sounded as if his mouth was full of cotton balls. "Doug, the crew is sick—Marsha, Wallace, Amanda."

"Oh, that's great."

She scowled. No compassion, probably worrying about the money he was losing.

"Listen, they're heading to a hospital in Belém, but it might take two days or so to get there. Depends on the weather and the river." She gave him the number for Captain Almeirão's satellite phone. "You can check with him later, when you're more awake. What? No. I'm staying behind. For a little while. No, I don't know the name of the village I'm in. Actually, the village doesn't have a name."

He said something she didn't pick up.

"I need to check out a few things, maybe get some more footage—I have Marsha's camera. We'll have enough for an episode in any event, not the entire series we'd planned, but it all won't be wasted. I'll make sure of that. Marsha? Yes. She's real sick, Doug. Yes, Wall is sick, too. Aren't you listening? What? Maybe Dengue fever. Look it up. I don't want to keep talking. No, I'm fine. Doug…I have to go. I want to keep the charge up on this phone so I can use it again. I'll call you later."

He was still talking, but she turned it off to conserve the battery, and zipped it into her duffel—underneath her clothes. She didn't want this phone to go missing. Then, despite thinking that she shouldn't be considering food, she went to find something to eat.

Instead, she found three black-as-night Dslala. The color was wholly unnatural and disturbing, as if they'd been dipped into a bottle of ink. Edgar and Moons were with them, the long sleeves of Edgar's T-shirt nudged up to his elbows, his lower arms covered solid with insect bites, looking like he'd walked into a nest.

"These men, Annja, have been looking for Baladi and F'yd since yesterday near the pharma camp. They said they saw us in the camp and almost joined us, but they don't like Dillon and his guys. Anyway, they came up with zilch."

"The two Dslala are still missing?"

"Yeah, these ones went dreaming last night, trying to find clues in some mystic vision," Edgar went on. "Baladi is this man's brother. He's worried."

"I'm worried, too," Moons said.

Edgar kept on speaking. "Turns our skin blue, turns their skin black. Man, that's really, really black. Moons would do it if it turned hers black. She thinks you look like a crayon."

"I didn't say that!" Moons spit out.

"Interesting," Annja said for want of anything else to say.

"Anyway, they turn black because they're naturally darker than us."

"I don't care what color they are, Edgar, what color I am. I care if they learned anything interesting."

"Zilch again," Edgar said. "It doesn't sound like they had good dreams. I can translate for you. They told me all about it and—"

"No." Annja'd had enough of the Dslala dreams. She stuffed her pockets full of fruit, waited until Edgar and Moons were occupied elsewhere, grabbed Marsha's camera bag, and slipped down the trail that would take her to the pharma camp.

Certainly she intended to get extra footage for the episode, but she would do a little investigating first. Being a busybody would keep her mind off her ailing companions. *Chasing History's Monsters* crew members had taken ill before on shoots. It happened. But Dengue? Annja shivered. If her well-wishing thoughts could increase the boat's speed, *Orellana's Prize* would be making good time to Belém. She intended to make good time to the pharma camp.

Although the vegetation did its best to snag at her feet, Annja kept a quick pace. She didn't have Marsha, Moons and Edgar to slow her down. The high-stepping was good, anchoring that welcome burn in her chest and making her muscles work. Rather than tire her, it proved invigorating. The birds were especially noisy this morning, the macaws a riot of blue, green and red. A pair of hyacinths circled above the path, probably curious about her. They were beautiful parrots, prized as pets elsewhere, and costing as much as a car. She thought people should leave such creatures in their natural habitat.

A breeze found its way down through a gap in the canopy, bringing the scent of rain and a mix of things she couldn't entirely place, animals maybe, mixed with rotting vegetation. She jumped at the first bang.

A few more bangs in succession, and Annja relaxed, finding some burst seed pods that had been launched from a possumwood tree. She kept a good speed, but she couldn't run; the rainforest prevented that with the myriad roots that spread across the ground coupled with the scattered snake holes. She paused to watch a large green and black snake slide across her path and into a hole, a bulge in its middle suggested it had recently dined on something. She put the snake at about eight feet long. Annja divided her attention between the ground and the way ahead and raised her knees as if she were in a marching band to avoid getting caught on the roots.

She was nearly to the camp when she noticed the sudden quiet. The birds weren't squawking anymore, and not a single monkey howled. She concentrated, feeling eyes on her, but not seeing any suspicious shadows. She'd learned long ago to realize that if she had the sense she was being watched—then she was indeed being watched.

But by whom?

Or what?

Shouldering the camera bag, she opened her hand and summoned the sword. Holding the blade low so it wouldn't catch the sunlight, Annja crept off the path and took a slightly winding route to the camp, the taller vegetation effectively cloaking her…but also probably cloaking the eyes she still felt.

Was she being stalked?

She moved slowly toward the camp, intending to come at it from the side nearest the big tent. A four-foot-high log wall would present no challenge. It was midmorning, and she saw only a little activity. The generator was running louder than it had yesterday, the incongruous sound probably what had quieted the wildlife. The sun fighting with the clouds, the area was well enough lit that she could see three figures moving around in the big tent. She noticed none in the other tents, but didn't have that good of a vantage point to be certain if they were empty. One man she hadn't seen on her previous trip was fussing with something on the table covered with chainsaws and machetes. There was a tarp on the ground next to it, in the event of more rain to keep the equipment from rusting. The skinny security guard was nowhere in sight; neither was the one Moons and Edgar had dubbed the big guy. The others? Maybe they had left earlier to gather plants…or to do whatever it was Dillon was trying to hide.

Certainly plants were part of this operation, but not all of it. Drug smuggling maybe, that was a good bet. South America had plenty of drug cartels, and maybe

Dillon's company was the front for one, shipping out illegal drugs along with legitimate medicinal samples. It could be a good cover and possibly go unnoticed by authorities on either end. Dillon certainly didn't want any authorities poking around out here—otherwise he would have reported Moons and Edgar. It was the fact that he hadn't reported the pair that made Annja certain something untoward was going on.

But what?

Annja loved a mystery, especially when it would keep her mind off her associates and what they were going through. She didn't have all the puzzle pieces yet, and so she couldn't fathom what the picture was supposed to look like, but she knew just enough to know that Dillon was not the righteous cure-finding man he let on he was. A glance at the sky; it was going to rain again and soon. The soft rumble of thunder punctuated that thought. She hunkered down to watch and took the camera out of the bag.

Two men wearing heavy flannel shirts emerged from one of the smaller tents, lights affixed to the tops of their hard hats, rollerblade pads on their knees. They tugged off their flannel shirts and shook them out and spread them on the empty table, like they were letting the rain wash them. They laughed, and the taller one slapped his fellow on the back.

Annja turned off the camera, stuck it back in the bag, and hid it in a hollow spot in a kapok tree. She'd need to get inside that smaller tent to see what they had been doing, and so she'd probably have to wait until nightfall.

Curiouser and curiouser. Flannel shirts in a tropical rainforest? Lights on their hard hats? And the kneepads… It spelled caving.

There was a cave under Dillon's camp. And that's why he didn't want the authorities here—he didn't want them seeing the cave, or maybe what was inside it. Annja considered herself a veteran caver. She was suddenly itching to do a little spelunking.

20

There was a loud bang, and Annja knew that wasn't from a possumwood tree.

"Hands up! And drop the machete."

Annja recognized the voice…Joe, the big guy. So much for her taking the stealth approach. His warning gunshot alerted the two men with the kneepads. She turned and saw that the Joe's gun was pointed straight at her, rain beading up and running off the barrel.

"Ham said your boat left at dawn. You should've been on it. Would've been healthier for you."

She could take him easily and without killing him, so she did just what he wanted. Annja dropped the sword. He came close, looking in the ferns and not seeing the weapon. She'd willed it away.

"Where is it?"

"Where is what?" She glanced over the barrier into the camp and saw that four men were there now, all watching.

"The machete," Joe said. He ran his foot through the ferns. "Where is it?"

"You're close enough," she said.

"Close enough?"

"For this." She kicked high, the hard heel of her boot connecting with his wrist. The gun went flying. Before he could react, she followed through with an old-fashioned uppercut to his jaw. It wasn't enough to drop him, but he was staggered. She turned sideways and drew her hand back, the sword forming. She swept it in, all her strength behind it, the flat of the blade striking him in the chest.

He'd been shouting something, but it came out a strangled, unintelligible sound that was cut off by a boom of thunder.

The shouts of the four in the clearing were quite clear, however. They were hollering "Ham!" She hadn't seen guns on them, but that didn't mean they didn't have them. And who knew how many more men were inside the tents?

She changed the grip on the sword and cracked the pommel on the side of Joe's head, dropping him. She didn't want to kill him. All life was precious—even his. Again, she wondered how many men were involved with Dillon's operation; she didn't want to face an army.

"Get her!" one of the men shouted. "Take my gun. Shoot her!"

Okay, at least one of them was armed.

"Put her out of our misery!" called another.

"Wake Ham! Someone wake Ham!"

She remembered that Hammond was the tall, skinny one that carried two guns.

"I'll get the boss. You get Ham."

Annja darted into the depths of the forest as thunder

rumbled loud enough to make the ground shiver. She hadn't seen Dillon, and she'd been watching the camp awhile. But obviously he was around somewhere. She ran to the northwest. There was a gap in the canopy and so the ground vegetation was thick and no paths evident. Annja couldn't effectively run here because the moss was deceptive, hiding snake burrows that her feet could sink into and roots that spread away from trees and tried to trip her. She dismissed the sword, as it was more trouble than help at the moment, getting snagged by vines and caught on low branches.

The air she sucked in was warm and wet, cloyingly humid. She heard the men behind her, ungainly and thrashing in their haste. It sounded like one of them fell. They were shouting to each other...helpful because she could angle away from their voices. She couldn't hear everything they were saying for the racket they made, but she caught pieces of it.

"—Creed, the television woman—"

"Boss didn't want her dead. He'd said—"

"Her boat left."

"Ham watched it."

"—take her alive."

"—made them sick, had to leave the—"

"No guarantees on—"

"Damn, look out—" Another man tripped and fell.

"Spread out and keep quiet."

They'd stopped talking. Now they were smartening up, but Annja had acute hearing and detected them working through the tight foliage.

When the ground cover started to clear, leaving

only moss and low ferns, she slowed and hugged one trunk after the next, some of them as big around as an elephant. Up against one, she registered how dry the bark was. The lower canopy in this spot was so thick that the rain wasn't reaching the ground. In fact, the way directly ahead was dark like a cave, the weave of branches so close, the air sickly sweet with death. There was little growing at ground level in that direction, not enough light stretching down…some seedlings, vines and patches of fungus, mostly bare earth. Near a cluster of seedlings she saw a monkey carcass. Large colorful insects feasted on it.

She hid in the darkest section, careful not to step on fallen branches that could snap and give her away. Annja didn't hear the men and wondered if she'd lost them; she hoped not. It took a moment for her eyes to adjust to the gloom.

Annja held herself still against the trunk of a "tourist tree," so called because its red, peeling bark was reminiscent of sun-burned tourists. Dillon's crew probably had been here, as half the trunk was stripped of its bark. At least they hadn't taken it all. She'd had tea made from such bark one night on the *Orellana*. The captain's chef had told her he always kept some on board because it was a good remedy for insect bites and sunburn. But he said it also made an excellent tea. She'd concurred; it had a rich, yet subtle flavor.

There! She heard a branch snap, someone coming closer. Annja wasn't running from the men—had that been her intent she would've headed to the Dslala village where there was safety in numbers. She was too curious about the hidden cave beneath Dillon's tents to take that tact. Rather, she was attempting a divide and conquer approach. She hoped to take them down and go back to the camp for further snooping.

She breathed shallowly and sorted through the sounds. Something was in the branches of this very tree, high overhead. Something small, judging by the slight noise, maybe a parrot or monkey that was otherwise being silent. It was probably watching her. There were a few barely audible thunks of what looked like pieces of overripe fruit falling from a nearby tree, a bang in the distance from a bursting possumwood pod. The ground trembled with a boom of thunder. And then came what she was listening for…the footfalls of someone trying to be quiet, but missing the mark because the ferns rustled and the ground crunched under his boots. Annja held her breath, opened her hand, summoned the sword, and waited.

He was one of the cavers, face smudged with dirt and sweat. He'd ditched the hard hat, but in his haste he hadn't taken off his kneepads. He was following a narrow trail she hadn't noticed, but it led by her tree. He had a machete in his right hand, a walkie-talkie in his left; it crackled faintly. Annja preferred a straight-on fight, but right now she just wanted to pick off these guys one by one. Focused, she stepped away from the trunk, eyes on the ground so she wouldn't step on anything that might give her away. Not on a twig or nut husk. Slow.

Slow.

She was behind him, shoulder brushing another

"tourist tree," the papery bark peeling. He was still oblivious, and he was actively searching, gazing to his right and left, then down at the trail like he was looking for tracks. He froze abruptly and Annja held her breath again. A few large drops of rain found their way through the tight trees and ran down her forehead. She could tell he was listening, too. Someone else was moving through the brush at a right angle and well ahead of them.

"Matt?" her quarry whispered. Whispers always seemed to carry. When he didn't get an answer, he held the walkie-talkie to his face and repeated the name. "Where are you? I've spotted a native, black as coal and carrying spears. No sign of the woman."

Annja took advantage of her quarry's distraction. She slipped behind him, raised the sword with both hands, and brought the pommel down on the back of his head. She'd not put everything into the blow—Annja just wanted him stunned, not dead. As he dropped to his knees, she belted him on the side of his head. He fell forward on the walkie-talkie, and she turned him over. He was breathing, but unconscious. She grabbed the radio and darted away.

"Jerry?" There was static and then the voice again. "Jerry, come in."

Annja turned down the volume and retraced her steps back to her "tourist tree." She could see the fallen man from here, and watched as a Dslala—one of the dreaming trio judging by his midnight-black skin—came upon him and knelt to investigate. The Dslala had a spear in one hand and a blowgun in the other, had a small pack on his back. He laid the weapons down and jiggled the man. She stopped herself from approaching. Annja didn't know a word of the Dslala language, and wanted to keep the tribesman out of her plans. He prodded the body harder and put his head to the man's chest. Then he swung the pack around and proceeded to take whatever the fallen man had in his pockets and put them in the pack. The Dslala tugged the man's belt off and strapped it around his own waist, took the machete, and left.

She smiled, and then doubled back to get closer to the camp again and find more of Dillon's men.

The rainforest was disconcerting, and she wasn't wholly sure she was headed in the right direction. Dillon's men had been this way at some time, however; she spotted a tree that had been thoroughly tapped for its sap, another that had vines harvested. Dillon obviously was culling plants for research; her brief tour of his laboratory tent proved that. But what was he doing with a hidden cave? Were the operations connected? She had to get underground and get some questions answered.

She hadn't traveled more than a dozen yards when she saw another of Dillon's men. He was wearing dark green coveralls. A radio was strapped to his waist, and he had a machete in each hand. Better than him having a gun—the noise from a gun would alert the others.

Annja inched toward him, easy because his back was to her. His head was cocked, listening, and he was ambling one way, and then the next, stepping over a fallen limb, poking at bushes with the machete, maybe thinking she was hiding in one, spooking a lizard and laughing as it scampered down the path. The ground rocked with thunder once more, and unseen birds started squawking, leaves overhead rustling and causing water they'd been catching to come down. The man pivoted, looking up, but catching sight of Annja.

"Got her!" he hollered. "I found the blue-skinned one!" He held the machetes close and charged, wisely picking his feet up as he went so he wouldn't trip.

Annja obliged him, summoning her sword, and in the same instant she wrapped her fingers around the pommel, bringing it down and around, catching one of his machetes. The machete spun away. The man blinked in surprise, but recovered, countered and took up a fencing pose as he jabbed forward with his remaining machete, forcing Annja back.

"Don't know where you got that," he said, a nod referring to her sword. "Nice one. I think I'll keep it when I'm done with you." He twirled the machete with practiced grace.

She was surprised; it looked like he had some skill. He lunged, another fencing move, a fast strike that she deflected with her sword. He stepped back and displayed an evil grin.

This was proving slightly more difficult. She'd hoped to clock him into unconsciousness like she had with the first guy she'd come across.

"Matt says to keep you alive. Boss doesn't want any blood in the camp." He lunged again and their blades caught, making a rasping sound as the edges slid against each other. His was a heavier weapon and not meant for being used in a duel. It was designed to help a traveler cut through the underbrush.

"Matt!" he hollered again, thumbing his walkie-talkie with his free hand. "I said I've got her and—"

Annja lunged and he quickly parried; she jumped back, came in again, and he managed to dodge her. That she wasn't trying to kill him made it more difficult. She looked for an opening so she could use her sword to knock the wind out of him. He had her at an advantage, as it became clear he was no longer following Matt's instructions to not hurt her.

She parried his next few blows, still looking for an opening and at the same time trying to wear him down. When his swing slowed she became the aggressor forcing him back until his free arm scraped against a tree. When he parried this time he didn't draw back. Instead he counterstriked, his machete sliding down her blade again and not giving her a chance to defend. The machete sliced through her shirt and drew a line of blood.

"Matt!" he tried again. This time the walkie-talkie crackled loudly.

"Coming!" a voice answered. "Keep the mic on and keep talking so we can find you." He tried a feint, but had telegraphed it, coming at her from a different angle.

She dodged and tried yet another move. This one was tricky, a counterattack in which Annja extended her right leg behind her and reached down with her free hand to catch herself from falling. Supported like a camera on a tripod, she aimed her blade up and jabbed him in the side. She could have run him all the way through, but her design was merely to wound him and put him in a panic.

It worked.

"Demon from hell!" The injury stoked some fire in him and he came at her faster, his grace discarded in lieu of more power in his swings.

Annja rotated her blade as she parried, then feinted herself, leaping to his left side and striking hard with the flat of her sword. The blow caught him in his sword arm and before he could raise the machete to parry her next swipe, she used a saber maneuver, a precision attack stop cut. He tried to block her, but she hit his arm again with such force he cried out, dropped the walkie-talkie, and shifted the machete to his other hand. In that instant she upped her tempo, caught his blade, and nearly wrenched it away.

"Damn you!" He hissed at her, sweat pouring in his narrowed eyes. "Demon!"

"I've been called worse." Annja did another stop cut, and when she pulled back she heard someone thrashing toward her. She needed to end this now, and so she gave him an opening, at the last moment dropping below his blade and attacking from beneath. She spun the sword and rammed him in the gut with the pommel, at the same time hooking her foot behind him and bringing him down. He tried to pull the machete up to counter, but she drove her heel onto his hand, hearing the crunch of his fingers as he howled.

The thrashing was louder. Her new assailant led with a gun and fired, the bullet hitting the tree at eye level, inches from Annja's face. She jumped behind the tree and then raced to the next, hoping her feet wouldn't get snagged by anything in the ground cover—she wasn't watching her step. A heartbeat later she realized her mistake. The tip of her boot caught under a knobby root and she went flying, the sword spinning away and disappearing. She rolled when she hit, a bullet spitting into the ground where she'd been a second before. Jumping to her feet, she cut to her right, thinking to come up on her new foe from another angle. She'd lost her sense of direction, the forest a blur of green and brown, the shadows so thick it looked like night was descending.

"I see her!" This from the gunman. "Len is down. But I see her!"

She couldn't tell if he was speaking into a walkie-talkie or if another of his buddies had arrived. Annja sprinted behind another tree, held her breath, and listened. Two sets of boots walking nearby, voices talking softly, no static from any walkie-talkies. Then something louder: "Len? He's bleeding, but it doesn't look bad. Do you still see her?"

"No, but she has to be close. Here, take my gun."

Two men, one gun. Easy odds. Annja kept listening, trying to place where they were in relation to her position, direction and distance. The rain must be coming down harder now, as a trickle was finding its way to the ground. Overhead something moved through the trees, rattling branches and making quick and harsh sounds... A few bangs followed and she couldn't tell if they were from a gun or possumwood pods bursting. She gave up trying to guess where the men were and looked out from behind her tree.

Nothing.

Wait, there was someone, but not one of Dillon's men. It was the Dslala she'd seen minutes ago. He was wearing the belt he'd taken, and the machete was hooked to it.

There was no sign of Len, but she saw the spot where she'd dropped him, and so his friends must have picked him up. She could still hear them talking. Annja edged out and picked a course perpendicular to the Dslala. Was he out here searching for his missing tribesman? Had his dream led him here? Her dream had led only to a nightmare…Charlemagne and Joan of Arc, Roux, a monstrous caiman and…a cave.

Dillon's cave?

Had the dream been a premonition?

She crouched behind the trunk of a tree thick with clusters of yellow-gold flowers. Its scent reminded her of cantaloupe. Some of the petals fluttered down like big snowflakes and caught in her hair and against her sweat-damp skin. Annja pressed on, thinking she was homing in on the voices.

"Len?"

"I'm all right," came the reply. They'd roused him.

"He can walk now. Take him back to camp. If you find Ham, send him out here. He'll track her. It's his fault she's here. Ham was supposed to chase 'em all out."

"Hey, Matt. I wouldn't worry about trying to take her alive. You see her, plug her between the eyes. She's gator bait as far as I'm concerned."

Again she wondered how many men were at the

pharma camp and what sort of firepower they had. Maybe she should revise her plan, skirt back to the Dslala village and pull out her sat phone and call for help, let the authorities know something was definitely wrong out here. Maybe…but first she'd get a look at Matt.

There were bushes to her left, where another gap in the canopy let enough light and rain down. The tallest was about three feet high, and warty gourds spread away from it on thick vines. It looked similar to something she'd seen growing near the Dslala village. Hunkering down, she skittered behind the bushes and came up at the trunk of a giant that stretched up out of sight. Some sort of tropical balsam, it was festooned with tiny white flowers; their perfume cut the stench from her sweat. From here, she could see Matt.

He was wearing khaki pants with kneepads, a long sleeved shirt tied around his waist. He had muscles and a tattoo on his arm that marked him as ex-military. She couldn't read the words with it, but she suspected he'd been a Marine. Interesting assortment of men Dillon had working to collect plant samples.

Matt had a Taurus in his right hand and was impatiently tapping it against his leg as he looked one way and then the next. He drew himself against a tree, pressing forward as if he was listening for something. Annja listened, too, but only heard something rustling the branches overhead and thrumming rain. He raised his gun and looked around the trunk, but away from her. That gave her an advantage and so she skittered closer. She was nearly on him when she saw him crouch and take up a classic firing pose. At the edge of her vision, she saw his target: the Dslala.

"No!" Annja hollered.

Matt spun and fired just as Annja sprang away, the bullet grazing her arm and feeling like fire. He fired again, but she was already moving, protecting herself behind a tree.

"I've got her!" he hollered. "She's pinned. What the—"

Annja heard the dull thud a body makes when it drops. She looked out from behind the trunk and saw Matt flat on his face, not moving. It didn't have the feel of a ruse, and the gun had slipped from his hand. She listened, looking in every direction quickly and seeing no one else. But she heard things—beyond the rain and the creatures moving through the canopy. Heavy footsteps crunching, another goon was coming closer.

Matt was breathing, but barely.

She squinted and shifted a few feet closer, and saw a dart protruding from the man's back. Annja released the sword and instantly it vanished. She pulled out the dart, but the poison obviously had been strong and quick and had done its work. He made a rasping sound and stopped breathing entirely. She rolled him over, concern for herself discarded. She tipped back his head, cupped a hand under his neck, and brought her mouth down on his, trying to breathe for him. His heart had stopped. She gave a chest compression and—

"Get away from him! Now!" The voice was familiar and Annja paused. She heard the click, a round chambering. "Get up."

One last compression and she complied. She rose to face Hammond who was bare-chested, wearing faded sweatpants and a scowl. He only had one gun this time, and it was pointed squarely at her.

"I can help him." She pointed to the downed man. "Let me try to help."

"Get away from him."

"Then you help him," Annja pleaded. "He's dying. It's poison. His heart has stopped."

"I saw your boat leave this morning. You should have been on it."

"That's what your friend told me earlier," she replied. "Let me help him."

"Dillon didn't want you dead, but he might have other ideas now." Hammond spat on the ground. She noticed a tattoo on his arm; it matched the one on the downed man. Dead man, she corrected herself. The poison was very fast-acting and his lips were already discoloring.

"Your friend's dead," she said. "You should have let me—"

"I got eyes," he retorted. "You might be joining him soon." He paused and cocked his head, listening for something. "Put your hands up. That's it. A little higher. We're gonna go back to the camp, see what Dillon wants to do with your sorry blue ass. I'm betting—" Hammond turned.

Annja saw the black-as-night Dslala at the same time Hammond did. The tribesman had a blowgun to his lips, his cheeks puffed, and he expelled air. The dart flew straight at Hammond. Annja dove at the mercenary to knock him out of the way.

All life was sacred to her, and though she'd killed more people in self-defense than she wanted to think about, she didn't want Hammond to die. She wanted him alive to question him. He had some of those precious puzzle pieces she was looking for. Annja barreled into him with enough force to push him aside…and put herself directly in the path of the dart. She felt it sink into the fleshy part of her upper arm, and she heard Hammond's gun go off, heard the whistle of another dart, which struck her in the back as she was going down.

Then she didn't hear or feel anything.

21

Roux wanted to quit this ridiculous notion. It was getting more expensive by the moment, not that he didn't have the money to cover it. He'd invested well through the centuries and was more than comfortable. But in a handful of days he'd shelled out thousands on what was probably a wild goose chase to find Annja Creed.

Annja would be all right. Somehow she always was. Sure, he'd gone looking for her before when he'd had a feeling that she was in trouble or could use his help. But it had never been this difficult to find her. It was a damn big river, and locating her somewhere on it would be like looking for that needle in a haystack—and a very giant haystack at that.

He suspected his efforts would be all for nothing and that she'd be safely ensconced in her New York City apartment before he got out of this insect-infested place.

Still, he paid the money to charter the tug, finding a captain and a mate that knew enough English. It was only a two-man crew. They were fishermen, and had at first thought that Roux wanted to go fishing.

He dropped his suitcase in the center of the deck and opened the maps he'd purchased.

Roux had asked enough questions on the docks and spread enough money around that he got the name of the captain of *Orellanna's Prize* and his likely course, a swollen tributary that led to only remote places.

"Sounds like where Annja would go," he told his captain. "So I want to go here." Roux stabbed a finger at a spot on one of the maps. It looked like a solid piece of green, no river that he could see. He scowled as rain started to fall on his map. He brushed the water away.

"There is nothing there," the captain returned. "River in the rainy season, solid ground otherwise. We have been that way, good fishing sometimes." He smiled. "Together we speared an arapaima as long as this boat on that piece of river."

That would be about ten feet, Roux mentally translated, a very big freshwater fish.

"Much money we sold that fish for. Took a picture." The captain reached in his wallet and pulled out a photograph with curled edges. The fish was probably longer than ten feet.

"Jonah's whale," Roux teased. "I certainly don't want to go fishing for something like that." *I am fishing for Annja Creed.*

"But along this tributary, other than big fish, there is nothing else." The captain leaned over the map to help shield it from the rain. "Now, here and here are interesting places I can take you. Some villages over there like tourists and have many trinkets—"

"No. This tributary," Roux was adamant. "I'm looking for something, maybe a village."

"It is your money." The captain worried at a wart on his thumb. "Okay. There are some villages, but they are small, very small, and have no names."

"That's fine. That's where I want to go."

Other boats, larger and in better repair, were leaving with tourists on them. Roux envied that there were metal or sturdy canvas roofs to keep the passengers relatively dry. But this was the first boat he'd found willing to take a lone man on a trip, and he was impatient enough not to look for something better.

"Long way, you are thinking," the captain said. "More than a day, maybe more than two or three."

"I'm paying you well enough."

"Yes, very well. But you will wait just a little while." He turned to his mate. "Bento, take some of this money and buy us some food. And a bottle for the evenings. Two bottles."

An hour later Roux was getting drenched and wondering if indeed he should have quit this nonsense and stayed at the hotel in Belém that he'd so quickly checked into and abandoned. That had been more money tossed at this silly venture.

BY THE AFTERNOON of the next day, Roux was certain he should have remained at the hotel—or back in France for that matter. The thread that connected him to Annja Creed was back. He closed his eyes, elbows on his knees, grateful the thin link had been reestablished. So very often he didn't realize the connection was there, as it drifted to the background of his life. He didn't let it drift this time, his mind keeping a firm grasp on it.

Was she all right?

Images flickered behind his eyes, as if he was having a dream while awake. He saw Annja, or was it Joan? No, both, the images next to each other, then one superimposed over the top, trading places in the corner of his mind. Joan was the youngest he'd ever seen her, innocent and determined. Annja was jaded but equally determined. The sword was held between them. Did the vision mean something? Should he turn around, content that he knew where she was?

"The village may have no name," Roux said. "But I know for certain where it is and where I want your boat to take me."

22

"She's dead, boss, that television woman." Hammond appeared to show some amount of care when he laid the body of his fellow ex-Marine on the empty table in the pharma camp clearing. The wind that found its way into the camp drove the rain sideways. It quickly washed the dirt off the body. Hammond rubbed at a stubborn spot on the man's forehead and straightened the legs and arms. "I watched the boat leave at dawn, didn't know that she wasn't on it. I'm thinking she must have been in the village. So the boat left without her. Probably wouldn't wait for her, as sick as those people must have been."

"Not good. Not good at all." Dillon shielded his eyes from the rain and looked in the direction Hammond had come, waves of concern rippling through him.

The surrounding rainforest was dark and seemed almost sinister. He'd go in looking for Annja's body himself if it wasn't so dangerous. Easy enough to get lost in the rainforest when there was daylight sneaking down. But with no light and in this weather? "You're certain she's dead? Absolute certain?"

Hammond laughed. "Oh, yeah. And the kick of it? The ironic thing was that she died saving me…or maybe she was just trying to throw off my aim so I didn't kill the native." He recounted the incident with the Dslala and the blowgun. "Poison. It's what got Matt. I guess the Dslala are angry about those two guys gone missing. Well, now there's another one missing. I plugged the blowgun dude."

"And left his body to be found?"

"I know where it is, boss. Not to worry. If it doesn't get eaten overnight, we'll take care of it in the morning. Gotta go back anyway."

"The Dslala don't know for certain their missing fellows were killed here." Dillon folded Matt's hands in front of him and straightened a ring on his right hand. He'd liked Matt, who'd served with Hammond during a tour. "I do not need an entire village of them provoked. I don't want them poking into our business."

"No, like I said, caiman eat the evidence." Hammond ran a hand through his hair. "I want Matt buried. He deserves better than to be eaten."

"Of course," Dillon said. "In the cave would be best." There was a section in the upper chamber with a dirt floor. They'd already buried two bodies there. "We can put him there, have a little ceremony if you'd like."

"Yeah, I was thinking that myself, the cave, next to Nancy. Your wife was the only one who'd play chess with him. It'd be appropriate, like their ghosts could have a game."

Dillon didn't believe in ghosts or any afterlife. It was all about the here and now, and when it was done, there was nothing else. "Yes, that would be fine. I think Nancy would have liked that."

A silence settled between the two. Lightning flickered overhead. The rain patted against the ground, flattening the reeds and grass and bouncing off the tarp. Dillon didn't mind the sound of the rain, which had become almost comforting to him. But he was getting weary of being wet so often.

"The Dslala with the blowgun?"

"Took two bullets, 'cause the television woman knocked my aim off the first one. Had a hard time seeing him, too, so dark in there, and he was black as night. I think he got Nate. Had Nate's brand-new leather belt on him and one of our machetes." Hammond tapped his waist. He was wearing the belt around his waist now, though the sweatpants had no loops for it. "I'm keeping it. I liked Nate well enough, and it don't need to stay on no damn dead native."

"No, I suppose not."

There was more silence, and this time Dillon broke it. "Can't trust the big cats to eat her, that Miss Creed. Or the Dslala."

"No, I suppose not," Hammond parroted. "Like I told you, I gotta go back in the morning. I already have that figured out, boss. Morning comes, me and Joe'll go get her and Nate. Couldn't carry them all back by myself, so I picked Matt out of respect." He spat at the ground. "Didn't want Matt getting chewed on. But that damn woman? I couldn't care less what tries to make a meal of her. But I get it, just in case someone goes looking, they don't need to find her. And we'll get the dead native while we're at it. Feed them to caiman and piranha. Except Nate. If we find him, we'll bury him in the cave, too."

Dillon nodded. His mood was darkening with the sky. He'd called his men in a while ago, not wanting to misplace any in the rainforest. He didn't have any particular attachment to them, but he needed their numbers to work this double operation. Down two men now— Nate and Matt—shifts would be adjusted to compensate. Everything had been going reasonably smoothly until Annja Creed and her crew showed up and set his nerves all a jangle. Would anyone come back looking for her? Her disappearance could be easily explained away; people went missing in the rainforest. But would they search? A celebrity, someone would come looking.

"Damn it all to hell," he said. "We'll have to go faster. Probably can't take everything. We'll go for the bigger pieces."

"Boss?" Hammond gave him a curious look.

"We need to put in a lot more hours in the cave," Dillon said. "I'll contact the labs in the morning. Tell them we've hit a snag with our plant harvest. I'll come up with a reason. Every effort goes into the cave in case we have to pull out."

"In case they come looking for her?"

"A celebrity? Someone will look for her. I just don't want anyone to find something we're trying to keep hidden," Dillon returned. "We cannot risk getting caught. How can we enjoy all our money if we're rotting in some South American prison?"

Hammond's expression turned grim. "Then if we

speed up production, how're we gonna ship it out of here? If we don't use the plants as cover—"

Dillon considered his options. The Brazilian government had only checked the transports going out the first month he was here. Everything all nicely labeled for research laboratories in Atlanta and Dallas, they fell to trusting him. He'd not had a single container inspected in the past ninety days.

"We'll still use the plants as cover," Dillon said. "Whatever snag I come up with to slow our shipments to the labs will become conveniently unsnagged. We just won't be shipping any plants. And our shipments won't be going to any laboratories." Dillon spun and walked through an ankle-deep puddle toward the tent near the generator. "Bring Matt's body, and let's bury him now." He looked over his shoulder. "Then we'll all put in a long shift tonight."

Hammond cradled the ex-Marine's body and followed.

23

She was in a cave; she could tell that by the scent of the place, damp and fusty; beneath her fingers she felt rock worn smooth by water. She pushed herself up and her eyes adjusted to the dimness. Light was meager, coming from luminous lichen high on the walls. She couldn't see the ceiling of the chamber; it stretched up as if to infinity. There were crude paintings of creatures she had no words for—monsters, grotesque beasts that resembled men only because they'd been drawn walking upright. There were bones, too, scattered on the floor like a child's toys. Should she take the time to put them together?

She wasn't alone. There was a man several feet away. He had long gray hair and looked like he might be a scholar, standing there studying her. He wasn't dressed for the cave, as he was wearing a navy suit with a striped red tie and shiny black shoes. His companion was not dressed for this place either. A mere slip of a girl, she was barefoot and wearing old, ripped clothing. A most unusual pair.

Did she know them?

Father-daughter?

Grandfather-granddaughter?

Should she talk to them? She opened her mouth, but no sound came out. She tried to approach them but discovered her feet would not move.

As she watched them, smoke curled up from the girl's feet, and bright red flowers spread away. Not flowers, flames. The smoke grew thicker and she thought it would choke her, but it didn't. She only smelled the musty scent of the old cave.

She wanted to scream at the man to help the girl. Her voice would not cooperate.

The elderly man did nothing except stare, and step farther away so the flames would not touch him. Again, Annja tried to move, and this time her feet glided forward over the smooth stone, the sensation against her soles oddly pleasing. One step, two, and then she was rushing toward the girl, intending to help her put out the fire. But in a heartbeat it had spread too quickly.

The girl was wholly engulfed, the blaze bright and fast, flaring white hot and then it was gone.

In its place a sword hovered, tip down. The Sword of Damocles?

"I'm dreaming," she said. "This isn't real."

She opened her eyes and found only darkness.

Dark.

Dark.

Dark.

"Death is close to life," someone had told her.

Was this death? Was death this lonely?

Instantly, she was not in a cave anymore, but she

might as well have been given how dark it was. She felt damp ground beneath her. Her face was pressed against the forest loam. She pushed up and rolled herself over.

She wasn't dead. She was confident death wouldn't feel like this. It was neither heaven nor hell. She didn't ache enough for this to be hell. It was a forest.

A sudden bang made her ask if the noise was gunfire. It was a familiar sound. If someone was shooting a gun, what were they firing at? There was nothing except utter blackness. What could they possibly see in order to shoot?

She breathed deep, pulling all the scents into her lungs. Plants, both vibrant and decaying, flowers, the musk of some animal, and blood. That latter scent was close. Was she bleeding? Sitting up and running her fingers up and down her legs and arms, she found a tear in her shirt and a tender streak where somehow she knew a bullet had passed by. It felt like the wound had closed. Still she smelled blood.

"Ouch." There were needles in her. One in her back, one in her arm. She tugged them out and dropped them.

On her hands and knees, she explored her surroundings, finding the tendril of a knobby root, spongy fungus, bones of a bird.

Definitely a forest.

But it was so dark.

Was she blind? Was that why the world was so black? She panicked at that thought and scrabbled around faster, not knowing what direction she crawled in and bumping into things. Her head struck a tree. She felt around the trunk, papery, shaggy bark that pulled off in her fingers. She remembered the bark being red and that she'd drank it.

A cat snarled; it didn't sound close, but it put her in more of a panic. Crawling faster, coming to another tree, she pulled herself up, tipped her head back. Water dribbled down and she opened her mouth for it.

"Ahhh." Shuffling now, slow baby steps because there seemed to be roots and fallen branches almost everywhere. After a time she walked with more confidence, taking longer strides that brought her into a massive spider web, the sticky mass cocooning her. She batted it away, fought through it and started peeling it off her, feeling spiders run down her face and over the backs of her hands. She wasn't afraid. Was that odd? That she wasn't afraid of the spiders? A little farther, taking smaller steps again and holding her fingers out to avoid more webs. "What?" Her feet connected with something that yielded a little.

She crouched and explored it with her hands. It was a man, naked, a shaved head. He wasn't breathing. Insects were crawling in his mouth and nose, and something had picked his eyes out. He smelled of being newly dead; his bowels had loosened. How did she know what new death smelled like?

There was a bullet wound in the center of his chest, and more bugs were feasting there, another wound of some sort in his shoulder. There was a hint of warmth to him, but not near as warm as a body should be. His limbs were stiff. Some warmth, and stiffness; he'd been dead probably eight hours, not more than twelve. How could she know that? Why would she know so much about death?

"Death and life are close," someone had told her.

She thought the body should have made her nervous, freak out, but it didn't. In fact, as the minutes flowed by, she started to relax. She was unfazed about dead bodies and spiders. What sort of person did that make her? A cat growled again, but a second joined it, creating a snarling chorus. There were two at least, maybe three, the sound was closer. Time to leave.

And go where in this dark?

It didn't matter, she decided, away from here. Pick a direction. To her right, wherever that would take her, as it was away from the cats and the body. The cats were coming closer, growling, snarling, probably hunting. Leave the body for them; let the dead man serve a purpose. Overhead a nightbird cried, the tone long and beautiful. There was rustling in the branches, something small moving around, a bird perhaps? Likely it was nothing that would threaten her. She slogged forward, and fought against fingers that grabbed her from all directions, spiky, bone-sharp fingers that she realized were low-hanging tree branches. She forced herself to breathe slower. Count to twenty. She remembered numbers, at least.

Questions tumbled through her head as she crept through the blackness.

How did she get here?

How long had she slept?

Would there be an end to the dark?

Please, don't let me be blind.

She thought she remembered other people, faces fleeting in her mind's eye, women and men, the old man again that she'd seen in the cave in her dream.

Where was here?

Who was she?

She should know at least that last thing, right? A name. She needed a name. She had one, didn't she? Didn't everyone have a name?

Villages with no names. People with no names. Someone had said that to her.

Orellana came to the fore, a pretty word. Was that it? Was that her name? Orellana? It must be; all the other names that floated by belonged to men and did not make sense: Ned, Wallace, Ken, Hammond, Matt. Did she know them? Had they come to these woods with her? Had they brought her here? Abandoned her?

Her stomach felt empty. Thirsty and hungry, she tamped down those sensations. Getting out of here— wherever here was—came first. Get out of the dark.

She didn't know how long she wandered, or if she was even going in a straight line. She supposed she might have been traveling in circles, but she hadn't come back to the body, hadn't crossed paths with the big cats, and the trees she brushed against were different here—vines growing down all of them, some fragrant, some reeking. The noises were soft, birds, bats, frogs; nothing sounded large or threatening.

She paused and rubbed her legs, the muscles starting to protest. She'd been walking a long while. A thought came and she searched her pockets, thinking she might find something to trigger a memory. There was nothing.

Farther and a band of gray encroached on the blackness.

Farther, and she came to a break in the canopy, where meager light fell with warm, soft rain. She stood in the center of it, letting it wash away the dirt and sweat, drinking it. Her clothes were so plastered against her they were a second skin, the water seeping into her boots. The leather was sodden. Birds soared across the scant space of sky, charcoal smudges against the gray. The air was fresher here, and she sucked it in so deep she thought her lungs were full.

When her legs cramped from standing so still for so long she picked a tree and climbed it—not so difficult a thing. She'd obviously done this before. She intended to wait for the better part of morning to come when a little color would creep in, hoping the rain might stop. Though everything seemed so terribly wet and verdant that maybe the rain never stopped.

She was at the lowest branch when she saw something move across the small clearing. It was a snake, big and long. As it slithered across the space she guessed it was more than twenty feet long. Anaconda…that she had a name for it and not for herself was perplexing. She almost went down to get a better look; she wasn't afraid of it.

Maybe she didn't fear anything. Maybe fear was a choice, and she'd banished it.

She must have dozed because the next thing she realized the sky was a pale blue and the rain had stopped. Her back ached from the position she'd wedged into against the trunk, and her neck felt stiff. She worked out a kink and climbed down and decided that she'd travel in the direction the snake had slithered. The forest was dark, but not black like last night; some light filtered down. A place of shadows, then. Where it was brightest she found a tall bush with glossy green leaves and fruit. Something had been eating it; she saw pieces of the skin on the ground.

So hungry. When had she eaten last?

Once more, names infiltrated her thoughts—Orellana again, Amanda, Marsha, Joan. The last name lingered. Was her name Joan? She rubbed at her temples. Joan sounded good, but it wasn't right. Orellana sounded better, like music.

What's wrong with me? she wanted to shout, but stopped herself. Something inside told her to be careful. The dead man she'd found last night…she wondered if she could find him again. Maybe he held a clue to her identity and then she could figure out why she was here, and just where "here" was.

Food first. The fruit was sweet and juicy, reminding her of strawberries, but it wasn't quite the same. The flavor was stronger because it was so fresh. She stuffed her face with it, and then pressed on, discarding the notion of searching for the dead man. Something bad had happened there, and she wanted no part of it.

Though she couldn't remember anything, she knew that she revered life.

Death waited back the way she'd come.

Still hungry, she found fist-sized fruit growing on a prickly vine. The vines nearby had been stripped, and some of the trees had been tapped. There were places where things had been dug up, some sort of roots collected judging by the size of the holes. Edible? Who'd been doing the digging? For some reason the "who" mattered. For some reason the "who" made her hands itch.

She had to work to open the pod. Inside was a yellow gelatinous pulp. Hesitating only a moment, she dug her fingers in and tasted. Not as sweet as the red fruit, but equally delicious. There was a veritable banquet in the forest.

Rainforest.

Suddenly she had a better word for this place.

Amazon.

An even better name.

She walked farther and came to a stream, orange-like fruit growing on vines that draped from branches into the water. Tiny monkeys played along the branches; watching her and quickly losing interest, they resumed their game. A bird the color of the fruit regarded her curiously and made a shrill sound.

She took off her boots and sat on the spongy bank. The light was even brighter here, the morning aging, and her heart seizing up when she saw her feet and hands. They were blue.

The panic she'd felt the night before returned and doubled, her throat tightening. She'd looked dark in the clearing, her hands dark when she'd foraged for fruit. But blue? She was ill, maybe dying.

Fear seized her, but she pushed it away.

She was not sick. She felt *good*. There was another explanation.

She gulped in the air and scrubbed at herself. People

were not blue. She might have no memory of herself, but she knew people did not come in this color. Maybe she was dreaming. Dreams could feel real, couldn't they? But this would be a nightmare.

No fear. She chose not to be afraid.

"Someone came this way." It was a man's voice. She jumped up and grabbed her boots, whirled toward the voice and listened. "She came this way. I was certain she was dead. She got hit by the poison dart, just like Matt. Two darts in her. Why the hell didn't the poison kill her? The poison took Matt and he was healthy as a bear."

"The poison should have killed her," a second man said.

"Matt had her beat in body weight by probably forty pounds."

"Maybe she didn't get as big a dose." This from the second man. "But you told the boss she was dead."

She moved behind a fern, staying in the stream, knowing there'd be no tracking her in the water. How did she know that?

"Yeah, I told the boss she was dead. She *should* be dead."

"Then she is dead, Ham."

"Like hell. Here's her footprints. And here, she stopped to eat."

She moved farther up the stream, quiet, listening, wondering how the men knew her…and did she in turn know them?

"Don't you get it? We just have to tell Dillon she's dead. Regardless of whether or not she's really dead, we have to say it. He's paranoid. He's going to send all of us out here looking for her. Can't have her running to the authorities, he'll say. And if he has us all out here, how are we going to get our treasure? And how are we going to make obscene amounts of money if we're not getting the treasure?"

She could tell the men had stopped. She stopped, too, breathing shallowly, feeling a snake float by at her ankles and forcing herself to be still.

"I don't like lying to the boss."

"And how is it lying, Ham? If she's not dead now, she's going to be. A woman by herself in the rainforest. Caiman, snakes, leopards, you name it. Oh, those pretty little frogs. Those frogs'll kill you quick as anything. Something's going to get her. If she's not dead now, she will be before the day is out."

"All right. All right, she's dead. We'll tell Dillon she's dead. He's going to want to see the body, though. We'll have to come up with a story."

"That's my Ham. We'll say we didn't find much of her, animals had gotten to her. And we tossed the pieces that were left in the river. Not enough to bring back. We'll haul Nate's bug-riddled carcass back, and the native, too. Two bug-infested corpses. That ought to satisfy Dillon, you think?"

"All right, we'll say we didn't find enough of her to bring back. I'm thinking I like the sound of that. I want Nate buried, like Matt. He deserves that. He doesn't deserve ending up in the belly of some critter."

"Okay, Ham. I'll help you bury him."

Ham. The man's name was Hammond, she remembered that much.

She also remembered that she most certainly didn't like him.

24

Roux had lived enough centuries and been to enough places that nothing really set him aback anymore. But the village he waded ashore to came close to doing just that. Few of the villagers wore clothes, and none of them appeared to speak English, French, Portuguese or any other language he tried…until finally a pair of Americans emerged from the forest. He talked the captain into tying the boat to a tree and waiting.

"For as long as it takes," Roux said. "I will pay you well, no matter how long this takes."

The captain agreed and settled back to nap.

"Yeah, we know Annja Creed," Moons said. "You her father?"

"No."

"Grand—"

"I'm a friend."

"She's awesome, Annja. Interviewed us for her television program. She's going to get the plight of the rainforest out there. She's going to help us spread the word. She's gonna help us bring down Dillon Pharmaceuticals."

Edgar elbowed her. "Annja said no guarantees."

Moons gave him a dirty look.

Roux endured their explanation of Annja going to the pharma camp with them. The woman—Moons she said her name was—struck him as a teenager, though he could tell she was in her mid-twenties. He politely listened while they expounded upon how badly the men at the pharmaceutical camp were hurting the rainforest by overharvesting. Then when they came up for air, he asked, "Where is Annja now?"

Moons and Edgar shrugged.

"I know she'll be coming back," Moons volunteered. "She stayed when the boat left, put her stuff in D'jok's hut, then took off into the forest, probably going back to that awful camp. We didn't see her leave, otherwise me and Edgar would have went with her. We went anyway, but she had a head start. Couldn't find her. Didn't see her at the camp, and we knew not to get too close. It's a big forest, and—"

"You could just wait with us," Edgar suggested. "She'll come back. You involved with her television show? Are you that producer Doug she mentioned?"

"Roux."

"Thought you sounded French," Moons said.

Roux asked to be shown to D'jok's hut, where he was relieved to find that the tribesman there could speak some English.

"I worry for Annja Creed," D'jok said. "One day gone and Annja Creed has not come back. More than one day gone now. But I think she will come back for this." He pointed to her duffel.

"Do you know why she left?" The "why" would help him pinpoint the "where." Roux felt the connection to her, but it didn't work as precisely as a homing beacon. He folded himself onto a woven mat. It was cool inside the hut, and it smelled pleasantly of cooking spices.

"Annja Creed left because she searches for something in the forest that she could not find in her dream." D'jok paused and fixed Roux with an unblinking stare. "Or maybe she finishes what the dream started. The dreams can be powerful. You can wait with my family, or—"

Roux thought about doing that. This was the largest rainforest in the world, and it would be very easy to get lost in it. Looking for Annja in the forest would be difficult, but there was the thread, and he still felt it. Maybe he could follow it, and they would find each other. He *should* wait right here.

But on the boat ride he'd told himself that he should have waited in Belém, or better yet remained in France. Annja always managed to take care of herself.

"I'm going to look for her," Roux told the old man.

"Then I will come as well. The forest is the world, and to find one woman in it could be unlikely."

"I know," Roux admitted. "But it is better than just sitting here."

"Yes," D'jok said. "And in the searching maybe I will not have time to worry so much about Annja Creed."

"Great, we'll join you," Moons chimed in. She'd poked her head inside the hut to eavesdrop.

Roux shook his head. "I think not, young woman." Before they headed out, he dug through his suitcase for a stash of food he'd bought in the hotel gift shop…bags of peanuts, granola bars, pretzels and candy. He put on a light cargo jacket and stuffed the food in the pockets. He was more than capable of roughing it. But he also knew to take precautions.

D'JOK SELECTED A tribeswoman to join them, the finest tracker in the village. They took the path created by the previous trips to the pharma camp. Roux didn't consider it much of a trail, but it was a little less overgrown than the surrounding ground.

"Are you the grandfather of Annja Creed?" D'jok asked after they'd traveled in silence for more than an hour.

"I am a friend."

"Then Annja Creed chooses her friends well."

Roux acknowledged that "choice" had nothing to do with it.

They reached the perimeter of the Dillon Pharmaceuticals camp by late afternoon, and Roux noticed two armed sentries patrolling just inside the barrier.

"Why does a pharmaceuticals company need guns?" he asked.

D'jok shrugged, held him back, and motioned that they should remain hidden. There was not another soul moving around, which Roux found unusual given the number of tents that indicated a good number of people must be about. Strange.

The tribeswoman skirted the camp to the north, Roux and D'jok in her wake.

"The men cannot see us here," D'jok said. "The forest is thick. I have not met those men, but I do not think I like them. Moons says they are bad. She says all of Dillon's men are bad."

The ground cover near the clearing was so thick Roux couldn't see what the tribeswoman was following. He knew the basics of tracking. As he was one of Joan of Arc's knights, the skills had come in handy centuries ago when pursuing the enemy and hunting game. He'd not had much cause to use those skills in the past few decades. He watched her intently. She was methodical, seeing things he couldn't, and was definitely following something. She talked softly in a pretty language he couldn't fathom.

He knew why Annja remained involved with *Chasing History's Monsters,* the tracker and this forest all part of it. She was an explorer at her heart, drinking in all the experiences and cultures the world spread before her. He envied her appetite. He'd lost that sense of wonder a very long time ago.

D'jok translated. "Annja Creed came this way, stopped here, then there." He moved aside the spreading leaves of a fern. Underneath was a camera bag. "Does this belong to Annja Creed?"

"I don't know." Roux plucked it out and swung it over his shoulder. "Just keep searching."

The afternoon stretched to twilight, when even Roux found tracks amid a spotty carpet of fungus. There had been considerable rain, but the weave of branches had kept the signs from washing away. There were two sets of heavy boot prints, and a set of thinner, smaller ones that he assumed were Annja's, a woman's in any event. A few yards away he saw blood on a patch of moss, more on a flowery plant, and evidence a body had lain there.

"Annja is all right," Roux said, kneeling. "This wasn't her." He wouldn't still feel the thread if it were, and it felt like that thread tugged him in the direction the tracker continued to go.

"No, it was not Annja Creed." D'jok looked grim as he held up a shell casing in one hand and a broken blowgun in the other. He let both drop. An hour later D'jok signaled an end to the day.

By midmorning of the following day, the tracker found Annja.

ROUX STARED. "She's blue."

Annja stared back and crouched defensively.

"Annja Creed dreamed," D'jok said. It took Roux a moment to realize that was an explanation for her skin color.

He still couldn't stop himself from staring. She looked...wrong, alien-like, as if she'd stepped off the set of a science fiction movie. Her expression was *wrong,* too. Roux had seen Annja during good and calamitous times and thought he knew all of her expressions. This was new and disturbing. "Annja, I've—"

She set her back to a tree; her gaze shifted right then left before settling on him. At first he thought she was frightened, but studying her eyes he realized she had a predator's look.

"Annja?"

"My name is Orellana," she said. "And I don't know you."

"That is not part of the dreaming," D'jok offered. "Dreaming makes you aware."

Roux said softly, "Annja and I will find our way back to your village. You can leave."

D'jok nodded and motioned for the tracker woman to follow him. "Annja Creed chose her friend well," he said.

"Annja," Roux tried one more time.

She was defiant. "Orellana. And I say again that I don't know you."

Roux guessed that this was going to be a very long, and potentially very bad day.

25

"I have never seen you before, old man." She folded her arms in front of her chest and blew out a breath, the air fluttering the strands of hair that had fallen into her eyes. But she had caught a glimpse of him in her dream. "And you should not be here. You are too old to be here. This forest is not a place for the old. You will die and be eaten in this forest."

"Thanks for that." The man sat cross-legged on a patch of fungus and rested his hands on his knees. A canvas and leather bag was next to him. She thought she'd seen the bag before, but couldn't be sure. "I feel old today, Annja. And you're making me feel even older, every one of the centuries that I'll admit to."

"Stop calling me that." She pushed her hair behind her ears and stuck her hands in her pockets, her thumbs rubbing over the stitching. The name wasn't familiar, but the more she looked at him…the more familiar he seemed. So she'd seen him before, other than in the dream. But where? "I am Orellana."

She could run, an old man like that—even though he looked fit—would not be able to keep up with her. She could lose him in this forest, lose herself, too. Let the big cats or the frogs get him. Had he been with the foul men, Hammond and the others? Probably not, he was too old and not dressed like them. His clothes, though casual, looked new, as if they'd just come from a store.

She remembered stores, and she remembered that she liked shopping.

"My name is Orellana." Or perhaps Amanda, or Marsha, as those names fluttered through her thoughts. But she liked the sound of Orellana, a little exotic. She was blue, after all, and exotic, too.

"Orellana was the name of the boat you rented, Annja." He brushed a large bug off his pants, and then waved away a cloud of gnats. "Don't you remember? You told me you rented a boat named *The Dependable,* but it wasn't so dependable and you settled for *Orellana's Gift* or something like that. No, *Orellana's Prize.* Then you mentioned the little biting insects. You were right about the insects. In all my centuries, I've not seen so many in one spot."

"My name is Orellana." She remained defiant, didn't want the old stranger to confuse her more than she already was. She wanted to ask him how she came to be out in the forest, but that would be showing uncertainty and weakness, and she refused to show him either of those traits. "My name is Orellana!"

"Fine." He let out a long breath and swatted at more insects. "Orellana, my name is Roux."

"As in rue the day you came to my forest?"

"Your forest?" He raised an eyebrow.

"My forest, and I rue the day you came here to bother me, old man."

"Something has disturbed your mind, muddled things for you. *Qu'est-ce qui vous est arrivé, Annja?*"

"My name is Orellana." And she didn't know what happened to her. Head pounding, thoughts still foggy, she could run away from this old, confusing man. But he wasn't a threat.

"Qué demonios le ha pasado a usted, Annja?"

He spoke a different language now, asking her the same question.

"Quid inferorum accidit tibi, Annja?"

And an ancient, dead language. Same question.

"I don't know," she admitted. "I don't know what happened. But my name is Orellana."

He cupped his face with his hands and muttered something softly in a language she didn't understand. Neither spoke for quite a while. She remained standing; the muscles in her legs began to cramp from not moving. Still insolent, she didn't budge. Her hands formed fists inside her pockets. She was angry, but it was unfocused, not angry at any one thing…just angry.

Three fast bangs blared from the forest.

The old man jumped to his feet with a speed that surprised her. He looked around and appeared to reach reflexively at his side for a gun, but she saw he didn't have one.

"No one is shooting," she told him. "It is seed pods from a possumwood tree." Someone told her the name of the tree and had showed her the pods, she remembered that. The face of that speaker was wrapped in fog. Her head pounded harder.

She saw the old man try to relax, but the muscles in his face remained tense.

"Can you call your sword…Orellana?"

"I don't have a sword." The moment she said it, she pictured one. But it didn't belong to her. Instead, she saw a girl on horseback holding it high and leading an army. The image was from centuries past, and her mind framed it in a picture on a wall in some museum. She wanted to ask him if he knew how she came to this forest and where she was from…and what her name was, since he insisted that he knew her. Orellana was only a word she liked the sound of. "I am losing my mind."

She slid down against the tree trunk and tears she fought against spilled down her cheeks.

"Then let me help you find it, Annja." The man knelt in front of her and his face filled her vision. He'd pulled over the canvas and leather bag and unzipped it, reached inside. "This is yours, right?"

"No." But it looked familiar. She focused on it so she would not have to look at the man. It smelled of leather and a perfume that didn't suit her. Was the man her father? Grandfather? It had a familial feel, but she didn't have a family, did she? She remembered that she didn't have a mother or a father…though everyone has those, right? But she didn't. "I lived in an orphanage."

"That's right." The man sagged back and futilely waved away more insects, smacked at some on his neck and apparently gave up. "In New Orleans."

"A long way from here." Finally, she asked, "How did I get here? To the Amazon?"

"On a boat named *Orellana's Prize*. But a plane before that."

"And here is? Where in the Amazon?"

He laughed. She liked the sound of his laughter. "I don't know."

"Then how did you get here?"

"Whatever happened to you, Annja? Who did this to you?"

TWO DAYS LATER she was asking the same questions, though more images and names were drifting through her consciousness. It felt as if someone was inside her head with a chisel, trying to break out. The throbbing and hammering filled her ears. It was a dull, constant pain that made it difficult to breathe. She'd asked the old man to leave her, but he refused.

"The camera," Roux pressed. "Please, at least look at it. Today. Look at it today."

She relented and flipped the viewer on the camera and played with the buttons, thinking that she should know how to work the device. After several attempts, and after nearly tossing the camera at a tree, the viewer came to life.

"Possumwood," she said, as she watched tiny figures on the viewer parade through the green of the forest. She turned on the volume, all the way up to be heard over a bunch of monkeys that arrived and hooted. "That's me...without the blue." She watched it all, and then watched it again, running the camera out of its charge. There were images of her blue, and one of her setting her hand against the camera.

"Now do you remember?"

"Only pieces," she said. "And not enough of them. And I certainly don't remember you."

"Great." He got to his feet and stretched, watched the monkeys. One of them had a big piece of fruit, and he pointed at it. "Is there something to eat around here?" They'd eaten everything he'd brought with him, even the candy. "I'm famished. And I can hear your stomach growling."

She smiled at that. "There's fruit. Quite a lot of it, and it's quite good. Better than the junk food you shared." She knew to call it junk food. And she also knew she'd just lied. The fruit was good, but the junk food…it had certainly tasted better.

"What I wouldn't give for lamb with ginger crust and a side of root vegetables at L'Astrance," he mused. "We ate there once, in Paris. Before you went off traipsing through the underground looking at ancient bones."

"I don't remember that either." But she was finally starting to trust him. She didn't think that he was lying, and she thought that he honestly did know her from somewhere. Annja, she tried the name on her lips.

Annja.

Someone had called her Annja Creed.

It niggled at her memory. She still liked the sound of Orellana better, but Annja sounded hard, almost unbreakable.

While he ate, she paced, replaying in her mind the video she'd just watched. Then other segments from films came to mind, ones that featured her. Vampiric goat-creatures in Mexico, mummies in Egypt, forgotten tombs in Thailand, ancient swords in Paris, and a pyramid at the bottom of a lake in Wisconsin. How was the latter possible? There were no pyramids in Wisconsin.

Fortunately he let her be and hadn't spoken to her for what she guessed was probably an hour. She caught him watching her once in a while, the look of a professor or a librarian, something scholarly.

"I was on a motorcycle," she said. "It was raining and a car was chasing me. It was in May, but I don't remember where I was going and why people were after me."

"People are often after you," he whispered. He picked up another piece of fruit, turning it over and over before taking a bite.

"I was on a different motorcycle, a passenger this time. There were kangaroos. It wasn't May."

He wiped at the juice dribbling on his chin, and then swatted away a swarm of gnats.

Another memory came. "I met Charlemagne."

He snorted, a sound like he was trying to swallow a chuckle. "I doubt that very much."

"No. I met Charlemagne. The king. I really met him. He was dead. He was as near to me as you are standing, but he said he was dead. He said that he had lived long enough and that he liked roast venison, and that he had saved just enough of France or something like that. I remember him clearly. We walked in the forest and talked about swords."

She watched the man's eyes widen. "You have a sword, Annja."

"No I don't."

Clearly, he looked exasperated.

"But Charlemagne and I talked about swords, and then he went away and a girl arrived. She was young and beautiful and wore clothes for a Renaissance fair. And talked about swords, too, me and her. Joan. Her name was Joan and she was French like you."

"Quelqu'un a complètement foiré avec votre tête, Annja."

"It's not like I can't understand you." She paced faster, wearing a muddy path through the fungus. "I know perfectly well what you are saying."

When he finished eating, they walked. Like a gentleman, he carried the camera bag. "I think I can find my way back to the little village. Maybe if we go there, that will help jog your memory."

It was getting dark.

Dark.

"I remember that traveling in the forest at night isn't the smartest idea. And I don't want to go back to the village." She didn't. While she didn't remember the village—she'd watched it on the camera's video screen—she didn't want to go there. "That's not going to help me remember anything. I know it won't help. I know!" She pounded at her head with an open palm, and the man grabbed her wrist.

"That's not going to help, either." He tipped his head back, eyes on a big red parrot. "I don't know where the hell I am anyway. I shouldn't have sent D'jok away. I'm not sure I could find the village."

"D'jok." Annja remembered that name. "He was the only Dslala in the village that spoke English."

"Yes!" The man grinned broadly and grabbed her shoulders. "This is a start. I'm Roux, Annja. Remember me?"

She was starting to, but again, only in pieces. It was a jumble of experiences and emotions regarding this man—respect, skepticism, affection, ire. He'd called her on a phone…how long ago? He'd told her to be well.

She wasn't well. She wasn't thinking straight.

They spent the night against the trunk of a kapok tree. It was a giant, at least ten feet in diameter and reaching up out of sight. It was the home of monkeys, parrots and all manner of frogs, and though the sounds of the animals were interesting and restful, she couldn't sleep. However, she noticed that Roux had no such problem. The old man softly snored, oblivious to the insects crawling all over him.

Roux? What sort of a name was that? French, certainly, and he'd talked about a French restaurant they'd dined at. Chunks of her memory were filled with images of the Eiffel Tower, the Arc de Triomphe, the Palace of Versailles, museums, and more disturbing ones—catacombs filled with skeletons. He'd mentioned her going underground in Paris to look at bones.

What *had* happened to her? Maybe she needed a hospital. Maybe there were drugs that could make everything right and make her remember.

Drugs.

Drugs from plants to cure all the world's most malicious ills.

More images flickered…plant samples, a tent, cartons labeled for Atlanta and Dallas and the CDC. There were men with guns, Hammond. She remembered that Hammond was linked to all of that. She needed to find the tent. Maybe the answers were there—the final piece of the puzzle that would complete the picture.

First, she'd try again to sleep. Just for a little while.

She was at the edge of it, just starting to doze, when she heard the snap of a branch. Despite the wetness of the forest, there were dry patches where the rain couldn't reach. Fallen branches were brittle there. And a large creature had just stepped on one.

Her eyes flew open. Less than a dozen feet away a pair of yellow-green dots glimmered in the darkness.

"Roux! We have company!" She leaped up, nudging the old man as she did.

The eyes belonged to a jaguar of impressive size, maybe three hundred pounds, muscles rippling in the faint light that stole down through a slit in the canopy. A beautiful and terrifying beast. It snarled, and saliva glistened in a string that dripped from its jaws to the forest floor.

"Oh, yes," her companion said. "The end to a wonderful day."

The end to a confusing life, she thought.

The cat snarled again and sniffed, pawed at the ground and padded a little closer. She saw its muscles bunch and it sprang right at her. Its claws sliced her arms, its jaw open. For an instant she shared its hot, rank breath. Then she dropped and opened her hand, a sword appearing in it. She swung, at the very last instant turning the blade so the flat of it struck the creature, and with enough force to make it lose its balance.

She pushed up and shoved Roux behind her and swung at the cat again, nearly connecting. Agile, it leaped away. But it wasn't leaving, not giving up so easily on a meal, and she hadn't really hurt it. She didn't want to hurt it. She recalled reading an article about their numbers dwindling. She'd read the article out of a magazine on the plane to Brazil!

Her memories flooded back as she swept the blade low, striking at its outstretched claw. That only seemed to anger it, and it came at her from another direction and managed to rake her leg, shearing through the denim of her jeans like it was tissue paper. The pain was intense and she felt the blood running down into her boot.

Shifting her grip, she leveled the blade at its shoulder when it came at her again, this time slicing it; she prayed the cut wasn't deep. She'd not put all her strength behind it. The jaguar's snarl was high-pitched and long, and from a distance the cry was answered. Jaguars were solitary, and so she didn't worry that there was a family of them coming her way. She turned the blade and struck the cat on the side of the head and became the aggressor, advancing on it this time. Three more swats, each stronger, and the jaguar wheeled and loped into the darkness.

"You're hurt," Roux said.

"I heal quickly."

"Welcome back, Annja."

26

For once she wished it was raining. But the sky was clear and a multitude of stars shimmered, some so faint they looked like diamond dust. She recognized the Southern Cross; stargazing in the southern hemisphere had always been a delight to Annja. She saw the constellation named Eridanus—appropriately, the river. And the brightest star in the cluster was called Achemar, meaning "end of the river."

She slunk into the clearing, her leg aching from the encounter with the jaguar. She'd made a makeshift bandage of her shirtsleeve and had argued with Roux that she didn't need medical treatment—for her leg or her memory problem. There wasn't any place to get either out here anyway. Her memory lapse? Bit of amnesia? She'd attributed that to the poison darts she'd caught when slamming into Hammond trying to prevent him from shooting the Dslala. The darts had been meant for Hammond. A dart had killed one of the other mercenaries; she was halfway surprised the poison hadn't killed her.

For once she was grateful for her blue skin. It let her

be a shadow among the shadows cast by the tents and the generator. The machine was silent, suggesting everyone slept. No one stirred inside the main tent. Annja ducked in and crouched, keeping as low as the tables. While there was enough starlight in the clearing for her to see by, not enough came in here. Still, she didn't want to take the chance that someone might see her shadow against the canvas.

She remembered where all the batteries were. Something made her crawl down the aisle until she felt the boxes. There was one open, and she reached inside, pulling out D batteries and sticking them in her pockets. Annja wanted to make sure that if she was lucky enough to find a hard hat with a light on it, she'd have enough batteries to keep it going. Caving could eat up hours and hours…and there was a cave around here somewhere. She was going to find it.

Back outside, she spotted a sentry patrolling the perimeter. She skittered to the generator, noticing cables like thick black snakes fed into the main tent and the next two larger tents. Nothing fed to the pup tents. She decided they served only for sleeping.

She listened against the canvas of the nearest tent, hearing only the sounds of the forest—nightbirds and leaves rustling in the slight breeze, frogs singing. Annja sucked in a breath and gingerly pulled the flap back. Again, it was too dark to see much—shadows that suggested a bench, a few crates, a jumble of things just inside. The air smelled different, and so curiosity tugged at her and pushed her inside. Her fingers played across the jumble of things. A flashlight! Looking outside for the sentry, as she about had his dull and predictable pattern memorized, she waited until he'd passed out of her line of sight and flicked the beam on, holding it close and pointing it low, shielding it with her free hand.

Annja was actually enjoying this bit of skullduggery. She was an adrenaline junkie, the danger of being discovered—and of potentially discovering something—made her heart race. The muted beam revealed kneepads, gloves and helmets, some with lights on the top…hence the need for the batteries. But so many batteries, Dillon certainly planned on being here a while. Nothing on the bench, nothing on the chest. It looked like one of those old sea chests, but it had shiny aluminum corners. She resisted the urge to open it. Instead, she directed her attention to a rent in the earth that cut down the center of the tent. Metal spikes were driven deep into the ground and were affixed to a rope ladder. Next to it was a pulley system.

The rent itself was roughly three feet wide at the greatest point and about five feet long, looking like an open mouth with jagged shards of rocks around it. She stared…it looked like the mouth of the huge caiman from her dreams. Annja strapped on one of the helmets, made sure the light worked, and turned off the flashlight and managed to wedge it in her pocket next to some of the batteries. Picking out the smallest kneepads she could find, and putting on a pair of gloves a few sizes too big, she crawled toward the opening and peered down, seeing a faint light and hearing soft sounds. Someone was down below.

She only debated for a moment. She didn't have all

the proper gear for caving, but this could be enough for a start. And she had something the men in this camp didn't—Joan of Arc's sword. That alone was enough comfort to nudge her onto the rope ladder.

Annja started down, turning the helmet light off and relying on her other senses. She remembered what D'jok had told her when she underwent the dreaming ritual. She smelled stone, decayed plants, a faint trace of chemicals reminiscent of a hospital. She heard a fluttering sound—bats; she'd been in enough caves to recognize that. Not many, at least not many were flying. She'd probably disturbed them when she'd started down.

The gloves were cumbersome, so she took them off and stuffed them into the waistband of her jeans, discovered the rope was damp—but what wasn't in the Amazon?—and continued down. The rungs were uneven, the rope ladder handmade. Some of the rungs were thicker than others; one dangled free and so she had to stretch her leg down to find the next one. The ladder swayed and she held still until it settled. The bats quieted, too, and now a new sound intruded. Water was dripping somewhere. The noise went on uninterrupted.

The dim light she'd spotted from above came from Coleman battery-powered lanterns on the cavern floor. So that's how he was using some of the batteries, and planned to keep using them for a long time apparently. Thousands of batteries. Four pickaxes lay near the closest lantern. She was about twenty feet below the rent. The clanking sounded like it was coming from down a corridor; she would investigate that later. First, she'd take stock of this chamber. She flicked on her helmet light and half expected to see cave paintings, like the ones from her dreams. She was disappointed. The chamber was roughly pear-shaped, about thirty feet long and half that wide, with a tunnel leading away...where the clanking came from. Water dripped down one wall, forming a muddy pool. Looking up, she could tell that the very top layer of the cavern was earth, only about a foot thick, beneath that and reaching to the floor was mica schist, a flaky thin rock that clearly had been dug at. The grooves were deep, and shards of mica formed drifts against the walls. There was a band of flint, too.

The bell-shaped section had a dirt floor, and there were three mounds; two were higher and fresher than the third. One had wilted flowers on it. Graves, but nothing to mark who was buried in them. In her caiman dream she'd seen the bodies of three villagers on the bank. Could these graves symbolize the three dead villagers on the bank...or was she only looking to read something into it, based on the dream?

She glanced up at the rent. How had Dillon found this cavern? By accident?

Annja was good at playing detective. Maybe Dillon and his crew had accidentally come upon it while harvesting their plants. He'd had to clear the trees to put up his tents. Maybe while bringing the trees down, they found the crevice. Maybe one of them had fallen into it; that notion seemed likely. Why else come down here unless it was to rescue whoever had fallen? And in the process, someone discovered something in the mica. There was clear evidence this chamber had been mined.

The clanking sound continued. She turned off the

helmet light and ever-so-quietly eased into the tunnel. The noise grew louder and echoed. It was a natural tunnel, formed by a river that must have run through here a long time past, the smoothness of the walls attesting to that. But it wasn't altogether smooth. There were places where the mica had been dug at. She edged closer to the sound and the light, some of her questions answered when the tunnel widened and she spotted two men ahead, striking small pickaxes against the wall at eye level. There was a bucket between them and when they'd work a piece of rock free, they'd put it in the bucket.

She inched closer still. They were gem mining. If it was a mineral like gold or silver, they wouldn't be so careful, and they'd possibly be using explosives. Closer and she saw the glint of green.

Emeralds.

Another puzzle piece fell into place.

Emeralds could be found across the globe. She'd tried her hand at prospecting once and came away with nothing, but had enjoyed the experience. The highest quality emeralds were said to come from Brazil and Colombia, the latter being the largest producer of the gem in the world. Dillon had found a vein, and he and his crew were poaching. They were probably smuggling the gems out amid their plant samples. Why take only a finder's fee for discovering a mine when you could plunder it and take everything?

A slick operation, making money from gems and plants, literally and figuratively rolling in the green. She would report him, of course, but she had to get back to the Dslala village and use her satellite phone to contact the authorities. Dillon was probably guilty of more than just smuggling—the three graves came to mind. As much as she wanted to linger and watch the miners, she knew the best course was to leave before she was discovered.

She paused at the graves, and then climbed the ladder, once again disturbing the bats that clung to the ceiling, and then crawling up into the tent. Annja doubted she'd been down there all that long; it would have been handy to consult a watch. But the watch led to her turning blue and having the cryptic dream about a cave. Instead of paintings, she'd discovered men mining for emeralds. In her dream she'd seen bones, and in reality there were graves down there…with bones in them. It seemed that everything was connected.

Listening before peeling back the flap, she didn't see the sentry. She waited. Frogs were trilling, sounding like birds, so loud that was all she heard. Several minutes must have passed before she saw the man walking the perimeter again. He was different, stouter, and wearing a ball cap. There must have been a shift change, and so this fellow was probably more alert. When he was at the edge of her vision, she started out, at the same time hearing voices behind her; at least one of the men who'd been mining was coming up the ladder.

Now! She ran in a half-crouch from the tent, past the generator, in front of the main tent, in which a low light now burned. Someone else was up. Faster and she was at the log wall and over it, ducking down on the other side and holding still. If they'd seen her an alarm would have sounded. She counted to twenty and felt her heart slow, and then she scampered into the forest.

In her haste she'd forgotten that she still had on the kneepads and the helmet. Did they take inventory? Didn't matter, she wasn't going to return them and risk being caught. She skirted the camp, trying to find the spot where she'd come in so she could better retrace her steps and find Roux. She didn't want to leave the old man out in the rainforest alone. What if another jaguar came his way? Would he spend eternity digesting in the belly of a great cat?

Annja saw a light come on in one of the small tents. It was one more signal for her to leave. She forged deeper into the forest directly away from the camp. She pulled out the flashlight she'd also forgotten to return and flicked it on. The vegetation was thick enough here that no one in the camp could see the beam. Traveling in the rainforest at night wasn't a good idea, but Annja mentally pictured where she'd left Roux. It took her more than an hour to find it.

"New accoutrements?" Roux pointed to her hard hat and kneepads. "They go well with your outfit."

"I'll tell you all about them on our way back to the village." Annja filled him in as they worked through the tangle of plants and eventually found the path to the Dslalas.

"I've a boat waiting," he said. "At least I hope it's still there. I've been gone a few days."

"And I've a satellite phone in D'jok's hut, which I will use before I crash. I am utterly exhausted."

"Call the authorities about the gem poachers, and

then let us get out of here, Annja. You can sleep on the boat."

It sounded like a good plan.

Until D'jok informed her that Moons and Edgar left the village shortly after Roux had, intent on visiting Dillon in the pharmaceuticals camp. They'd not yet come back. Neither had a tribesman who'd also gone to investigate.

"I worry for them, Annja Creed," D'jok said. "Days gone."

She'd not slept in more than twenty-four hours. "The phone's in my duffel, Roux."

"You're going back to the camp?" he asked.

Annja didn't answer; she was already jogging back down the trail.

27

No skullduggery this time. Despite the hazards of tree roots and snake holes she kept a fast pace, knees high. Annja thought as many times as she'd been up and down this path she probably had every obstacle memorized. Parrots swooped low, a small severe macaw flying alongside her for at least a mile before it found something more interesting. The sounds were a pleasant, sonorous buzz. The air felt muggy, almost heavy, and then a mile later it was drizzling.

When this business in the Amazon was done, maybe she'd come up with a *Chasing History's Monsters* idea for some arid desert. Heat would be good right now, instead of the humid dampness of this place.

The run helped shake some of her fatigue, and the pain in her leg, merely a dull ache now—almost healed—helped keep her focused. What would have happened, she wondered, if Roux hadn't appeared and jogged her memory? Would it have come back on its own? Maybe, she'd like to think that would have happened. Or would Orellana have started a new life for herself in some nameless village along the river? The latter possibility wouldn't have been so horrible. A simple life surrounded by nature had its appeal. D'jok's tribe might have welcomed her as a resident.

The pharma camp came into view and she stopped, her thoughts redirected to Moons and Edgar. Had they pushed Dillon too far? Had he done something to them? She had a feeling in her gut that there was a good chance the pair had been killed. The rain was coming steady now. There were two sentries both outside the barrier, one definitely familiar—Hammond. He sneered when she brazenly approached him.

"You should be dead," he said. "I'd left you for dead."

A snappy reply hung on the end of her tongue. She ignored it and said, "I want to see Arthur Dillon."

"I suppose you do."

Her skin crawled the way he studied her. It felt like insects scampering over every inch of her. "It's about Becca Mooney and—"

"The troublemakers? They're with Mr. Dillon."

So they were alive.

"Hammond, I said I want to see Arthur—"

Hammond had his finger on the trigger; the gun was still tucked in his waistband. Annja saw his eyes change, the pupils shrinking as the gun came up. She didn't know if he was going to shoot her or simply threaten her. The sword was instantly in her hand and she brought it around at waist level.

"Where the hell did that—"

She struck the gun the moment it went off, his shot going wild and then the gun flying. She'd sliced his hand in the process, showing him less concern than she had the jaguar.

"Mitch!" Hammond shouted. "Mitch!"

The other sentry was already running toward her, firing as he came, striking her in the hip. Annja slipped behind Hammond, putting him between her and the gunman.

Hammond hollered and jumped aside. "Mitch! Watch where you're aiming!"

Despite the threat of Annja's sword Hammond came at her with a roundhouse kick, the steel toe of his boot connecting with her wrist and loosening her grip. The sword came out of her hand.

"Hands up! High!" This came from the other sentry. "Now or I'll blow your brains out!"

Annja held her hands up.

Hammond backed up a few steps, clearly wary of her. He looked at the ground. "Where's the sword?"

"What sword?" Annja's hip was coated with blood, the bullet evidently hitting a big vein. She felt blood flowing down her leg. Maybe it was a worse hit than she'd first thought. "I don't see a—"

Her knees buckled and Hammond retrieved his gun before scooping her up. "Mitch, she had a sword. You find it, and you get a hold of Mr. Dillon. Then you meet me inside."

Annja could have fought him—she told herself she could have, but her muscles protested too much. This was her fault, coming here already spent, not taking the best tactical approach and blatantly strolling up to the camp so sure of herself. Arrogant, she'd been foolishly arrogant. If she hadn't been so tired, she would have been sharper, and she wouldn't be carried into a tent and laid on a cot.

"Mitch!" Hammond bellowed.

She took stock of her surroundings. She was in the second of the medium-sized tents, the one she hadn't looked in the other night. There were two cots, an assortment of crates, two-way radio, boxes of cartridges and a case of chocolate bars. She couldn't see beyond that; Hammond's broad frame blocked her view. She struggled to sit up, but his beefy hands held her shoulders down.

"Mitch!" he bellowed again. A shadow loomed in the doorway.

"No machete. Couldn't find it."

"It wasn't a machete. It was a big ass sword," Hammond reminded him.

"Fine. No sword. I think you were imagining things. Too much whiskey last night? Dillon's on the radio. He's staying down in the mine. Says to patch her up if you can. He wants to talk to her. And if you can't patch her up—"

"Yeah, yeah, I know. Drop her down the hole or feed her to the caimans."

The image of the monstrous caiman from Annja's dream swam through her memory.

"Listen, Mitch. Get that first aid kit, the big one, and find me…uh, the scope goggles. There's some tweezers and razor blades. Bring me those, too." Hammond looked at her. "I'd rather you just die and I dump you in the river. Some satisfaction in feeding caiman, but the boss says otherwise, for now."

Mitch returned.

"You hold her." Hammond patted her front pockets and looked inside. "Batteries? A crap load of batteries. What do you need those for?" He dumped them and pulled down her jeans. "Oh, that don't look good. You're watching me, right, Mitch? I'll give this a go, but I'm thinking she's caiman bait. Looks like you nicked her superficial femoral. She dies, I'm telling the boss on you."

So he had some medical training to throw out a term like superficial femoral. Annja ground her teeth together as she felt him slice into her with a razor blade. Then he poked around with tweezers. It hurt worse than getting shot. He'd not done anything to first clean the wound.

"Tough cookie," Mitch muttered under his breath. "She hasn't hollered yet."

Hammond fumbled for something in the first aid kit, all the while keeping pressure on her wound. Agony. Annja settled on that word. She was in agony. Then she felt a needle. He was suturing her vein, applying more pressure.

"It's holding." Hammond waited and then eased up on the pressure. "Had to do this outside of Kabul a couple of times." Next he was stitching her up. "This could work. Might hold, might not."

He poured something on her that stung. A few seconds later, he patted it dry and put a bandage on her, tugged her jeans back up. "I always cleaned the wounds there first, though. She might have some infection in there." He stood. "Done. She probably ought to lie there awhile before we take her to Dillon. Don't need to rip my stitches."

"Should you give her something? You know, for pain?"

Annja saw Hammond's smile. "Nah. I had a sergeant once who told me pain lets you know you're still kicking. You sit with her. I'm going back on patrol. And I'm going to find me that damn sword. I'll find it, and I'm going to keep it."

Annja intended to wait for an opening, overpower her guard and confront Dillon. Instead, she woke up some hours later when Mitch tugged her to her feet.

"Boss is taking a break. Says he wants to see you now."

In a way, Annja was getting what she wanted—an audience with Arthur Dillon. She had hoped it would have been under different circumstances.

28

At the bottom of the rope ladder, Mitch tied her hands together with a thin cord. She saw fresh wildflowers on the oldest grave, in place of the wilted ones she'd noticed before. Of the three bodies, one had meant something to somebody at the camp. Three buckets were filled to the brim with emerald chunks. No one else was in the chamber, but she heard music and the constant clanking coming from the corridor. Mitch had a gun to her back and pushed her forward. She was still sore, but it wasn't terrible. She healed quickly, and this time was no exception.

The mine was better lit than on her previous foray. Four large battery-powered lanterns in this chamber, and as she walked by the light made her shadow dance on the opposite wall. More light came from the corridor ahead.

She could take her escort, whirl and grab the gun and turn it on him. She wouldn't even need the sword. But she decided to play along. She wanted to find Moons and Edgar. Besides, she wanted to talk to Dillon.

As she was prodded along, Annja discovered that

Dillon was the source of the music. He was singing as he worked the pick against the wall. Three other miners worked farther down. Dillon had a good voice, but the words sounded haunted in the close confines of the tunnel. The tink-tink-tink oddly syncopated accompaniment.

She'd heard it before, an old Swedish hymn that mentioned the pearl of great price.

He finished and smiled sadly at her. "In a church in Melbourne, there is a remarkable stained-glass window depicting Jesus and the parable of the pearl." Dillon's eyes took on a rheumy look, as if he was lost in a memory. "Nancy and I were vacationing in the city. Nancy was my wife for eighteen years. She was devout and insisted on attending church, that one because of its windows. Incidentally, that day, the pastor included that verse in his sermon. Do you know the one?"

Annja didn't answer.

The silence seemed to not sit well with Dillon. "I've memorized the lines," he said, and quoted them to her. "In that time, pearls had a much greater value than today, but it means—"

"I know what it means. It illustrates the value of finding your way to the kingdom of heaven, and that the merchant gave up everything to get there, to be closer to God and to be saved."

"If you believe in God and that sort of thing, Miss Creed. If God and heaven exist, I suspect I'll see neither, given the things I've done in my life, especially recently. No matter, I have found my pearl of great price here in the Amazon. It is right here, and it is an emerald. My deal of a lifetime so to speak." Dillon tapped the wall with the vein he'd been mining.

"This belongs to Brazil. You're poaching."

"Do you know much about gemstones, Miss Creed?" He waited for an answer. "No? I didn't either initially, but my wife knew a lot, and through our years together she shared her knowledge. I used to call her my magpie because she adored shiny baubles. Every birthday, anniversary, was a reason to add another piece of jewelry to her cabinet. In the lean years, it was small things." Again Annja saw Dillon become lost in a memory, but the wistfulness left and his eyes took on a bitter shine. "Let me explain then why this is my pearl. The clarity of the stones in this vein is amazing, the color intense. But what makes this find so staggering is the size of the pieces we're pulling from these walls."

He reached into the bucket and held one up, shining the light from his helmet so she could get a better look. It was thick, bright and beautiful.

"If a one-carat stone is of such a quality that it sells for six thousand, some would think that a five-carat stone would sell for thirty thousand…five times the initial amount, right? No. The larger stone is far rarer, and it would instead be worth ninety thousand. The stones we are pulling, Miss Creed, a few of them are five carats. Only a few. Ten carats, twenty carats, thirty…most of them fall into that range."

Annja looked past him and watched the men carefully chipping away, putting emerald chunks in their bucket. There was more clanking coming from where the tunnel narrowed and curved. How many men did he have working down here?

"The largest jeweler-cut emerald that I know of is called the Mogul, at two hundred and seventeen carats. In the Viennese Treasury sits a vase carved from a single emerald, that's more than two thousand carats. An uncut crystal from Colombia sits at nearly fourteen hundred carats. And most impressive is the Bahia emerald, an eight-hundred-and-forty-pound cluster. There's more."

She noticed that his voice grew louder, the words carefully spaced out as if he placed importance on each syllable and wanted her to miss nothing.

"Much more, Miss Creed."

"I get it," Annja said flatly. "You're getting stinking rich."

"Our first shipment brought us forty million." Dillon had a smug look on his face. "Forty million."

Annja knew he wanted her to acknowledge his prowess. She wouldn't give him that satisfaction.

"I have three more shipments of equal size ready to go. Packed. Waiting. And I'll have more and more after that, the good lord willing as they say, and the Amazon doesn't rise and drown us. Though you have thrown an unfortunate wrinkle into our work. You've made things less certain."

Mitch pushed the gun against her back. "Yeah, now we're working fast. Real fast, since we don't know how much longer we're going to have this place."

Dillon set his pick down. "Who have you told, Miss Creed?"

Annja mulled her answer. If she said no one, they wouldn't need her alive, or need Moons or Edgar. He probably intended to kill her anyway, as much as he'd shown her about his illicit operation. "What makes you think I even knew about this mine?"

"You didn't notice the security cameras, Miss Creed? I trust my men, I really do. But…one can never be sure with all these emeralds. I saw you on the footage, snooping down here, creeping like some spy. I know the lighting isn't the best, but you're the only blue woman I've seen since setting up my camp. There's no mistaking it. You were here yesterday."

She hoped Roux had gotten through to someone on the satellite phone, and that the authorities were indeed sending someone out here. Time to change the subject. "Becca Mooney and her friend Edgar. Are they here?"

Dillon wanted to talk about emeralds. "I have a fellow in Belém, my partner, who is custom-cutting some of the stones for us. We're using my company to get the emeralds out, his connections to sell everything. He is passionate about his art."

Annja at least understood that part. She was passionate about staying alive.

"Let me show you one of his finished pieces."

"Is this one of those before-I-kill-you moments?" Annja had held her tongue long enough. "Because that is what you're going to do with me."

He ignored her and reached into the collar of his shirt, tugging up a leather cord. Dangling from it a woman's gold ring with a large emerald anchored into a simple setting. "I had him make this, a keepsake for me, something I would have given to Nancy. I thought I should have something both of this place and to remind me of her. It will be the only emerald I intend to keep, actually, a ten-carat fancy cut. The rest of this…I am trading for money." The light played along the ring and set dizzying spots of green reflecting like a prism. "My pearl of great price, Miss Creed, is not just this emerald keepsake, but this entire emerald mine."

"And what great price are Becca and Edgar paying?"

Dillon pointedly dismissed her. "The emeralds in this vein, in all the veins we've mined down here, are special. Their color and clarity certainly, but it goes beyond that. And it took my partner in the city to point it out. Come, let me show you more. Mitch, if you'll bring her along?"

Dillon turned sideways to squeeze past his men. When he reached the narrowest part he slowly forced his way through.

Annja felt the sword hovering, knew she could use it to cut the cord that tied her wrists. This could be a good place to strike, where it was so narrow that only one man could get to her from either side. Those odds would be in her favor. She could cut down as many as she had to here. Yet she waited, curious. She needed to find Moons and Edgar.

"How did you find this place?" she asked. "I suspect you weren't looking for it."

Dillon motioned for Annja to come forward through the narrow passage. "It was an accident. My wife, Nancy, found it, actually. We were clearing some scrub to put up a tent and the ground gave way beneath her."

"The grave with the flowers." Annja walked into a large chamber, the floor of which sloped down.

"Yes. We thought she might survive the fall. She lived nearly an entire day afterward. Hammond was a medic, and took good care of her. But there was internal bleeding."

"You could have called a helicopter, gotten her to a hospital."

"It wouldn't have come in time. The cost you pay for working in such a remote place."

"A high cost for your 'pearl of great price,'" Annja said. Despite the poor light she saw Dillon's angry expression.

"This way."

Mitch nudged her.

The tinking sound was loud now and there was more light ahead, around an outcropping. On the other side, the chamber stretched away into darkness. But the part she could see—illuminated by three more battery-powered lanterns and the helmet lights of the miners—was staggering.

The very large emeralds Dillon had mentioned...the piece they were carefully working their way around well might exceed any he'd described.

"My pearl of a very, very great price," he said proudly.

Picking at the wall were five of his men in the customary coveralls and with hard hats. Working with them was Moons and Edgar. A sixth henchman had a gun pointed at the couple.

"This pearl is priceless," he said. "This emerald is like no other in all the world."

29

"Can you possibly imagine what an emerald weighing hundreds of pounds would be worth, Miss Creed?" He let the thought hang for a moment. "My men and I will never want for anything. I will set them up for the rest of their lives. Half divided by them, half for me and my partner. All that money—"

She thought the faraway look in his eye was like a man gazing on his beloved. She shuddered.

"You'll never get a stone that big out of here." She'd remembered the size of the shipping crates.

"We just have to get it up top, Miss Creed. Two days ago I took pictures and my partner has sent them on to our bidders, and terms of the sale require the buyer to come get this monster. Men with the money to buy this…they have the resources to come in here, whether they have to grease the government's sweaty palms or use other means. We've teased our bidders with these photos. We've had on nibble as high as four billion. So many zeroes." The faraway look intensified. "Of course, selling this will be the last thing we do before we pull up stakes."

The noise continued—the sound of the pickaxes, the water dripping, the labored breathing of the henchmen, all added to the greedy scene Dillon had orchestrated. Annja's head ached and she mulled over the possibilities of how to best these men without putting Moons and Edgar in jeopardy.

"This will not go unfound," she said. Conversation… she wanted to keep Dillon talking, get as much information as possible. "Somehow word of all of this will get out, your buyers, the laboratories you've been using to help smuggle the poached stones. And the money—that much money is going to be noticed by someone. Brazil, America, you'll be hunted and arrested. Besides, you have blood on your hands—"

He beamed. "Blood emeralds. I like the sound of that, Miss Creed. Not the same connotation as blood diamonds, and a far better ring to it, don't you think?" He fingered the ring hanging from his neck. "Oh, I know word of this monster gem will surface. But my men and I have no worries about ever being caught. My partner has all the contingencies covered. I chose him well. No law will be able to reach me." He took a step closer and she smelled him, sweat mixed the heady loam of the rainforest, and under that an expensive cologne. "There are places in this world, opulent, civil places that will welcome us. My money is already safely there, waiting for me, waiting to be added to. I've a place in mind where there is no extradition, where I will be embraced and protected, and where I will live like an emperor." He tucked the emerald ring back under his shirt.

He would kill her, and Moons and Edgar, maybe

some of his men in the mix before it was all done. Arthur Dillon might not have started out evil. She remembered that on their first meeting he'd talked about a brother dying of bone cancer, his grandfather with Alzheimer's, and that he'd melanoma himself. He might have started out altruistic, truly searching for cures in the rainforest. But the glitter of the emeralds had wholly corrupted him.

Now it was a matter of finding the right opening to take him down.

"And so I am presented with the complication of you." Dillon stroked his chin. "I value life, Miss Creed. I truly do. Life is so very short as it is, and I hate to even contemplate the prospect of taking anyone's last breath. You say I have blood on my hands. Maybe? But not of my doing. A few natives…but they forced the issue, and I didn't pull the trigger."

He turned away from her and Annja felt the sword in her mind, considered this an opportunity. But there was the henchman watching Moons and Edgar, and one man still held a gun to her back.

She would have to wait, biding her time.

Dillon stepped between two of his men and touched the massive gem in the wall. "I wonder how deep it goes into the rock? How big she really is and how many billions she will bring?" He retreated so the men could continue chipping away. They were all being so careful, even Moons and Edgar, Annja noticed. None of them wanted to mar the stone. The radio at his waist crackled and he answered it. He spoke softly, but Annja caught some of it.

"How many—"

A crackling response she couldn't make out.

"—are you sure there's only one?"

Another indecipherable response.

"You've got to be kidding me," Dillon grumbled. "Be certain there's only one. Be certain! Bring him down now."

One more response.

"Yes. Alive." He hooked the radio to his belt and spun. "Another complication."

"Let them go," Annja suggested, nodding toward Moons and Edgar. "You don't need any more blood on—"

"I really don't want to kill anyone," Dillon said. The look in his eyes seemed chaotic as he glanced around the cavernous chamber, his finger circling the button on the radio like it was a worry stone. "Diseases kill enough people. Cancer."

"I thought you were hell-bent on finding a cure for cancer and Alzheimer's. Don't those things matter to you anymore?"

His expression of anger sent a shiver down her back. "I intend to use some of my money to pursue those cures, Miss Creed. Green is the answer, the right amount of money, the right plants. I will not give up while I breathe. I will find cures. All this money…it will make everything easier, finding the solutions for the world's most horrible diseases, and in the process I'll live like a king. Life will be much more pleasant all the way around, eh?" He rubbed his chin again and

Annja noticed scars there and on the side of his face, souvenirs of his melanoma. "I don't want to kill you."

But he was going to try, she thought. Still, now wasn't the time to make a break for freedom, as Moons and Edgar likely wouldn't fare well. She had to put them first. "Then keep them here, Moons and Edgar, helping you with the emeralds." She inclined her head toward the two. "Keep them until you quit the mine. When that giant emerald gets air-lifted out of here, you could let them go."

"I'd like to do that," Dillon said. "Truly, I would. And I had considered that. But they're such troublemakers. I think I will have to—"

Moons turned and Annja saw that her dirty face was streaked from where she'd been crying. Edgar stopped for just a moment, but then kept going with the pick. The other miners hadn't missed a beat either.

"We won't be trouble, me and Edgar. We won't say anything. I promise. I don't care about your emeralds. I was only worried about the forest. Don't you see—"

Dillon let her prattle on. Moons started crying again, and Edgar hesitated, but kept working. There were foot-falls nearby, shuffling and cursing.

"Regardez salaud! Vous porcs immondes!"

Annja's throat tightened. That was Roux's voice. He'd followed her to the camp, just like he'd followed her to Brazil. When he emerged through the narrow opening, she noted his bruised and scraped face, wrists bound in front of him and hands bloody—it threw another wrench into the situation. Hammond was behind him, a sneer on his hard face, two Taurus pistols in his hands, and helmet light shining in her eyes.

"Here's your other complication, Mr. Dillon. He was alone. And, yeah, I'm sure of it."

Annja squinted through the light and got a closer look at Roux. They'd beaten him. Roux could well hold his own in a fight, and he'd certainly done some damage to Hammond. The thug's lip was swollen and the nose canted to the side—broken. Dried blood was caked under his nostrils. No doubt he'd cleaned himself up a little before coming down here. Roux had done a number on him.

"Guy wouldn't give a name, but I figure he was with the television woman."

"Miss Creed," Dillon said. "Call her Miss Creed, Ham."

"He has to be with her. Just look at him, groomed, like he's a producer type. Never saw him on their boat." Hammond clocked Roux hard enough on the back of the head to drop him. Roux landed on his knees and let out a groan. Annja wanted to shout at her friend. *Why did you come here? Why didn't you protect yourself, stay hidden until the authorities arrived?* But she kept her mouth shut and focused on the sword, keeping it at bay.

She mentally calculated the distance to Hammond, to the guy watching Moons and Edgar, figuring angles of attack and likely outcomes. Moons and Edgar could be shot before she could get to the gun pointed at them.

Moons was still blabbering away. "In fact, we'll keep mining for you. We're young and able. Look how we've helped so far."

"Shut up," Edgar whispered.

"We've been working nonstop since—"

"Enough!" Dillon shouted. The workmen stopped, too.

Annja felt the gun pressed harder into her back.

"I don't want your blood on my hands, sir. So I'm not going to kill you," Dillon said. "I'll let the river do that." He motioned to Hammond who tugged Roux to his feet. The other henchmen grabbed Moons and Edgar.

Had she waited too late to act? Moons and Edgar were forced down the passage first, then Roux with Hammond behind him. It had to be now, she thought. In a heartbeat the sword was in her hand. And in the same heartbeat the butt of the gun was slammed into the side of her head.

30

Annja heard voices as she began to regain consciousness. Charlemagne? Joan of Arc? No, those were from
a dream. And it would be so good to be deep in that
dream right now, walking in the forest with King Charlemagne and talking about swords and saving France.
No one else in the world to bother them.

Annja concentrated and fought to clear her head.
She wanted to take in the real conversation swirling
around her. She recognized Roux's voice and Hammond's. Moons's, too, the girl sounding panic-stricken,
and then she heard scuffling.

Annja struggled to open her eyes but the memory of
pressure underwater forced her down.

The noises all spun together.

She shouted at herself to wake up.

Had a punch been thrown? Hopefully Roux had
thrown it; the old man was good in a fight. Another
punch. A grunt. A groan. More scuffling.

Edgar was shouting. Dillon was saying something
about a crevice.

"Throw them down the hole." It was Hammond's voice.

Just as her eyes fluttered open she felt someone kick her side…then again. Fully conscious now and flailing to grab onto something, she could only see rock and the glow of lanterns. Another kick. She was rolling and then falling. The sword was in one hand and her free hand was waving around for a purchase. She couldn't see anyone to swing the blade at.

It was all dark.

Dark.

Oh, but she hated that word.

Falling fast, Annja caught only a musty scent of old wood. In a heartbeat she plunged and hit the ground. The impact sent the sword from her hand and tore the breath from her lungs. Every inch of her ached.

She pushed herself to her knees; there was a body under her—Moons. The girl had fallen on her stomach, and the hard hat with the light…that was where the pale beam came from. Fortunate the light hadn't broken. It sent a beam across the stone floor that was littered with rocks, dead leaves and bones. Bones were everywhere. How many people had Dillon dumped in this hole?

From overhead came the screech of bats disturbed by all the action. Dillon had tossed them in a cave.

Down the hole, Hammond had said. This had to be below the emerald mine.

Annja gently turned Moons over, setting the hard hat where the beam illuminated the girl. Annja felt for a pulse, just as she heard voices from above.

"Please don't do—" It was Edgar's voice.

There was the flapping of material and a dull thud. The bats shrieked louder.

Annja, still feeling for a pulse on Moons and finding none, saw Edgar flat on his back only a few feet away. They'd dumped him down here, too. His helmet had rolled away and was rocking, its light playing shadows on the cave wall.

Edgar twitched, moaned, and his eyes closed.

No pulse on Moons, but Annja knew CPR. She wasn't going to give up on the girl.

"Look out below!" Hammond shouted.

There was more flapping material, another body coming down. Annja had just enough time to reach over and pull Edgar out of the way. Roux, his hands still tied, landed where Edgar had been. Roux wasn't moving, but Annja wasn't worried about him—somehow he'd always survived.

Annja cursed. Above her there was scant light, but Annja could make out Hammond's face leering through the hole in the floor. The hole was barely big enough for a body to pass through it. Hammond rolled something over the top, covering the hole. The bats started to settle down.

Annja swore again as she felt Edgar's neck to make certain he was alive. She found a steady pulse. She turned all her attention to Moons.

Annja alternated chest compressions with mouth-to-mouth resuscitation. The routine became a mantra... thirty compressions, two breaths, thirty compressions, two breaths. Annja had remarkable stamina, but even she was wearing down. Such a dangerous situation was taking its ugly toll.

"Don't die on me," Annja pleaded. "Don't die, Moons." A first responder kept up lifesaving techniques until either the professionals arrived or the victim started breathing.

Thirty compressions. Two breaths.

"Don't die."

But Moons was dead. Annja went at it minutes longer before rocking back on her haunches, spent and furious, acknowledging the girl's lifeless body.

"You say you don't want to kill anyone, Dillon? You might not have pushed her, but this blood is on you." Tears of rage and sorrow welled in her eyes as she shuffled on her knees to Edgar. She felt his head, neck, back. He seemed to be intact, but definitely unconscious—fortunate for him at the moment. "You're the real monster," Annja continued to rant; she needed to vent her ire. Every profane word she knew spilled out in rapid succession. "I came to the Amazon looking for monsters, and I found one. I found the king of all monsters."

Edgar's arm was bent at an odd angle. Definitely broken. Maybe he'd put out his arm to stop his fall, a reflexive action. Annja stretched and grabbed Edgar's helmet, sitting it so that it highlighted his arm.

"That's definitely not good." She ripped the sleeve off his shirt so she could get a better look. Gingerly feeling it, she figured it was broken in more than one place. Edgar needed an emergency room. Annja had first aid training, but this damage went beyond her expertise. She muttered another string of foul words aimed at Dillon and then took a glance at some of the bones in the cavern, finding four that looked like ribs and that would work as splints.

She began to treat Edgar's arm when she saw that Roux was stirring. "This is going to hurt, Edgar. Please stay unconscious a while longer." She did her best to re-align the bones in his arm, the humerous first, splinting it with two ribs, tying them with the discarded shirt-sleeve.

She tugged off Moons's shirt and ripped it into strips, then took off Moons's belt. It took Annja considerably longer to work on Edgar's lower arm, splinted it, wrapped it with the T-shirt strips, and then used the belt as a sling to help immobilize it. Finally, she retrieved Moons's fanny pack and looked inside for anything useful. She found a pocketknife and stuffed it into her already-overstuffed pockets. The fanny pack became a makeshift pillow she gently placed under Edgar's head. Still, he hadn't moved. Angling the light, she opened his eyelids; the pupils were uneven. Great, a concussion.

"Annja." Roux had come to. "Annja—"

"I heard you, give me a moment."

"Annja, my legs are broken."

Annja suspected the only reason she hadn't broken any bones was that Moons had cushioned her fall. She picked up one of the hard hats, put it on, adjusted the light and checked on her next patient, using the pocketknife to free his hands.

Roux's legs were twisted at odd angles, not the way legs were meant to bend. A bone protruded from his skin and jeans in one spot, the denim dark with blood that continued to gush. He'd propped himself up on his elbows.

"What am I supposed to—"

"You may have to set them, Annja. I can do it if I have to, but—" A pause. "But if you don't mind—"

Had this happened to him before? She went to work, noting that his hands were clenched into fists and an expression of pure pain crossed his face. He refused to cry out. "Do I splint them?"

"No." His hands unclenched slightly, and then formed fists again. "Just leave me be awhile."

She stepped away. Though she was curious, she nevertheless didn't want to watch him regenerate or be reborn or whatever it was that happened to always save him. Let that be his mystery. Her mystery remained how Joan's sword had come to her. The sword was still within reach, she knew, but she had no cause to call it at the moment. Now that her companions had been tended to, it was time to check out her surroundings.

Up was first, since that was where she needed to go. Up to get out of here. Her hip still bothered her where she'd been shot, but it was dull and annoying and wasn't bad enough to stop her. The beam barely reached the ceiling, which she guessed was thirty feet up, maybe a little more. The hole had been covered, and there was no way—short of flying—to reach it. That opening, the only one that she could see, was too far from the walls, which looked impossible to climb anyway, all smooth and covered with…paintings.

Am I dreaming?

Annja literally pinched herself, thinking maybe the

whole episode of falling through the hole…was another nightmare, an extension of the Dslala dreaming ritual. No such luck. This was all achingly real.

But the paintings…she'd seen them before, in a dream. Primitive, but discernible, remarkably preserved, the colors—red, black and violet reasonably bright. They depicted amazing beasts. In one the creature was on all fours, slothlike, but not sloth-sized as an almost stick figure of a man was in front of it. In the next series, it showed the creature rising up and standing on its hind legs. In the next, it showed the creature breaking something large, maybe a log or a tree. There were other creatures depicted, half-men half-fish, birds with the heads of men, jaguars with the heads of men and more.

The bones. She padded closer to a pile and moved them around with the toe of her boot. Some were human, or at least similar to human—she couldn't be certain without closer examination. But a couple of the skulls were abnormally large and shaped oddly, like the combination of a cow and an ape. Perhaps the beasts depicted on the wall. She sensed that this place was ancient, though people had been down here recently. Annja saw that some of the smaller bones had been shattered, as if someone had walked on them. And a callous soul had dropped a chocolate bar wrapper. Dillon's men, or maybe Dillon himself had come down here to make sure there were no emerald veins.

Emeralds were found closer to the surface.

She explored further, certain that she'd been here

before—or rather it felt like that, familiar, yet discomforting, too.

"I dreamed this."

"Pardon?" Roux was on his feet, brushing off the dust and dirt, scowling at the blood on his jeans. She watched him shift his weight from one foot to the next, testing each leg. "Annja, did I hear you right? Did you say you dreamed all of this?"

"Yes. No." She shook her head and continued to prod the bones with her foot. "The Dslala dreaming experience, it is supposedly a mystical mind-expanding thing. I guess it was for me. Charlemagne, Joan of Arc. You were there, too. And there was this monstrous caiman. But I'm thinking the caiman represented Dillon. I felt like I was drowning, fighting him…fighting the caiman. I got free and found this cave. *This cave*." She pointed to the paintings and turned her head so the light on her helmet showcased them. "I'm not kidding, Roux. I saw these exact paintings in that dream." She dropped her gaze, the light falling on the bones.

There were several of the large cow-ape looking skulls. She waded in and picked one up. It was heavy. Her thumb rubbed across the surface, smooth and the shade of eggshells. "I'm taking this with us."

"With us?" Roux snatched up the other hard hat and put it on. He walked around the cavern, and then looked up. "We're not getting out that way. Not unless we can sprout wings or magically levitate."

"You're funny, old man. But we are getting out." Annja carried the skull over to Edgar and checked on him again. "We'll have to wait until he comes round."

She shivered. This far down, it was a little cold. She'd seen some decayed plants and retrieved them, putting them in a pile. Next, she found broken roots. Then back to the wall. She waded through the bones and hunted for small rocks.

"What are you doing?" Roux had taken his rain jacket off and respectfully placed it over Moons's face.

"I want to keep Edgar warm. I'm starting a fire." She sat next to the pile of broken roots and plant matter, rock chip in one hand. Annja opened her other hand and the sword appeared. "This blade is steel, and this is a piece of flint."

"Yes. Very clever."

Annja carefully arranged all the bits and pieces. Flint in her left hand, she awkwardly held the sword and struck it down on the edge of the rock. It took only a few tries for a spark to fly and catch the tinder. She leaned over it and blew gentle puffs until a flame grew, and then added her kindling.

"You could've managed it, too," she said, warming her hands over it.

"But I, dear Annja, didn't have the steel."

"This won't burn all that long unless we can add to it. We need to keep it small anyway, don't need smoke choking us." She saw Roux scanning the ground and coming up with more roots. "Great. Hey, you stay with him all right? I'll be back."

"You going to find us a way out?" Roux broke up the leaves and sticks he'd found and added them to the fire.

"That's my plan." She looked at him for a moment. He turned the light off on his helmet, letting the light from the small fire suffice. "For whatever reason, when I'd snuck into their camp yesterday I stuffed my pockets with batteries. I've got a dozen." The flashlights on the helmet required two, and that's how many she passed Roux. "Maybe some little voice in my head told me to take them."

"Joan heard voices, too," Roux said softly.

Annja didn't have anything to say to that. She turned and struck out toward where the shadows were the thickest, a niggling memory of her dream tugging her.

31

Annja was an experienced caver, and well aware of the rules…take nothing but pictures, well, she didn't have a camera, leave only footprints, and kill nothing but your own time. She had no intention of harming the cave's inhabitants. Bats, there were a good number of them, evidenced by the squeaks and rustling. She saw a few large spiders, a salamander-like creature and tiny insects.

The bats were what intrigued her. They might not have come in the same way she did. In fact, she prayed they hadn't. They might be able to show her a way out. There were more paintings along the wall, showing more versions of what Annja guessed was a mapinguari. She wished she had a camera, but maybe…if she could get through this, she could come back and record these for *Chasing History's Monsters*.

Take nothing but pictures?

Annja hoped to break that rule and take out one of the unusual skulls.

There was no way to judge the time, her watch gone in the trade; she hadn't thought to see if Moons or Edgar had one for the borrowing. Exhaustion couldn't serve as a measure; she was already past the point of exhaustion and knew if she wasn't moving, she'd be sleeping soundly. The floor of the cave sloped down dramatically now and there were no more paintings or bones in this section.

She walked through a stony corridor now, the ceiling higher than the beam of her light would reach, the walls steep and smooth and fifteen feet apart. If they were narrower, she could climb them with her legs and arms extended and sort of walk up the walls. There were no handholds that she could see. The place had been formed by a river.

Her footfalls echoed eerily, and she could hear her breath. She wondered if Edgar had come to. It would be better for his own health and well-being if he did; however, he'd then be faced with his friend's death. Annja was glad she was away from the situation—she had enough of her own emotions to deal with.

Annja had to brace herself against wall when the floor sloped down at an even steeper grade. She almost stopped and turned back, needing to go up, not down. But she heard more bats ahead, and that presented more possibilities. She also noticed more paintings.

The archaeologist in her would have spent as much time as possible reveling in the discovery. These paintings were more intricate than the others, but in the same style and colors, suggesting the same relative time period, but more accomplished artists. No bones in here, but there were shaped rocks—primitive tools, a great find. She couldn't help herself to take a brief look, her practiced eye noticing stone awls, scrapers, hammers and spear heads. They must have hunted game in the area and processed it, ground grains with some of the tools. Some were large. She'd seen enough Paleolithic relics to place these in the same area, about ten thousand years old when they'd likely went after large prey such as mammoths.

And maybe smaller game like mapinguaries, she thought.

She estimated she'd traveled two or three miles from Roux and Edgar, through the twists and turns it had taken. Now she stood at a wide point, roughly egg-shaped and with three tunnels leading away and looking to stretch ever downward.

"I shouldn't be here alone." It was the first basic rule of caving that she was violating. Two cavers were barely adequate—one to spot for and aid the other; but three should be the minimum, as well as three sources of light. Annja had one light, and it was fading. She replaced the batteries. Eight fresh batteries remaining.

She had no gear, no ropes, no jacket, and it was beyond chilly. She was cold. Annja could climb without ropes, provided she could find some hand- and footholds, but Edgar? The situation was starting to look more desperate.

Fatigued, hungry and with her optimism fading, Annja nevertheless pressed on.

Three tunnels, all pointing down.

"I need to go up." She needed to get back to Roux and Edgar. But when she looked up again all she saw were walls that had been washed smooth by a river a long time ago and darkness.

She selected the tunnel to her right. Annja had no idea what direction she traveled, other than down. She'd gotten turned around in the number of curves the corridor had taken. West, she guessed, but ultimately the direction didn't matter.

Down and down and down, an abrupt turn to the right and down so steeply now that she slid.

"Wonderful. Now how am I going to get back up? How in the—"

Then she heard it. The fluttering of wings and rushing water.

But the river was farther below, not above where the Amazon flowed.

A river under the river?

Down to go up.

Somewhere below was a way out.

Please, Annja thought, *let there be a way out.*

32

Roux explored the cavern, collecting anything that looked like it might burn—roots, bits of plants and two broken planks that must have been dropped down here by the miners. They'd probably done a little exploring themselves and discovered no veins of emeralds. He also discovered a fairly recent corpse amid the bones where Annja hadn't searched.

The man, once young and fit, had probably been dead two days, maybe three. Roux had been around corpses enough to hazard a good guess. The chill of the cavern had helped preserve the body.

The dead man looked like one of Dillon's crew, dressed in coveralls. Two bullet holes in his chest, all the pockets on the coveralls ripped, back and front, big pockets on the thighs shredded, fingers broken… maybe from the fall, but Roux didn't think so. His mind played over the possibilities. Maybe the man had gotten greedy and tried to keep some of the emeralds, the pockets ripped to check for pilfered stones.

Since Roux had nothing better to do at the moment, and since he'd been long inured to the condition of corpses, he searched the body, thinking maybe he might find something useful. Under the coveralls the man had worn a T-shirt and boxers. The boots had steel toes and were expensive looking. He tugged these off, wondering if they might suit the unconscious man better than the flimsy things he was wearing. Provided Edgar ever regained consciousness.

Roux smiled grimly. As he removed the boots from the dead man, uncut emeralds fell out and onto the ground. There had been a dozen pieces in one boot, three in the other, all of which he pocketed, the fading light from his helmet wasn't enough to let him properly inspect the gems. The dead man did not need them, but Roux might.

His fellow thieves had killed him because he'd broken their code. But a handful of gems were not worth more than a man's—even a thief's—life.

Man's cruelty never ceased to surprise Roux. But in all the centuries he'd never come to understand where the evil came from. Why was there such darkness in some men's souls and only light in others? Roux knew his own soul held a mix of darkness and light that sometimes battled each other. Always the light managed to prevail, but that hint of darkness provided a balance, and it was why the poached stones were now in his pockets.

He'd only seen light in Joan's soul.

In Annja's? She had both, and it was probably that blend that gave her such fire and drove her. He rolled the dead body over, seeing bugs clustered around the exit wound in the corpse's back.

Annja had been so confident about finding a way

out. Gone eight hours now, he prayed she actually could. Roux didn't fear death. He'd "died" so many times or came close to it, that staring the Grim Reaper in the face was old hat. But he feared being trapped down here.

He worried that if Annja did not prevail this cavern would be permanent; his company—Annja and the young man still unconscious—would eventually die. Roux would be left alone. Would he go mad? He shuddered and paced, watched the fire die down and fed it a little more. And when the fire was out and the batteries dead, would he spend eternity in darkness?

He would have liked to dump everything he'd gathered onto the fire and make it rage to match his spirit and keep him and Edgar warm. But he needed to conserve his bounty. The fire would remain small to extend its life. He flipped off his helmet light again. The batteries were dying and he wanted to conserve those. Annja had given him two more, but he could suffice by the meager firelight.

Roux cursed himself for coming here. In France he'd been worried about Annja; he feared that fate was telling him something had gone horribly wrong and that she was in jeopardy. He didn't want to lose Annja as he had Joan. A failed knight once, he did not want to repeat the experience.

And so he was here, in this damnable cave.

And so here he was wondering if that warning he'd felt wasn't so much about Annja's fate, but about his own…a hint that his existence was the thing in jeopardy.

If he hadn't come to Brazil and subsequently found Annja stumbling around in the rainforest, she might not have regained her memory. She wouldn't have charged back to Dillon's camp in search of Moons and Edgar, nor would she have wound up captured and thrown down here. If he hadn't followed her, he'd not be here either. Moons might be alive.

Had he set all these unfortunate things into motion? Or was he merely playing a role that had been assigned to him? Roux glanced at some of the cave paintings, knowing Annja had been excited by them. They were mildly interesting, but did not intrigue him.

He returned to the fire and stared into it, in his mind's eye seeing Joan burning at the stake. Roux closed his eyes and let a more pleasant recollection consume him. Joan had been an amazing commander, aggressive and smart. He'd ridden with her on many campaigns, winning most of them. And he'd traveled with her to places far and wide—all of them surrendering when she'd approached, banner held high. They hadn't wanted to fight her.

Wise, Roux reflected, she was a remarkably skilled swordswoman, whether fighting on foot or from horseback. And tactics? She knew precisely how to direct an army and how to orchestrate her gunpowder artillery, the cannons that had so often made a difference in the battles.

But when the odds had become overwhelming, when she did not have access to those cannons…that was when the defeats had come about. Those were the battles she shouldn't have joined. So while her aggression and skill made her formidable, Roux also knew she had weaknesses. Those traits had led to her capture.

Annja had those traits. They'd led to her capture by Dillon.

Gone eight hours? Maybe he should go in search of her.

Instead, he lost himself in another memory. Charles VII wanted the city of Troyes to surrender, but after days of intense negotiations, it was clear that wasn't about to happen. Roux had been in the room when Charles asked Joan her opinion. She didn't hesitate.

"Nous devons commencer le siège," she'd said.

Charles agreed to the siege and designated Joan in charge of it. Roux walked with her that night as she placed the cannons and directed her army and her knights to fill the ditches that circled the city.

At dawn, Joan yelled for their forces to attack.

Without a single cannon firing, the city yielded. Roux knew it was the mere sight of her forces that made the enemy's troops surrender.

Annja lacked the cannons, but she had her own heavy artillery…laptops and the internet, satellite phones and a cadre of archaeologist peers throughout the world to call upon. But just as Joan saw defeat in battles where she lacked her best weapons, so, too, Annja was now missing hers. She had only her wits and Joan's sword.

Would that be enough?

SIXTEEN HOURS GONE and Edgar woke up. He grieved over Moons, and then Roux moved the woman's body into the space with the other corpse, hiding death from their view, if not their thoughts.

He listened politely while Edgar alternately mourned

Moons, complained about how much his arm hurt, and spilled his life story. So many people talked endlessly when they were frightened, as if their words could keep the terror away. And while Roux listened, taking in only bits and pieces, he continued to ruminate about Joan and Annja, cannons and computers.

Eighteen hours gone.

Twenty.

"Roux." Annja's voice was a whisper. She looked beaten, defeated, a mere stick of a woman. She stood far enough away from the tiny fire that he couldn't see her eyes, only the shadowed sockets. "I might have found a way out of here." She collapsed on the stone and he went to her, picked her up and laid her next to the fire, adding the last bit of kindling.

He watched her sleep until the fire went out and the cavern was plunged into blackness.

33

"Stop complaining." Roux sent Edgar a withering look, but Annja knew the expression was lost on the young man.

Edgar was shuffling along with his face down, grumbling about wearing a dead man's shoes.

She stepped ahead of the pair. The cavern was large enough that they could walk side-by-side, but she opted for a little solitude and so walked faster than was comfortable for either of them. Still, she could hear Edgar.

"My arm, it hurts like nothing I've felt before. Like sometimes I can't feel it, sometimes like an elephant stepped on it. And it's cold down here. You'd think under a tropical rainforest it would be warm, same latitude and everything."

Annja agreed with Roux—Edgar prattled so he wouldn't have to think. If his tongue stopped wagging he'd have to face up to how unfortunate Becca Mooney had been and the dire predicament they were all in. Bats scattered as the three of them followed Annja's earlier path, disturbed by their noise and the light on her helmet and Roux's. She took a large step to avoid a slick patch, though she couldn't avoid the stench that made her eyes water.

"And these boots, they're tight. Sure, they're better than what I had. But they belonged to one of Dillon's goons, and—"

Even Annja reached a point where her patience wore thin. "Edgar, if you're so uncomfortable, maybe you should wait for Roux and I back in the hole that Dillon dropped us in. You can safeguard my mapinguari skull." That had actually occurred to her at the outset, leaving him back there. But she wouldn't have left Edgar a light and doubted he could handle the dark for what might be days.

"And starve? Die of thirst? Because you might not come back for who knows how long…provided that you *can* find a means to escape this place, and then provided that you can find the camp and get past Dillon's goons, and get a rope down to me. I don't think so."

It was Annja's intent to get out of this cave, reach the authorities, and have them deal with Dillon's goons. Roux had told her that he tried to call them on her satellite phone, but the charge was gone and he had no way to remedy that. It had been why he'd come after her and been subsequently captured. There was no other cavalry coming. They'd already been down here going on two days—or was it three?—and Edgar was right—he could starve by the time she or someone else could get back here.

"So I'll deal with tight boots, and I guess I'll manage with my arm and the cold and—"

"You're breathing," Roux said. "Be happy that you're breathing."

"Yeah, and I'm in pain."

"Pain is your body's way of letting you know you're alive. Deal with it."

Annja smiled. Roux had used a similar line on her shortly after they'd met.

Edgar continued to talk, but changed the subject to the rainforest and how Dillon had not been content to steal the plants from the Dslala but to steal emeralds from the Brazilians. She ignored his chatter and instead focused on the primitive paintings that lined the walls. She thought of the *Chasing History's Monsters* crew and hoped they'd recovered by now from whatever struck them.

At the section of the tunnel that grew wide and offered the three tunnels, Annja told them, "This one. It's the one I took and heard the water." She replaced the batteries in her light, leaving her with four. Roux's light was starting to fade, and she passed him two batteries, which he pocketed. "Edgar, wait here, and I'm going to investigate these other tunnels. They might—"

"You heard water. That'd be the way to go," Edgar said.

That had been Annja's instinct, too, but… "The slope is very steep, like a sliding board, Edgar. If Roux and I get you down there, it might be too difficult to get you back up." She had a difficult time making it back up herself. "I think—"

"—that water's the way to go," Edgar persisted.

"Probably. But you could do with a few hours' rest."

Annja pointed to the ground, and she took off down the center tunnel. She was back four hours later; the passageway had ended in a dead end.

There was one more tunnel to check out, and it, too, led to a dead end.

"The water's the way to go," Edgar said. From the looks of the bags under his eyes she'd doubted he'd slept while she was gone.

Roux's light died and he replaced the batteries. She had only two spare batteries remaining.

"Then let's be about it, all right?"

Annja led the way, and Roux kept his light off. Edgar kept his mouth shut, apparently concentrating on staying on his feet. More than once he fell, however, nearly bowling Annja down with him when the ground sloped so steeply and the rocks were too smooth to grab on to.

"This is deep," Roux said. "I've been in caves in Turkey, Annja, and I thought they were deep." Did she detect hesitation in his voice? "I can hear water."

Annja could, too, but they hadn't reached it yet. Still, the tunnel led down.

She'd explored part of the Huautla cave system in Oaxaca, Mexico, during her *Chasing History's Monsters* program on the chupacabra. Some of the area residents thought the chupacabra dwelled in the caves, escaping notice by all but a few ranchers working in the evenings. That cave had been discovered in the 1960s, and supposedly its seventeen entrance points and many different routes made it convenient for the chupacabra— Annja had never managed to see one. The cave was one of the deepest in the world.

Though she had no way to measure this, Annja wondered if this one was deeper.

Her light was dimming and her feet ached, her leg muscles burning by the time they reached the water, the sound of it a roar echoing against the close walls. It was black like oil, flat and flowing under a rocky ceiling they had to stoop to get below. It looked like water flowing through some irrigation tube. Her feeble light couldn't reach to the other side, and so she replaced the last two batteries.

"Holy crap," Edgar said. "Don't you realize what this is?"

Annja registered that his once pain-etched face was replaced with a look of wonder. No, it had passed that. It was bliss. Like the young man had reached Nirvana.

Edgar dropped down on his knees and touched the water with his good hand. He shivered. "This is amazing. Do you have anything that can take a picture? Cell phone? Camera? Where's that video camera you had?"

"Nothing," Annja said. "I have nothing."

"So what is this?" Roux touched the tip of his boot to the water. "Some underground tributary of the Amazon?"

Edgar nodded, his eyes still wide in awe.

"Looks like a way out to me." Annja wanted to be *in* the river and on their way. But a brief rest would do Edgar good. Let him continue to be amazed for a little while.

Annja paid attention to the current. It didn't look as swift as the Amazon far above them, but if there was an undercurrent, it might sabotage their escape.

Edgar prattled on about how they were going to be in the history books. "We're the first people in the whole world to see this."

But they weren't the first. There were more of the primitive paintings down here, fainter than the ones above, the water and moisture taking their color.

"Interesting," Roux said. But his expression told Annja he wasn't at all interested.

"Let's just hope this leads us to safety," Annja said. Again she thought of Marsha and Wallace and the others.

"It must join up with another tributary, or the source, somewhere." Edgar stood, staring in the direction of the flowing water.

"Yes, one could hope." This from Roux.

"The River Styx," Annja mused. It was the main river in the mythological underworld. Acheron, Cocytus, Lethe and the Phlegeton, all underground water routes lost to time, but preserved in fables.

Edgar looked at Annja and then Roux, and back again. "Just wow. Wow. Who knows where this could actually lead?" He slapped a hand to his forehead and turned to Roux. "Do you know what this means?"

"That we can get out of here."

Edgar made a face. "Well, yes. If it doesn't slam us up against a wall of porous rock and kill us."

"Best pray that is so," Roux said. "There has been a fair amount of death on this trip already. Try not to add to it."

Annja noted Roux's frustration with Edgar, and their delay here. She was feeling the same about both.

"I am. I am, believe me. We've gotta survive this… so that I can write about it, all of it. I know how to get back here…with cameras. I can go to the Nature Conservancy and write my own ticket. They'll hire me in a heartbeat. Hell, I could probably get on with—"

Annja nudged him. "How about we 'get on with' getting out of here?"

34

This would be dangerous and desperate, but it would be their only chance. There'd be no chance if they stayed in the cavern and hoped someone would come rescue them. Dillon and his thugs had left them there to die. Joining the tributary would be exciting and frightening, too, and Annja had to admit that she was looking forward to that.

A life lived on the edge was sweeter, and the sense of peril would help keep her awake and alert.

She took off her boots and set them at the edge of the water.

"I didn't like these anyway," Edgar said, pulling at his boots and kicking them aside. He gave her a weak smile. "Stiff boots from a stiff. Moons would've thought that was funny." He had to work at getting rid of his socks. He declined Annja's offer of assistance. "If we don't make it back here some future explorer is really gonna puzzle over the shoes."

"We'll make it back." Annja was hoping to have the adventurous Marsha in the film crew.

Roux kept his boots on, but Annja saw him loosen

the laces, probably in case they became too cumbersome in the river and he wanted to divest himself of them later.

She stepped into the water and almost lost her balance; straight down it was an unexpected drop-off. Annja was suddenly in waist-high water. And it was cold, but after a moment she adjusted. Edgar accepted her help this time and he settled in next to her. She grabbed his hand and interlaced their fingers.

"We stay together, all right?"

He nodded.

"The current doesn't look fast, but—"

"I know. There might be undercurrents." Edgar frowned and stepped forward cautiously.

Roux slipped in behind them. She saw the old man shiver.

"We could walk, I suppose," Roux said. "Shallow enough. Right here it's shallow enough."

"Take too long," Edgar said. "Take too much energy. Feel like I'm starving right now. And I'm so damn tired. And my arm hurts and…oh, never mind."

Annja certainly felt like she was starving. She hadn't eaten in two, maybe three days, possibly four? Time was a blur. Maybe there were fish here they could eat. She'd been thinking about that, summoning her sword and spearing something, not worrying that Edgar would see the weapon appear. She'd had sushi before, could well eat raw fish to survive.

Roux seemed to have the same idea. "Maybe there are fish that we could—"

"No." Edgar made a face. "I'm not eating raw fish.

And I'm praying, actually, that there aren't any fish in this place. Bad enough the sorts of fish in the Amazon. Piranha, to start with."

Annja's dream came back in full force, the piranha that had bitten at her. That hadn't been real, though, the fish and the caiman, all in her head and nurtured by whatever she'd swallowed in the shaman's hut. She wished she was back in that hut right now, or that this was another dream.

"Fish with teeth and—" Edgar droned on.

Meanwhile, Annja was getting used to the feel of the current and walking with it. If there were any fish here, they would probably be small, about the size of her hand…blindfish, cavefish, she'd seen them when caving in other parts of the world. They looked almost alien in appearance.

She led Edgar farther out, the cold water swirling around her shoulders now. Annja hadn't expected it to be quite this cold. It smelled so different than the Amazon far above them. The water smelled fresh, no scent of dirt or plants and animals to compete with it. Stone, though, she could smell the stone. She breathed deep and even and started to float, tightening her grip on Edgar's hand as she tipped her head back. He finally stopped talking; she felt the added turbulence in the water from his legs moving as he treaded lightly next to her. The light from her helmet played along the rocky ceiling and the far wall—the primitive cave paintings of the legendary mapinguari seeming to move in slow dance steps.

She shared Edgar's joy at the discovery of this place,

though the cave paintings were far more significant to her. Those paintings…and the creatures who were only rumored to exist. They were a real treasure.

Annja focused on the images here and pictured the ones she'd seen earlier that were particularly strong, the colors still reasonably bright. It was something to keep her mind occupied and away from the unfortunate possibilities of this water ride.

How old were the images?

That would take scientific means—radioactive carbon dating. Clay, charcoal and plants had probably provided the pigments in this cave. The very earliest paintings were all one color, so Annja guessed these were somewhere between twenty thousand and eight thousand BC…*old*.

Annja wanted to survive as much to tell the world about these cave paintings as she did to stop Dillon. The man had to be locked up for the rest of his life. She *had* to survive, as she had work to do. Finding her way back to Arthur Dillon was at the top of her list.

It was all so eerie. For a change Edgar was not talking; the only sound was the water carrying them and lapping at its limestone banks. The noise was loud at times and distorting. Her ears filled with water, slightly uncomfortable. She wished she'd thought to ask Edgar or Roux the time when they went in, so she could tell how long the trip was taking. She could ask them now, in the event one of them had a waterproof watch…but that might only cause depression. She had a feeling this trip was going to take a while. It occurred to her that she should be more frightened than she was, that she should be contemplating death. But she wasn't, and she didn't.

The tunnel changed direction, angling steeply away and rising, the speed of the current increasing. It went faster still when the cavern widened to give the tributary more room and the ceiling rose so high Annja couldn't see it. The smell was awful and she breathed as little as possible and heard Roux making a gagging sound. There were bats in here; she heard them flying. By the sounds and smell she guessed there were hundreds or maybe thousands. She tried to swim toward the edge, while still keeping hold of Edgar, figuring that the bats would have gotten in here somehow. He was dead weight, passed out and floating; her fingers ached from holding on to him.

"Edgar!"

He stirred.

"Come with me."

"God, that smell!" He cooperated and they headed toward the river's edge. It looked like there was enough of a ledge to crawl up on. Maybe the bats had come in through the ceiling somewhere. That possibility was something Annja wanted to explore.

"The ground is too slick to grab onto," Edgar said, trying to climb up on the ledge.

Annja changed her mind and tugged Edgar back toward the center of the tributary.

"Okay. That was a mistake." Annja took small quick breaths; they were all she could handle.

The stench was from the guano, a rancid, overpowering ammonia smell. Enough of it and it could rot sheet-rock, and it harbored disease.

"That was lovely, Annja," Roux said. He was treading with one hand cupped over his mouth. "Let's not repeat that, all right?"

She leaned back and let the water carry her. It felt as if it was going slower; ahead the channel narrowed. Edgar squealed when he was battered up against one side of the rock wall. Annja was scraped, too. The channel curved abruptly, straightened for only a short distance and then followed an "S" pattern. At the same time the ceiling came lower and lower, her light brighter against the stone. The air was fresh, but close.

And then everything went dark when the batteries died.

Now, Annja allowed more fear to seep in. Her heart beat faster.

"Crap," Edgar said. He squeezed Annja's hand tighter. "Just crap."

Everything sounded louder, though Annja figured that wasn't really the case, just that she was perceiving it that way because she couldn't see. D'jok had been right—limit one sense and the others magnify what they take in.

"Roux?" She wanted to make sure he was nearby. "Roux!"

No answer.

Again she was thrown against a rock wall and felt like a discarded doll battered by cruel elements. Edgar let go of her hand and she flailed around trying to find him.

Nothing, nothing…there! She grabbed his shirt and pulled him to her. He wasn't moving on his own and she shielded him as best she could from the wall as they continued through the channel. Holding him with one hand, she felt his head with the other, making sure he stayed above the surface. She could feel warm blood. He'd hit his head.

"Edgar!"

Definitely unconscious, but he was breathing. Annja concentrated on keeping Edgar's face tipped up. The blood flowed over her fingers; it was a bad wound. His broken arm floated free; the belt that had held it close to him had come undone. Nothing to be done about it, she knew, just keep him from drowning.

"Roux!" she tried once more. "Can you hear me, Roux?"

Still no answer, only the sound of the water. Annja lost her hard hat the next time she struck the wall, and her hair floated free, tangling in front of her face. Had she been foolish to talk Edgar and Roux into this? Had there been another way out of Dillon's deathtrap, and she'd been too exhausted to see it? Should they have waited in the cavern and hoped for a rescue from some outside source… would her *Chasing History's Monsters* crew have let the authorities know she was with the Dslala? The Dslala somehow coming to their aid? Should they have waited?

"No one saves us but ourselves. No one can and no one may. We ourselves must walk the path." The words had been attributed to Buddha. One of the caretakers at the orphanage in New Orleans had been Buddhist.

Annja had found comfort in those words as a child, and that quote in particular had always stayed with her. "No one saves us but ourselves." The river had been their best opportunity. Waiting for any help could have meant waiting to die.

She couldn't judge the time; it felt like hours had passed, maybe more…maybe days. She felt numb from the cold and lack of food, the water seeming ethereal as it carried her. She'd managed to angle herself so she was floating on her back and didn't have to tread; her legs had gotten too tired. All her effort was directed at staying awake and keeping her and Edgar's heads up. He floated limp next to her. Sometimes water filled her mouth. It was fresh and clean, cold, and she gulped it down. Let it fill her belly and trick her body into thinking she'd had something to eat. Wasn't that a dieter's trick? Drink water before a meal so you don't eat as much? Your stomach thinking it's already sated? Annja had been blessed with a metabolism that made counting calories unnecessary.

Her mind started to wander, images of the orphanage popping in, some of the children morphing into miniature Buddhas. "No one saves us but ourselves," they chanted in unison. Then Charlemagne and his army thundered on horseback through the streets of New Orleans and chased the little Buddhas away. Hallucinating. Delirious.

"Stay with me," she whispered to Edgar. "Stay—"

Annja's face scraped hard against rocks directly overhead and she had just enough time to suck in some air. The space above the river had vanished. Keeping one hand on Edgar, she floundered around with her free hand, hoping to find a pocket of air. Desperate, she started treading, trying to reach what might pass for the bank, praying to find a ledge to pull them up on, mounds of guano be damned.

But there was nothing, and the channel only tightened. It felt as if they being pushed through a garden hose. Once more her dream rushed back, being pulled down by a caiman, down and down. But this time there was no down, only being tossed about by water. Like the tributary had become angry and was lashing out. There was life in the ink; she felt things brushing up against her and guessed they were fish.

Then abruptly Annja felt herself flying, and she wrapped her arms around Edgar in a vise grip. Air was all around her and she took in great gulps of it. She could still hear the water, thundering, a recognizable sound—a waterfall. She and Edgar plummeted, striking water again and going under, the gushing torrent of the falls thrusting them to the unforgiving bottom.

No. No. No, her mind shouted. *Don't—*

Annja blacked out.

35

Annja tasted blood. She ran her tongue around inside her mouth and discovered she'd broken a tooth—fixable. She was probably fixable, too; she was alive. The waterfall had wedged her between two rocks. Her face felt as if it was on fire. Maybe she'd broken her nose. She gingerly touched it. Yes, a broken nose, a gash on her cheek, another one above her right eye.

Pain was the body's way of letting you know you're alive…hmm.

She'd expected to drown, maybe meeting Joan of Arc face-to-face, but not this, not…nothingness. That part of the very rocky tunnel the channel flowed through had opened up to provide a miracle. Air, and lots of it. Fresh air.

"Roux." The word came out too softly to be heard over the rushing water. The tributary sounded like thunder, and it surged past her. She didn't want to go any farther into the abyss, wherever this current traveled to. There was real fresh air here, and that meant it was coming in from somewhere.

Everything was black. "Roux!" she tried again, rewarded with a mouthful of cold water. "Edgar!"

Had they been carried ahead? Had they been crushed by rocks? Or had they drowned? Rather, had Edgar drowned?

"Edgar!"

She could only hear the water.

Annja felt weak, battered by the rocks and river, no food for days. How long had she and Edgar and Roux been at this? More than a day at least; she didn't need a watch to tell her that. But how much longer?

Her arms felt practically useless, yet she managed to wrap one around a rock to anchor her and stretch out the other to do a little exploring. The current threatened to dislodge her, but Annja was persistent. Doug had once complimented her on it. That was one of the few days she hadn't argued with him over something.

What is…there! She grabbed onto a rock sticking up and out of the water like a stalagmite. She pulled herself toward it and wrapped her arms around it. Her face pressed against it; its odor was strong. It was indeed a stalagmite. She stretched out again, fingers brushing another. Annja pushed off against her post, and with hands outstretched caught another one and held on with every ounce of power she had left.

"Roux!" No reply. Nothing. "Edgar!"

Stretching out, she found the next stalagmite much closer this time. Annja didn't know where she was going, but it felt good to be out of the current for now.

Another stalagmite, and then she felt a rocky ledge.

She pulled herself up on it, and crawled farther away from the water. The farther she went, the better she felt.

Annja stretched out on her back and shivered, listened to the water and thought about Edgar and Roux, Moons who'd died before they even reached the underground tributary. Mostly she thought about Dillon; wanting to bring him to justice gave her strength. She must have dozed for a while because she was dry now, although her hair was still damp.

She got to her feet, shaky, the muscles in her legs feeling like noodles. Wobbly, she took a few steps, small and shuffling, not wanting to end up back in the river if she could help it.

"Edgar!" Her voice had more power now and it came back at her, reflecting off a wall she could see. "Edgar! Roux!"

She thought she heard something.

"Roux?" She took another step forward and strained to hear anything besides the waterfall. "Edgar!"

She did hear something, a moan. Her name? Someone said her name.

"Roux!"

"I'm here. You don't have to shout."

"Where are you?"

A chuckle. "Don't know. Can't see a damn thing."

"Keep talking."

He did and she carefully walked in that direction, realizing the ledge she was on was more than a ledge, the size undeterminable. Annja slipped in guano, picked herself up and continued on. Her limbs ached and she felt so empty inside.

Finally, she bumped into the old man. He was seated, back to a stalagmite.

"You stink," he said.

"Thanks." She had to admit the guano-smeared clothes smelled awful. "Edgar?"

"He's not here."

She crouched down next to Roux.

"Seriously, you stink."

"I had a hold of him," Annja said. "Then we went under."

They didn't say anything for a while. She listened to the river and the gentle flutter of the bats moving overhead.

"I've felt around every inch of this spot, as much as I could," Roux said. "Searching for you. For Edgar. I don't know how long I've been here. You were going to ask me that next, right? I lost my watch in the river. Edgar got lost in the river."

"I had a hold of him and—"

"Not your fault, Annja. It was a miracle he hadn't died earlier, when Dillon's man pushed him through the hole. He should have died then, when the girl did. Would've been more merciful."

Roux sounded thoroughly defeated, and Annja imagined a sorrowful expression on his face. He was probably thinking that she would die here, just like Moons had, and like Edgar most certainly had. If she didn't die of starvation…she'd passed the point of feeling ravenous. Now she just felt weak and numb, her fingers and lips trembling; serious hunger, her head dully pounding.

"I'm not going to die here," she said to herself as much as to Roux.

She'd been listening closely to the bats, and they were leaving.

And she was going to follow them out of this place.

Annja had a hard time standing, her legs not cooperating. She pulled herself up by finding breaks in the rock. Listening to the shrieking bats, she followed them, hands out in front of her like a mummy in an old black-and-white film. She found another stone wall and could hear no more flying bats. However many there had been, they were all gone.

And they'd left through a hole very high up.

The moon must be full and bright for it to shine down. It was a spotlight that didn't reach her, and yet it reached far enough to give her hope.

"I'm not dying down here, Roux. Do you hear me?"

He mumbled something. Sounded like swearwords, but in German.

"I'm climbing out. You can come with me if you'd like." At least, Annja hoped she was climbing out. She felt the wall, searching for dry spots and other good places to hold. So much was too slippery, but she persisted, keeping the faint overhead light in view. Finally she found a deep enough niche to wedge her fingers into. She started up. "I'm serious, Roux, I'm getting out of here." She heard some shuffling, the sound of him cracking into another stalagmite, heard him fall.

"Verdammt!"

Annja wasn't fluent in German, but she knew that word.

"I'm not waiting, Roux." But she was, climbing slowly, talking as she went—about the river and the cave paintings, staying away from the depressing subject of Edgar and Moons. She heard him climbing below her. Despite his age—real or otherwise—she knew him to be athletic. Roux probably didn't share her total exhaustion; her legs felt like lead as she pulled one up over the other, searching for spots to wedge her toes in. Too, Roux had kept his boots on. She could hear the scraping sound of the leather against the rock.

He fell once, and she hung suspended, waiting for him to start again. "I could come back for you," she offered. "Find ropes, people to help, old—" She stopped herself from calling him "old man" again.

"Just climb." She could tell his words came out between clenched teeth. His cursing continued, louder and with more variation.

After many minutes, Annja found a wide enough ledge to rest her knees; her face pressed against the stone, she took several deep breaths. She was starting to doubt this route; giving herself to the river and seeing if she'd survive the rest might have been the better route. If she fell from this height…she'd be done.

Annja waited. The fates had smiled on her so far, giving her a rock wall with plenty of hand- and footholds. Otherwise, she never would have been able to attempt this climb. It felt like forever before Roux joined her. She pulled him up to her perch. His breath was ragged and he didn't talk. After a short while, she broke the silence.

"I need to rest," Annja said. "Before I start up again. Is that all right with you?"

"Yes." It was a whisper.

ANNJA AWOKE TO the sound of bat wings flapping, the air rushing against her face. Maybe it was almost daylight above. She didn't feel any better for having rested; her legs still felt like weights when she managed to stand. Looking straight up, she thought she saw a hint of light...or rather less black.

Annja consoled herself, took a deep breath and began climbing again. One hand, one foot, over and over again. She still couldn't hear Roux; for now, she would go on alone. But then she heard...thunder? Rain, she didn't need. Wet rock would make the climb even more difficult, and it had been difficult enough.

"Move. Move. Move." She gritted her teeth and increased her rate of ascent. The spot of light she'd seen above only a few minutes ago was gone; no doubt the sky—however high up—had gone dark with clouds. What were those curse words Roux had used? Her stomach, legs, every inch of her ached. Her fingers and feet were bloody from cutting them on the rock. Annja let anger fuel her; an image of Dillon flashed in front of her eyes. "Move. Move. Move!"

It was raining.

She'd poked her head out of the hole like a rabbit, and scrambled topside. She lay on her belly, peering down into the darkness, listening for Roux. The hole she'd climbed out of wasn't large, and she used her body to shield as much of it as she could, trying to keep the hand- and footholds dry for him.

"Roux?" She risked after a minute or two. "Are you there?"

There was silence. The tempo of the rain increased, drumming against her back.

"Roux! Roux! Roux, are you—"

"Of course I'm here," he hollered. His voice sounded distant. "Where else do you think I would've gone to?"

Annja shut up and waited, listening to the thunder, dozing, and then waking when Roux's hands reached up and out of the hole. Reflexively, she grabbed him, holding as tight as she could manage.

"Pull harder!" Roux commanded. "C'mon, Annja!"

She heaved and got him halfway out, and he struggled himself the rest of the way. He rolled onto his back and she took stock of him. His clothes were shredded, his face and hands crisscrossed with cuts. The rain pelted down on him.

"The next time—" he began. "The next time I worry about you I am staying in France."

"Probably a good idea," she said. Annja lay at a right angle from him, too worn out to move. In the time since she'd inherited Joan of Arc's sword, she'd been shot at, chased, attacked with all manner of weapons. Someone even tried to do her in with explosives. She'd never been tossed down a hole in a tropical rainforest before with the intent of letting her die there.

Dillon had almost succeeded.

"Do you want to stay here, Roux? Mend or whatever it is you do while I go for help?"

"No," he answered curtly. "I'm going with you."

But he didn't. He remained flat on his back, the rain pattering against him.

She struggled to her feet, picked a direction, and struck out. Annja would come back for him later, after she figured out where in the world she'd just arrived.

36

The rain didn't last long. It was long enough though to wash most of the blood and guano off her. She couldn't imagine what she must look like. And she felt even worse. Still, she persisted.

The clouds thinning, Annja could tell it was close to sunset.

She'd expected trees. She was after all in the middle of the rainforest. She wanted to see the tall buildings of Belém. Annja had hoped the water ride had taken them toward the big city. At least the temperature was delightfully warm. She'd almost forgotten what warm had felt like.

Annja was slogging through soggy savanna, so she really had no clue where she'd come out. The ground was relatively flat; there were trees in the distance and the outline of a barn and a house.

"I'm not in Manhattan anymore," Annja quipped. She shuffled toward a fence and hitched herself over it, fell in a swath of mud and for a moment contemplated just lying there for a while. But there was Roux to think about, and Dillon to bring to justice. On her feet, she kept going, and she passed a herd of water buffalos. She'd made it across the pasture and over the other side of the fence when her legs gave out.

A farmer coming in from the barn saw her.

PORTUGUESE, HE KNEW just enough Spanish to carry on a casual conversation. She used his shower, and gorged herself on bread and boiled chuchu while his teenage son went in search of Roux. The farmer loaned her a pair of his son's blue jeans and a well-worn plaid shirt. The high-top tennis shoes were too large, but she didn't care at this point.

She thanked him profusely and let him fuss over the cuts on her face and tape her nose. The farmer said one year in veterinary school had proved helpful with wounded livestock.

"Me siento como ganado heridos," Annja said. In English her words meant that she felt like wounded livestock. He pressed, and she gave him the very condensed, edited version of her exploits. That she'd been pushed into a cavern and a long while later had found a way out onto his property.

"Necesitas un medico."

She didn't have time for a hospital or a doctor, she thought. Annja shook her head. "I will be fine. *Voy a estar bien.*"

He scowled like he didn't believe her, went to the refrigerator and brought back two bottles of DaDo Bier. Annja did not refuse the hospitality.

"Dónde estamos? Esta casa?" Annja wanted to know just where she was.

The farmer—Duarte Cruz, as he introduced himself—disappeared for several minutes, coming back with a laptop so large and old Annja thought it could be displayed in a museum. He strung the power cord to an outlet.

"Wireless," he said, grinning. He scooted it around in front of her, leaned over her shoulder and impatiently waited for the machine to start up. He spoke to her in Portuguese, but she had no idea what he had said. Maybe something about the machine's sluggishness?

"Ah! *Veja? Ele funciona.*" He drummed his fingers and switched to Spanish. *"Ven? Va."*

Yes, she could see that it worked. His thick, calloused fingers typed in a series of letters, hit return, and a map of Brazil popped up. He zoomed in on the map, presumably to the spot where they were.

So this was where she'd crawled out of the earth.

She was on the largest island in the world that was surrounded by freshwater, the Amazon flowing around it; the largest city, which Duarte said was *no legos*—not far—was called Breves.

Looking over her shoulder, Duarte pointed at the word *Breves. "Tem um hospital,"* he said.

"Don't need one. I will be fine," she replied. *"Voy a estar bien."* Eventually she would be fine. The meal had gone a long way to help, but she hurt all over. The only reason she hadn't keeled over from exhaustion was because nervous energy had taken over. She had so much to do that she didn't have time for sleep. Besides, she'd napped some on the rocky ledge, and that had also helped.

The island was almost directly on the equator. Belém

sat to the south, across the Para River. She clicked a link to Breves, no English page available; she found one in Spanish and discovered the town did a reasonable tourist business because of its beautiful beach. That meant there would be boats. She needed a way to get back to the nameless Dslala village. Her passport, papers, her satellite phone, Marsha's camera...all of it was there. And Dillon's camp was down a well-worn path that extended from the village.

"Duarte—" Annja indicated the chair next to her. He sat. She finally took stock of him. Middle-aged, skin weathered from the sun, black hair streaked with gray, a careworn face. He wasn't a poor man judging by the house and his clothes, but neither was he rich. Generous, though, and thoughtful; he'd taken her in. "I need to tell you where I've been," she said. And not the condensed, edited version, either. She was halfway through her story about Arthur Dillon and his pharmaceutical and gem operation when Roux and Duarte's son stumbled in.

The cuts were gone on the old man's face, but he was filthy and raggedy looking. Introductions were made, more bread and boiled chuchus were served, and Annja finished her story.

"A polícia. Eu vou chamar a polícia para você." Duarte went to a black, rotary wall-mounted phone.

"The police will be a start," Annja said to Roux. "We'll see if Mr. Cruz will let us spend the night. I need to crash a few hours, talk him into taking us into the city tomorrow. He said it isn't far. I'll make arrangements to pay him something. I'll have it wired later. And I've got to rent a helicopter." She dropped her chin in her hands. "With no money, no ID, no passport, I have to get back to the village." She was talking to herself, continuing to ramble as her voice fell to a whisper.

Duarte scowled and held the receiver away from his mouth. *"Estou na espera."*

His son was hovering and translated his words into English. "My father says he is on hold."

Roux took another helping of the boiled chuchu and liberally sprinkled salt and pepper on it. Annja watched him eat and turned back to the laptop, finding Duarte's email program and dropping a quick note to Doug to let him know she was all right.

"This is delicious," Roux told the boy. "I don't know what it is, but—"

"Vegetables. My father, he raises buffalo for the money, but he is a vegetarian. We grow a lot of chuchu for ourselves." The boy shrugged. "Go figure, eh?" He came close to the table. "He'll give you a ride into town in the morning. You two can sleep in my sister's room. She is away at school. And you do not need to pay us. We are just happy to help you."

Duarte spoke into the receiver. *"Ah...finalmente alguém para conversar."* Obviously someone had answered, and he started talking anxiously. Annja picked out the word *pharmaceuticals,* and understood *assassinato*—murder. Then he was put on hold again, apparently transferred, and he repeated the conversation.

Roux reached into the pocket of his jeans and pulled

out three stones. "We'll pay you and your father, Herberto."

Annja mentally chastised herself for not asking the teen's name.

Roux set the emeralds on the table. "They're uncut, and though I don't know the value of such, I suspect by their size and their variety that they ought to be enough to buy you a new computer and a better truck. You told me on the way here that yours is in bad shape."

"On its last wheel, you might say." The boy smiled warmly. "Thank you, Mr. Roux. Thank you ever so much."

"Herberto, do you have a shower I might avail myself of?" Roux asked.

"Sim," Herberto answered, gesturing for Roux to come with him. "And I will find you something else to wear." Roux plopped one more emerald on the table.

Annja stared at the gems, wondering when Roux had gotten them. Inside the mine, probably picked them off the floor. Pieces of rock, beautiful certainly, valuable, undeniably. But the lives Dillon took because of them were worth far more. Dillon would answer for what he'd done.

37

When Annja was driven to get something done, time crawled and nothing was adequate.

The ride to the city in Duarte's rusting pickup was rocky and took too long, though she held her tongue the entire ride and effusively thanked the farmer for his kindness and generosity. And while Breves was a large city as far as the island of Marajó was concerned, it wasn't quite large enough to suit her needs. Tourism was big business here, but that didn't include a place to rent a helicopter, or a store to buy a satellite phone so she could talk to Doug and Wallace.

"I need to talk to Doug, not just an email," she told Roux. She wanted to know whether Wallace and the others had come through the malady that struck days ago and had made it back to New York. "Maybe Marsha's still in the hospital in Belém?"

Annja had to think of her priorities. Yes, she could spend her time finding out about Marsha—a situation Annja could do nothing about, or she could pursue Dillon, something she definitely could do something about. So that's what she settled on.

The boats available were smaller than she'd hoped and lacked large motors—she wanted to get back to the Dslala village quickly. Her heart raced due to her frustration, and she anxiously cast her eyes across the river to Belém, where there might be a helicopter available, and perhaps faster boats.

"There is the notion of a bird in the hand," Roux said.

He looked much better this morning, well groomed and dressed as she'd never seen him—faded olive trousers that were about four inches too short and a blue and red plaid work shirt. He looked like a retired farmer. But she looked no better—save that she was no longer blue. The die had washed off during her long spell in the underwater tributary.

Appearance didn't matter, though, not while there was Dillon to deal with. She'd stopped in the police station right away, found an English-speaking officer and related much the same information Duarte had in his phone call the previous night. The officer confirmed that several agencies in Brazil had been notified and that likely that the authorities were either already at the site or on their way.

That helped mollify her, but like everything else this morning, it wasn't enough. Annja was obsessed with seeing this for herself. Besides, there was the matter of reclaiming her passport and duffel.

"The bird in the hand," Roux repeated.

She got in the boat he'd arranged, a small weather-beaten tug. She discarded the notion of looking for faster transportation across the river in Belém, as that might end up eating more time and for no better results.

"The bird in the hand doesn't have a name painted on its side," Annja said, as she settled in and started waving away the clouds of insects. She was surprised Roux continued to accompany her. She was safe, she was going to fly back to New York after this business was done, and he seemed miserable with all the insects and his ill-fitting clothes. Too, if he had any more of those emeralds, he could cash them in somewhere and fly back to Paris in the first-class section that he so coveted. He'd spent a walnut-sized emerald arranging for this boat, food and bottled water. Did the boatman—Jorges Inacio—have the savvy to turn that emerald into a far better boat when this little trip was over?

The hours melted, three days actually, as her recollection of the tributary to reach the unnamed village was not perfect. Inacio had to do a little searching and backtracking.

Eventually, the shore began to look familiar to her. Annja stood in shock; the scent of burned bodies hit her as if she'd run into a concrete wall. Wisps of smoke twisted up from the ruins of the Dslala village.

Inacio spoke low and rapidly in Portuguese and steered toward the shore, cutting back on the engine then stopping it as the nose ran aground. He canted the motor up so the propeller would not become stuck in the mire.

Roux was the first over the side, grabbing the rope and looping it around a tree hanging low over the river.

Inacio continued to talk, crossed himself, and kissed a small silver crucifix that dangled from a cord around his neck.

Annja got out, the water swirling around her boots and seeping in through cuts in the leather. A few feet away a small turtle poked its head up; it looked like the one from her dream.

The bodies had been stacked like chopped wood where the central cook fire had been. They still smoldered. No smoke came from the huts that had also burned. The closest ones had burned down to the ground.

Annja helped Inacio out of the boat, and she watched as he tested the rope Roux had tied, making certain it was secure. He continued to talk in a hushed tone. He was praying. The rest of his words were drowned out by a pair of howler monkeys erupting in full voice and scaring a flock of sun conures.

Numb, she walked toward the pile of bodies, almost three dozen of them, adults and children. Annja stretched out her hands, feeling a hint of warmth. They'd been burned yesterday, possibly as long as two days ago.

Behind her, Roux and Inacio talked and sifted through the wreckage of the closest hut. Annja walked toward one hut farther away, where D'jok and his family had lived. The blackened reeds were cold, and when she picked up some they felt damp and crumbled in her fingers. This fire had happened first; no smoke came from it or any of the other destroyed huts, no hot spots. How long ago? How long had she been in the river? She'd not asked the date or looked for a calendar in Duarte's farmhouse. She'd not thought to ask the police at the station in Breves. Then, days and dates really hadn't mattered.

How long ago had she been in Dillon's emerald mine?

She nudged the pieces of the hut around with her boot, seeing her blackened satellite phone and the buckles from her duffel and Marsha's camera bag. She stooped and picked up the charred video camera. All the footage Marsha had taken—gone. But the loss was inconsequential.

Her lungs stung from the tragic scents and her eyes watered.

Dillon's men had done this—that was the only answer. And the rains had put the fires out. Why? Why kill these beautiful people and destroy their homes? What threat could they have posed…could the children have posed…that warranted this?

She pulled in a deep breath, the acrid air festering in her throat and stoking her ire.

Annja went from hut to hut, purposefully staying away from Roux and Inacio, wanting some time alone. While Dillon had no doubt burned this place and killed—or had ordered the killings—he hadn't gotten all of them. She knew this because she knew he wouldn't have had the decency to build a pyre for them. They'd have been left for the big cats and the caiman. There'd been roughly seventy people in this community, and half of them were no more. Half must have escaped. Maybe they'd burned their kinsmen.

Had they then gotten to safety?

"Annja!" Roux pointed toward a trail. "This way." He started down it without waiting for her.

Inacio crossed himself again and followed.

She took another look at the smoldering pile of bodies, and then went after them.

The shaman's hut was intact, and D'jok, as black as ink, stood outside it. He'd been dipped in huito.

"I waited for you, Annja Creed," he said. "I dreamed that you would come back."

"Tell me what happened," she said. Annja knew what had happened, that Dillon's men had come here. But she wanted every last horrible detail for the record.

D'jok held up his hand and spread his fingers. "Five days ago," he began. "The men came with anger and guns and fire." The Dslala had sent a band of tribesmen to the pharma camp in search of Edgar and Moons and a few of their own who had not returned. It had been a confrontation with awful repercussions.

"Some of those men died," D'jok said. "But more of ours. So many guns."

"Were you there? Did you—" A scarlet macaw screeched and swooped low, took another pass and flew toward the river. A monkey howled long and loud, and it was quickly answered.

"I ran, Annja Creed. I lived." D'jok's face looked like it was carved from a piece of rock, no muscles twitching, eyes like marbles and unblinking. "My family did not. The men came with anger and so many guns and fire. Like hunters circling a caiman they circled us, yelling their angry words. I begged them, Annja Creed, to save the children. I told them we were sorry and would leave them alone, that we would leave this place forever."

"Everyone," Roux ventured. "Did they kill everyone here?"

D'jok shook his head; his face remained implacable. "They did not. They did not follow the ones who ran into the river. I ran into the river. They burned our homes, Annja Creed. And they left us in the river." He paused and watched a small orange parrot on a thin branch overhead. "They left us in the river because their guns were empty. So very angry to use all the bullets. So very, very angry to kill children."

Inacio shook his head and kissed his crucifix. He shuffled back toward the burned village.

"How many survived?" Annja feared the river and its creatures almost as much as gunfire.

D'jok's expression finally broke and tears welled in the corners of his eyes. "Nine, Annja Creed. Only nine, and me. All gone into the forest now. Gone to find a new place."

"Will you follow them?"

"No. This is my home. I dreamed that I should stay here. I dreamed that you would come back, Annja Creed. I dreamed that I should tell you about the angry men."

He'd been the one to gather the bodies and burn them, Annja realized, not wanting the caiman or scavengers to get them. He would have to burn them again and again to reduce them to something manageable. Joan of Arc had been burned three times; the French authorities had not wanted anything left to be buried.

"That must have been five days ago." Annja's words

were hoarse; her mouth was desert dry. "Did anyone come to go after Dillon?"

He shrugged. "There have been helicopters, Annja Creed. So maybe yes. I will not go back to that evil place. But I dreamed that you would."

"You dreamed correctly, D'jok." She turned to Roux. "Would you—"

"Help him with the bodies? They need to be burned again."

"Please."

He nodded. "Unfortunately I know how bodies burn, Annja. Yes, I will help him."

"Talk Inacio—"

"—into keeping the boat here. I'll do that, too."

She watched the orange bird and listened to the wind tease the leaves. Then she started off through the forest in the direction of Dillon's camp.

"And we will wait for you," Roux said.

38

Annja took the path that Edgar and Moons had forged. It was late afternoon, and even at her best speed she wouldn't reach Dillon's camp before sunset. There might be nothing there; the Brazilian cops or government officers might have found the place and swooped in. Based on her description of the approximate location, coupled with Dillon's permits on file, they could have found him.

D'jok said he'd heard helicopters, too.

This could well be an unnecessary waste of time.

But Annja had to see for herself.

The miles melted with her quick pace, though she stumbled several times in her haste, her feet catching on tree roots that snaked across the ground, tangling in vines, the forest rising thick all around her. Once she stepped in a hole, the burrow of some creature, and twisted her ankle. A minor sprain. She kept going, though a little slower and with a little more care.

The sky was clear, no hint of rain, and the air was filled with the scent of damp ground, flowers and suddenly something truly awful. She skidded to a stop.

What was that stench? Not fire, like back at the village. Something that she couldn't put a name to. Dead fish? Maybe a honking big barrel full of dead fish. The hair on the back of her neck stood at attention and she held her hand down to her side, calling the sword. There was movement to her right, something rustling the branches, causing one of them to snap. A wuffling sound like a horse might make, then a shrill, earsplitting shriek.

Annja crouched and faced the source of the stench and the ruckus, seeing a shape through the foliage, a massive shadow that came closer. It pushed aside saplings and trundled into view.

Her mouth fell open.

The beast resembled both monkey and sloth. As it came closer still she saw that its front legs were longer than the back ones. That its back sloped and it was covered with thick, matted fur. In places the fur was missing, perhaps from a battle with a big cat. When it turned slightly, Annja saw where claws had raked it. The exposed skin looked thick and bumpy like an alligator's.

"Crap," Annja breathed. "Just crap."

The creature's snout was long and sharply tapered at the end and filled with tiny jagged teeth that glistened in the sun.

It reared back on its hind legs, and Annja involuntarily trembled. It was taller than her by at least a foot. It shrieked again and reached down with a three-toed foot, wrapped its claws around a young tree and pulled, uprooting it. Turning and squarely facing Annja, the beast ripped the tree in two in a powerful display of strength, shrieked again. The beast belched a sulfurous cloud of vileness and made Annja gag.

This was a mapinguari, one of the beasts she'd come to the Amazon to find. It was both beautiful and horrible, and here Annja was without a photographer or a camera, no means of recording the creature for posterity. But perhaps that was why nature had allowed her this glimpse, because she could not record it.

It was real, not a myth. The descriptions the villagers had provided of it had not been adequate. Her stomach roiled as another puff of ghastly stench came her way.

A number of the monsters her program chased were mere legends. Some she believed had existed; some she was certain were pure fabrications embellished by popular media. But to see one face-to-face. It was no more than a dozen feet away.

"Incredible," she said. Annja wished Roux—wished anybody—was here with her to validate the encounter. A sighting like this should be shared. She could slay the beast, or try to. It truly looked formidable and might do her in. But if she killed it, the thing's carcass would be her proof, one of history's monsters that she'd chased and caught!

Annja dismissed the sword and held her hands to her sides.

There'd been no reports of mapinguaries attacking people. And she wasn't about to make a trophy of one just for her television program.

"You are incredible," she told it.

The mapinguari shrieked again and dropped down to all fours. It swung its head back and forth, snout raking through the bushes. It opened its maw to show its bright white teeth, and then it clumsily turned and headed back into the foliage, in the direction of the river.

Annja held her breath and watched until she could no longer see even its shadowy shape and could no longer hear its thrashing through the underbrush. The birds started up again. She stood quiet for several more minutes, taking deep breaths. The freshness of the rainforest air had returned. If only Marsha or Wallace had been here to record this, not just for *Chasing History's Monsters,* but just to have a visual record of this creature.

And since the mapinguari was real, perhaps the other Amazon creatures she'd come in search of were, too.

Somehow Annja would talk Doug into financing a return trip. But she suspected she'd not see a creature like this ever again.

The sun had set by the time she reached Dillon's camp. The surrounding forest was dark, but the cloudless twilight sky over the clearing revealed the remnants of a battle. A half-dozen Dslala tribesmen lay outside the log perimeter, bodies riddled with bullets and insects. From the smell and look of them, they'd been dead for several days. A few of the bodies had gaping holes in them, scavengers come to dine. She knelt at the closest body and quickly backed away, a snake slithered over the torso.

D'jok had said five days; that would be about right.

She climbed the log wall rather than walk around to the barbed wire gate. There were another half-dozen Dslala tribesmen in here, bodies in the same horrible state—masses of maggots, some bloated with gasses.

The smell was intense and the insects swarmed around the corpses. There were fatalities on Dillon's side, too; she saw four men, all in coveralls, some with kneepads, two with helmets on as if they'd come up from the mine to join the fight.

Annja padded closer, wanting to see how they'd died. Poison darts, each of Dillon's men, the darts still in them. Their eyes were hollow sockets and pieces of their faces were gone. She looked away and toward the tents. No one else had been here yet. Maybe they hadn't found the place, or maybe her report and the one Duarte had made on the phone from his farmhouse were in a stack on someone's desk.

When she got back to Belém she'd find someone to do something about all of this. She was nothing if not persistent.

"Dillon!" she hollered. Hand out to her side, she felt the sword poised at the ready. "Dillon, you monster!" His wasn't one of the bodies, and neither was Hammond's.

D'jok had heard helicopters. Maybe Dillon had hitched a ride out with one of his so-called plant shipments.

"Dillon!"

The tent canvas flapped in the wind that gusted. There was no one in the main tent, which had been stripped of its computer, microscopes and various other devices. Cases of batteries remained. The drawers of a file cabinet were open, and the cabinet itself leaned forward, unbalanced. Whatever files that had been in it were gone. She went back outside, took a helmet off one of the dead men, scraped out the insects, and turned on its light. Back inside the main tent, she searched more thoroughly. The light died and she replaced the batteries, stuffed a few more batteries in her pockets, and continued to rummage around.

Nothing useful. She'd hoped to spot forgotten jump drives or other computer-related items so she could follow Dillon's electronic trail.

Next tent, and the next, and the next. All of them empty, a place of ghosts. And in the growing darkness, it was a place of eerie shadows. The insect chorus started, frogs and nightbirds joining in. Faintly she heard a big cat snarl. She brushed away mosquitoes the size of quarters.

Beyond the perimeter she saw where helicopters had landed fairly recently, the marks still evident in the damp ground. Two helicopters of different sizes, one quite large by the print it left. Dillon probably needed it to take his men out of here…though he'd had fewer to accommodate after the fight with the Dslala.

Annja returned to the camp and took down all of the sleeping tents and one of the larger ones. She wanted the nylon cords from them. Inside the tent that covered the crevice to the emerald mine, Annja sat and worked on the cords, tying them together, making a harness for herself, tying another length together and looping that over her arm. Outside, she tied one of the ropes to the generator and tugged fiercely; it would hold. They'd taken the rope ladder with them. She found another helmet inside the tent, and opted for it, as it didn't stink of a dead man. She put it on, tested the light, and went down the hole.

She noticed a difference right away; two more graves had been added, and there was a mound of wilted wild-flowers on the oldest. At least Dillon, or his men, had enough respect to bury some of their dead. But they'd left others up top to rot, and so they'd left the camp in a hurry. He'd mentioned to her and Marsha that he had a small camp twenty or thirty miles due west. Maybe she'd go there next. But first a little more exploring.

Picks had been abandoned, buckets—but these were empty. There were a few small chunks of emerald-laced rocks along the wall where the men had been work-ing. Undoubtedly valuable, the smallest pieces weren't valuable enough for Dillon. Farther along and she saw a gaping hole in the wall where the massive emerald had been. They'd managed to get it out…unfortunately, Annja thought. They'd also managed to pretty well strip most of the thick emerald veins, though dozens of smaller veins had been left untouched. She imag-ined they'd been working around the clock and could almost picture Dillon's face red with rage that he'd had to abandon this pot of gold.

She picked a sturdy outcropping, looped the other cord around it and tied it tight, tugging repeatedly to make sure it would hold. Annja didn't want to risk get-ting trapped in the cavern below. Yes, the underground tributary was a way out, but that wasn't a ride she ever wanted to repeat.

Down again.

The light dimmed and Annja replaced the batteries.

My kingdom for a camera, she thought, as she stared at the walls with all their primitive paintings and at the bones of the ancient beasts. She allowed herself a few minutes to ogle the cave paintings, the one bright spot in this otherwise beyond-miserable day.

Then she went to the center of the cavern, where she'd left the mapinguari skull. Next, she found Moons's body. Because it was cooler here, the girl's body wasn't too badly decomposed. Annja could deal with it. She gathered up the body and managed to get it to the level above.

Annja went back for the mapinguari skull. She'd only take the one, and leave all the rest of the bones behind.

Wait...one more notion. Annja retraced her steps and returned to the area the men had been mining, picked up a few small emeralds and put them in her pocket. They were for Moons, to pay for getting her body back to her parents, which wouldn't be cheap, and to pay for a proper burial.

Then back up top. She laid Moons's body in the tent, the skull next to it, and looked outside.

Annja might make it back to the shaman's hut by midnight if she started now. But it would be slower going with Moons's body. Annja wasn't going to leave her here to rot with the dead Dslala and Dillon's men. Waiting until the morning might be prudent. But there wasn't a trace of rain in the air, and she'd made the trip between the village and this camp enough times to find her way even in pitch darkness. She went outside and took the canvas and poles from one of the smaller tents and fashioned a litter, wrapped Moons's body in another section of canvas and tied it to the litter. Then she sat the skull on top of that.

Annja was halfway to the barbed wire gate when she saw him.

"Hammond."

"Should've shot you before I tossed you into the hole. I had bullets then." Hammond's twin machetes gleamed in the starlight.

"Where's Dillon?"

Hammond chuckled. "Gone."

Annja could smell Hammond, though he was nearly two dozen feet away. He stank of sweat, strong enough for her to pick it up despite the reek of the corpses. He was filthy, his skin streaked with mud, dried blood and other stains, his face a mass of scratches.

"So the master left the dog behind." Annja was taunting him. "Did he leave you any scraps? Or did he take all the money and gems for himself?"

Hammond's lip curled. "I stayed to clean up some loose ends. I just didn't expect—"

"—me to be one of them?"

"No," Hammond admitted. "I expected you to be dead."

"Where's Dillon?" she tried again.

"A long way from here."

Annja dropped the litter poles and stepped aside as he rushed her, summoned her sword and brought it around, catching both his blades as he swept them in, meaning to cut her in half.

"Where the hell did the sword come from?"

"You wouldn't understand," Annja said. She skittered back to give herself more room and get Hammond away from Moons's body. She wanted it to remain in reasonably good condition. "This sword, it belonged to Joan of Arc."

He spit at her and shifted his grip on each machete. Hammond wasn't usually clumsy; Annja had noted earlier that he was rather stealthy, but clearly he wasn't used to using machetes as weapons, and he obviously didn't know any of the rudiments of fencing. Still, he was angry and determined, and that combination was dangerous.

"Tell me where Dillon is." Annja set her jaw and locked eyes with his. Hammond's expression was cold.

"Safe," Hammond said. "Where no one can get to him."

"You going to join him?" Annja circled slowly, and he turned to keep her in front of him.

"I like it here." Hammond gestured with a machete to her sword. "And I'm liking that weapon. It will look good hanging from my brand-new belt, don't you think?"

"Charlemagne held this sword when he was a young boy," Annja said. She didn't mind recounting the rest of the sword's history for Hammond. The moment she saw him by the barbed wire gate, she knew what the outcome would be. Hammond wouldn't be telling any of her secrets.

He rushed in and cleaved with both machetes, and Annja parried one blade, catching it on the edge of her sword, the metal squealing, then hooking it at the handle and yanking, hurling the machete away. The other blade she'd managed to dodge, but she felt the air from his swing.

"You're going to die!"

"You've tried a few times already," she said. Annja danced to his right, and then came up behind him. He spun and jabbed at her, but she leaped back and caught the edge of his machete, rode her sword down along it and drove forward. Her sword plunged into his side.

Hammond screamed in pain and pulled the machete back and up above his head, clearly intending to drive it down on her. Annja stepped in close as she pulled her sword out, and then whirled around behind him. Hammond cleaved the air.

"Over here," Annja said.

He turned, leaning to his right, favoring his wounded side.

"I don't suppose you'll just give up. Surrender."

He charged her.

"I didn't think so." She pivoted and swept her blade in, the edge slicing deep into his stomach. He let go of the machete and dropped to his knees, held his hands close as if trying to keep the blood from coming out.

"Where's Dillon?" Annja asked.

"A long way from here. You'll never find him." Hammond pitched forward, dead.

Annja dismissed the sword, tossed the hard hat on the ground and picked up the ends of the litter.

"I will find him," Annja said.

She repeated the mantra all the way back to the village. It was almost dawn before she made it there to see D'jok and Roux.

"I dreamed you would succeed, Annja Creed. And I dreamed that you will return."

She held his hand tightly. "I will, my friend." Annja would return with archaeologists and another film crew, finishing her planned series and participate in a dig. "And maybe…maybe I will dream with you."

39

Annja rented a sailboat, but ended up taking down the sail and paddling most of the way when the wind died. She'd set off from Coron, where she'd flown in late yesterday—the largest town on the island of Busuanga in the Philippines. She intended to fly out of there tomorrow afternoon, catch a connecting flight to Manila, and then off to Belém again; it would be a long flight with a couple more connections. There'd be a lengthy layover, too.

But that's what it was like when flying to and from the remotest of places. It took her more than two hours to reach the private island of Innaapupan, roughly two hundred and fifty acres, all of it considered virgin…no development, a place untouched.

Her arms ached from the workout, but it was a good feeling, and she relished the sun on her face and the salt-tinged scent of the sea air.

The beach she landed at had powdery white sand that glistened like fresh snow under the noon sun. She pulled the boat up, canted it, and tied the rope to a big piece of heavy driftwood. Annja stared out across the brilliant blue water, seeing other smaller islands nearby, one of them called Lamay, a place with people and amenities, or so said the brochure at the airport. Snorkeling was supposedly good around that island.

The handful of other islands she could see ranged from five to ten acres, like dots of ink on a map that most eyes would overlook. But Dillon hadn't overlooked them—he'd bought six of them; this was the largest of the lot.

That's how Annja had tracked him.

A cop she'd met a little more than a year ago in Madison, Wisconsin—she'd been in the city attending an archaeology conference that turned into quite the adventure—told her it was always about the money.

And while she didn't think it was entirely about the money in Arthur Dillon's case, taking the cop's advice worked. She followed the money. Despite her most diligent efforts and calling in favors, she hadn't been able to track the sale of the massive emerald. Maybe it hadn't been sold. Brazilian officials—who eventually arrived at Dillon's camp and the mine beneath it—could not find it either or prove its existence. But they had managed to catch Dillon's British partner who'd been living in Belém. If the Brit knew about the massive gem, he wasn't saying.

Still, she followed the money, studying expensive transactions in places beyond the reach of the Brazilian government. One transaction raised a big red flag: the purchase of six islands dotted with tropical rainforest. Dillon had paid forty-two million dollars for them.

She'd followed the money and found Dillon's goal

of finding cures for the world's most horrid diseases. Annja believed he'd been sincere about his desire to eradicate cancer and other maladies during his lifetime, no matter how twisted his methods.

And now she followed a path that led away from the beach and into the trees. Another boat had been pulled farther up on the beach and turned over. The name on the side, though upside down, was clearly legible. *Nancy's Emerald Dream*. A nice touch.

She found his tent about a hundred yards from shore. It was one of those luxury models that probably cost a few grand. An outdoor grill next to it, a lounge chair and umbrella to cut the sun, a small table with a pitcher of tea.

He wasn't inside. The tent was divided down the middle, half a laboratory, with some of the same equipment she'd seen at his site in the Amazon, a small generator under a counter, but it wasn't turned on. The other half was living space, a comfortable looking bed, an easy chair, lanterns on a bookcase stuffed with a mix of biology books and mysteries.

She went back outside, sat on the lounge chair and waited.

Dillon arrived about a half hour later, carrying a canvas bag probably filled with plants he'd harvested. His tanned face appeared to pale when he saw her.

Annja got up.

"You're—"

"—trespassing, I know. This is private property. You own this island, you own other islands. I looked on one of those first."

"I could kill you." Dillon dropped the bag and reached into his pocket. Even here, he carried a gun.

"You could try," she said. The sword hovered, waiting. She kept her hands in her pockets. "Hasn't there been enough deaths? The Dslala. Edgar. Moons. Your people." She paused and studied him, inhaled and picked up the scent of his sunscreen. He'd had a bout with melanoma, he'd told her. Of course he'd wear sunscreen. He still had that spot on his hand, no larger, but it looked worrisome. Maybe he'd get it taken care of in prison. "I killed Hammond."

The gun wavered for a moment, and Dillon squared his shoulders.

"In hindsight, I didn't have to." Annja continued confessing, spilling out the thoughts that had been tumbling through her head since that night at his abandoned pharma campsite. "I could've taken him without killing him. Looking back now, I should have. But I was tired and full of righteous anger and out for vengeance. But vengeance was really not mine to take." She quoted a piece of scripture to him; she knew he would appreciate. "I don't always follow the directions."

"Get off my island." Dillon gestured with the gun. "Get off!"

"I will," Annja said. "But you're coming with me. Brazilian law doesn't apply here. That helped me find you, by the way, looking where their justice couldn't reach. I'm going to take you where their justice reaches just fine."

Dillon fired.

Annja had noticed his finger twitch, and in that

heartbeat she reacted. She dropped in a crouch, pulled her hands from her pockets and summoned her sword.

Dillon gasped, the instant of surprise giving Annja an advantage. She pushed off and raised her leg, twisted and kicked his gun hand. He kept hold of it, but she followed through, bringing the pommel of the sword down hard. She heard fingers crack. The gun dropped.

"I can save us!" Dillon screeched. He swung at her and connected square in her stomach.

The blow was harder than Annja had anticipated, Dillon was clearly fit. He got in another blow before she leveled the sword and turned the blade so the flat of it caught him in the ribcage. She swung again with more power and felt his body give. She'd broken a few ribs.

"Maybe you could," she said. "Maybe you could find a cure for something."

Dillon feinted and she almost fell for it. His uppercut grazed her cheek. He recovered and came at her again, but she pivoted as he closed, stepped back and hit him with the flat of the blade again.

"Maybe you're right, Dillon, that the answers are in the plants. And as much as I'd like those answers to be found, pray that someone can do it…that someone can't be you." She switched the sword to her left hand and rose on the ball of her foot, spinning and kicking and catching him in the chest. The impact sent him against his grill. He grabbed at it to stay on his feet, and she kicked again, this time against his knee. He cried out.

"You've too much blood on your hands, Dillon. You have to answer for it."

He was in pain, tears thick in his eyes and his lips

twisted in an ugly grimace. His knuckles were white; he was holding on to the grill that tight.

"I can pay you, Miss Creed. I can make you rich. There's still plenty of money left from the emeralds. You'd never have to worry—"

"There's not enough money in the world to make me look the other way." Annja pictured the bodies of the dead Dslala and Moons, pictured Edgar drowning. She stepped in and brought the pommel of her sword against the side of his head. He collapsed, woozy and half conscious.

She reached into the "V" of his shirt. Dangling from a cord around his neck was a woman's gold ring with a large emerald anchored into a simple setting. She tugged it free.

"Something to remind me of you," Annja said.

Then she dragged him to her sailboat.

She'd easily make her flight tomorrow.

And she'd be in what amounted to Coron's downtown by dinnertime. There was a little restaurant near the airport she'd spotted, a sign advertising Philippine specialties. It had been a long while since she'd had a big plate of adobo, slow-cooked pork and chicken, crisped and oh-so-amazingly spiced. Her stomach growled in anticipation.

* * * * *

ALEX ARCHER
GRENDEL'S CURSE

A politically ordered excavation unearths more than expected

Skalunda Barrow, rumored to be the final resting place of the legendary Nordic hero Beowulf, is being excavated, thanks to charismatic—and right-wing extremist—politician Karl Thorssen, and archaeologist Annja Creed can't wait. But with the potential to uncover Hrunting and Nægling, two mythical swords the politician would kill to possess, the dig rapidly becomes heated. As Thorssen realizes the power of possessing Nægling, he is quick to show how far he will go to achieve his rabid ambitions. And when Thorssen marks Annja for death, the only way she can survive is to find a sword of her own.

Available May wherever books and ebooks are sold.

JAMES AXLER

DEATH LANDS

End Program

Newfound hope quickly deteriorates into a fight to save mankind

Built upon a predark military installation, Progress, California, could be the utopia Ryan Cawdor and companions have been seeking. Compared to the Deathlands, the tortured remains of a nuke-altered civilization, Progress represents a fresh start. The successful replacement of Ryan's missing eye nearly convinces the group that their days of hell are over—until they discover the high tech in Progress is actually designed to destroy, not enhance, civilization. The companions must find a way to stop Ryan from becoming a willing pawn in the eradication of mankind....

Available May wherever books and ebooks are sold.

The
Don Pendleton's
Executioner®
PATRIOT STRIKE

Superpatriots decide Texas should secede with a bang

After the murder of a Texas Ranger, Mack Bolan is called in to investigate. Working under the radar with the dead Ranger's sister, he quickly learns that rumors of missing fissile material falling into the wrong hands are true. The terrorists, die-hard Americans, are plotting to use the dirty bomb to remove Texas from the Union. As the countdown to D-day begins, the only option is to take the bait of the superpatriots and shut them down from the inside. You don't mess with Texas. Unless you're the Executioner.

GOLD EAGLE®

GEX425

Available April wherever books and ebooks are sold.